"Where are you—from," Sarah asked. . . .

Spock shook his head wearily. "The name of the planet would mean nothing to you. Your astronomers have not even discovered the star yet."

"I see." She looked down at her folded hands where they rested on the handle of the door. Then she looked up at him again. "I knew at the dance, you see."

Spock's eyebrow lifted, startled. Sarah smiled a little.

She reached out and took his hand in her long slim fingers . . . then she released it and her fingers brushed lightly against his cheek. "That's fever-hot," she said clinically. "A hundred and three, a hundred and four. A—one of us—would have been raving. You were clearly having the time of your life. . . . When you took my hand for the grand right and left, I noticed the scars on your hand had turned a sort of apple-green."

"In the future," he found himself saying tiredly, "I must remember to avoid dancing. . . ."

Look for *Star Trek* fiction from Pocket Books

ISHMAEL

BARBARA HAMBLY

A STAR TREK® NOVEL

PUBLISHED BY POCKET BOOKS NEW YORK

Another *Original* publication of POCKET BOOKS

POCKET BOOKS, a division of Simon & Schuster, Inc.
1230 Avenue of the Americas, New York, N.Y. 10020

This book is Published by Pocket Books, a Division of
Simon & Schuster, Inc. Under exclusive License from
Paramount Pictures Corporation, The Trademark Owner.

ISBN: 0-671-66089-6

First Pocket Books Science Fiction printing May 1985

10 9 8 7 6 5 4

For M. Shannon, Nedra, and Tom

ISHMAEL

Chapter 1

THE SOFT, INQUIRING NOTE OF THE DOOR SIGNAL threaded apologetically into the dimness. Captain James T. Kirk, lying on his neat bunk looking at the ceiling of his quarters, almost didn't answer it, except that as Captain of the U.S.S. *Enterprise* he felt obligated to do so, even when officially off duty and presumably asleep.

He had not slept in two nights now. It was, he guessed, close to the end of the third. He had dozed, restlessly, skimming the surface of dreams that repeated the same scenes over and over in a nightmare treadmill of doubts and grief. And the dreams always ended the same way: with that implacable riddle, and final silence stretching away into the darkness of space.

He hoped, for the thousandth time, that Spock was dead.

He should be, he told himself. *Twenty-four hours is a long time.*

But the other half of his mind whispered treacherously, *He's tough. And the Klingons are very skillful about things like that. Twenty-four hours isn't all that long.*

Kirk closed his eyes, as if that could blot out some hellish inner vision, then opened them again and looked up at the ceiling in the dark. He had stared at it for most of this watch. But if the neutral, shadowy pearl of that surface held any comfort, or any answer, it had not so far manifested them.

The door signal bleeped again. Kirk sighed. It was 0400 hours, the depths of the *Enterprise*'s artificial night. But then, most of the crew would know that Kirk wasn't sleeping, and why. He touched the switch beside the bed.

Bones McCoy stood silhouetted in the light of the corridor. "When you didn't answer you got my hopes up," he remarked accusingly, stepping inside. The door slid shut behind him. "Jim, let me . . ."

Kirk rolled to a sitting position on the rumpled bunk. "If you're going to offer me a sedative again I'll have you clapped in irons," he said tiredly. "I don't need a sedative, I just—need to think."

McCoy's sharp blue gaze flickered over him, once, like a tricorder taking a reading, and a corner of his mouth twisted down. "If that's what thinking's done for you I'd recommend the sedative, but it's up to you." The small glow of the entryway light brushed an edge of blue from his uniform jersey as he passed under it; then he came to stand beside Kirk's bunk, looking down at his friend. He said quietly, "There was nothing you could have done, Jim."

"I know." Kirk sighed, and ran a tired hand through his hair. "It's just that I keep thinking that there should have been."

On the other side of the room a small green light winked on. Automatically Kirk got to his feet and crossed to the desk. He touched a switch. "Kirk here."

"Captain?" The night communications officer didn't seem surprised to find him awake at 0400 hours either. "We've got Starbase Twelve on visual, sir. ETA 1200."

"Pipe in visual, Lieutenant."

The small screen above the desk widened into life.

Kirk stood in silence for a long time, gazing at the aphotic depths of interstellar space. Remote and un-twinkling in the frozen emptiness of that terrible vac-uum, stars stared back at him.

Against those endless light-years of nothing, Star-base Twelve hung like a magic Christmas-tree orna-ment, the gnawed rock ball of the original planetoid sewn over with a silver mesh of the lights of the surface works. An attendant swarm of docked space-craft surrounded the base like the flashing halo of electrons around an atomic nucleus. There was some-thing warm about it, welcoming—the fires of home.

It had been on Starbase Twelve, thought Kirk, that he had seen Spock for the last time.

Like a lot of last times, he hadn't expected it to be the last, had not even remotely dreamed of the possi-bility. Starbase Twelve was a completely routine stop, to deliver a couple of highly ranked astrophysicists and a load of scientific equipment to record the effects of the passage of a wandering white dwarf star through the so-called Tau Eridani Cloud—that vast, amor-phous region of ion storms and unexplained gravita-tional anomalies which was Starbase Twelve's *raison d'être*. That evening in the Wonder Bar there had been absolutely no thought in his mind that Spock might not be on the bridge of the *Enterprise* when they left.

Gazing at the image of the base in the blackness of

the tiny screen, he felt like a man who has lost a hand, but continues to reach for things with the stump.

The memory of the Wonder Bar was vividly clear in his mind, cozy and dim and overpriced, with the tinkle of ragtime music in the background and the sweet taste of Aldebaran Depth Charges on his lips. He'd been there with Maria Kellogg, an old friend from his Academy days. McCoy had offered to squire Lieutenant Uhura. Spock had arrived alone, as he was generally alone; and, as usual, he did not drink, saying that if he wished to consume alcohol he could manufacture it far more cheaply in the laboratories of the *Enterprise,* and have a guarantee of quality as well.

"You could probably metabolize it more efficiently if you took it intravenously, too," commented McCoy, and Spock raised a prim eyebrow.

"So I could," he agreed in his most correct voice. "But it has always escaped me why anyone would wish to metabolize alcohol in the first place, much less to do so in the company of strangers who have, perhaps, overmetabolized."

At the bar on the other side of the grottolike room, a Gwirinthan astro-gravitational mathematician slid from its barstool to the floor with a squashy thump.

"And yet here you are," Uhura teased him.

"Indeed," Spock replied. "Where else would I find such an unparalleled opportunity to observe the vagaries of human behavior?"

Uhura laughed, her dark eyes sparkling warmly. Spock leaned back a little in his chair, silhouetted against the red lights of the main room; a tall, thin, catlike shape, watching the human race in all its irrational glory with well-concealed fascination.

Kirk had seen him do this, on hundreds of shore leaves, and on countless evenings in a corner of the main rec room on the *Enterprise* while Uhura played her harp or Ensign Reilley sang Irish ballads: Spock the observer, the outsider. A Vulcan forced to deal with humans, a cold logician stranded amid the chattering welter of random emotion.

But Spock had saved Kirk's life and soul and sanity more times than Kirk cared to think about; put himself in danger against hope and logic in situations where Kirk knew his own survival had been despaired of. And all out of an emotion that Spock would have denied to the death that he felt.

A couple of Hokas waddled by, elaborately robed for one of their endless games. Over by the bar voices were raised as a scruffy-looking spice smuggler got involved in an argument over a girl with a pair of brown-uniformed pilots from some down-at-the-heels migrant fleet. McCoy, mellowed with good bourbon, raised his glass and commented, "You've got to admit, Spock, you'll never find anything like this in all your logic."

"A fact which I find most comforting," the Vulcan replied. "There are times, Doctor, when I feel as though I had been shanghaied by a shipful of Hokas—except that in the case of Hokas, once one has understood the rules of their current system of make-believe, one is fairly certain of what they will do next."

Kirk concealed his snort of laughter at McCoy's outraged expression behind another Aldebaran Depth Charge. The comparison with that fanciful teddy-bear race was hardly a flattering one. The girl by the bar, he noticed, had watched calmly as the altercation between the pilots and smuggler had degenerated almost to the point of fisticuffs, then finished her drink and departed on the arm of a tall, curly-haired man in the eccentric garb typical of space-tramps—the combatants had continued their quarrel undeterred.

Thinking back on that evening, Kirk could not remember anyone mentioning the Klingon ore transport at all.

He'd made a mental note of it when he'd seen it listed on the base manifest, as a possible source of crew conflicts. It hadn't seriously concerned him, though. Ore transports, though gigantic, are far too thinly manned to cause much trouble even had its whole crew come ashore at once. The crew of this one had kept to their ship.

Maybe, like Sherlock Holmes's dog, that was what had tipped off Spock. Something had.

Kirk had been preparing to meet Maria Kellogg the next morning when Spock had contacted him. "Power readouts on the ore transport are running suspiciously high," that deep, rather harsh voice had said over the communicator. "There would also seem to be about twice the usual number of crewmen listed. I should like to have a look at the inside of that vessel."

"You have a hunch something's up?" Kirk threw an uneasy glance at the chronometer, settled in its wall niche slightly to the left of the door. The visiting officers' quarters, like most of the older part of Starbase Twelve, had been remodeled from the far more ancient tunnelings that dated back to the days when the long-vanished Karsid Empire had used this planetoid as a base. Thus the rooms all had the slightly awkward feel of space created for nonhuman proportions, the wall niches all about half a meter lower or higher than they should have been. The chronometer itself said 1000 hours. Spock, Kirk thought, must have been up early. More likely he had sat up late the night before, scanning the readouts for the other ships on the base, curious about which governments were sending what kind of scientific crews to watch the

latest fluctuations of the Tau Eridani Cloud and looking for the names of scientists whom he knew.

Instead he had found—what?

"Captain," said Spock severely, "Vulcans do not
have 'hunches.' There are enough subliminal clues to
add up to a high order of probability that something is,
as you say, 'up.' The base manifest lists the ship
simply as an ore transport. The Klingons might be
using it for scientific observation of the Tau Eridani
Cloud, but why would they do so when they already
have two legitimate research teams working on the
base?"

Kirk's mind snapped suddenly to something else,
with an almost audible mental *click*. "And the Klingon
cruiser *Rapache* is due within eight hours," he said.
"ETA 1800, departure two hours later—no shore
leaves."

"And the ore transport is scheduled to depart at
1800 hours," said Spock's voice thoughtfully. "Fascinating."

Personally, Kirk felt less fascinated than he did
suspicious and apprehensive. But then, Spock was
capable of being sincerely intrigued by processes si-
multaneously with being sincerely appalled by possible results. Kirk's own mind was already scouting the
ground, ticking off possibilities. Starbase Twelve was
in Free Space; not even the base commander had the
authority to inspect a properly registered ship. Moreover, on what grounds could he base the request for
such a search? That his instincts, and Spock's instincts, told him that something was afoot? And even if
a search was made, who else on the base had Spock's
triple grounding in abstract scientific theory, Klingon
computer systems and the workings of the Klingon
military mind?

All this went through his mind in a matter of seconds. Then he said, "Can you get on board?"

"Affirmative, Captain. I have made arrangements to go aboard as part of the base technical crew. Our access will theoretically be limited to a very small area of the ship, but it will be possible for me to tap into the computer database."

After a long moment Kirk said quietly, "Mr. Spock—you know what that's called."

"As I will be uniformed as a starbase technician, I believe 'espionage' is the correct term, Captain."

Kirk was silent, rapidly weighing alternatives in his mind and discarding them just as quickly. Kirk had had enough run-ins with alien weapons technology to know that the possibilities were hideously infinite, and the populated heart of the Federation was not so far away as to be out of danger if the Klingons had achieved some kind of major breakthrough. Yet the price of capture was unthinkable, not only to the lone spy himself, but to whoever had sent him. The Klingons had gone to a deal of trouble to keep secret whatever it was they had on the transport—how much more would they go to?

We can't know that, Kirk thought ironically, *until we know what the thing is.*

"Mr. Spock . . ." He hesitated. The knowledge that the risks involved in investigating the transport weighed small against the potential risks of not investigating made it no easier. If anything went wrong, he thought—if Spock didn't manage to get off the transport, if he was caught in an area of the ship where he had no right to be, if the Klingons even suspected the motives behind that Vulcan technician's nosiness—there would be absolutely nothing that Kirk could do to bail him out. "Be careful."

"Espionage is not something that one does carelessly, Captain," Spock replied, after due consideration. "I will rendezvous with you at 1400 hours. Spock out."

Kirk realized he was still staring half-hypnotized at the small darkness of his cabin viewscreen and the glittering ball of lights that hung suspended in its center. He rubbed his eyes tiredly, and turned to see McCoy still behind him, one shoulder propped against the partition that divided the desk area from the rest of his quarters. The doctor's cynical features looked very worn in the reflected glow from the screen.

Kirk said quietly, "To this day I don't know what I could have done differently."

"Nothing," said McCoy.

"Nothing," Kirk repeated bitterly. "If I had done nothing we'd be exactly where we are now with regards to that transport. Only Spock would still be with us." He turned to the galley-pipeline mechanism in a corner of the office cubicle, and prodded the coffee button. It didn't always work, and occasionally what was delivered more closely resembled something that came out of reactor-coolant coils than a coffeepot, but at the moment Kirk was in no mood to seek out the more palatable alternatives available in the rec room or the galley. "You want some coffee, Bones? It's nearly 0500 now and staying up looks simpler than getting up."

The corner of McCoy's mouth turned down again as the pipeline made an indescribable noise and produced a cup of faintly steaming black fluid. "You can put a relief on standby until we reach the base, you know," he reminded him.

"To do what? Hold the con while I stay here and look at the ceiling some more?" Kirk turned away, leaving the coffee untasted to prowl across the narrow confines of his quarters. "I'll be fine, Bones," he added, more quietly. "It's just that—I'll be fine."

McCoy watched him keenly from where he still stood beside the desk. Then he said, "What about Spock's transmissions?"

Kirk paused in his pacing, his back to the doctor. McCoy's clinical eye observed the straight line of the spine under the gold jersey, the tightening of the shoulder muscles and the way they relaxed suddenly in a long sigh as the captain turned back toward him. Kirk's face, usually a little boyish, looked haggard. "You know, Bones, if it weren't for those transmissions sometimes I'd think that transport never existed at all?"

McCoy carried the coffee over to him. "Here," he said. "Drink this if you're determined to pollute your bloodstream rather than get the sleep you need. I'll be back in a few hours with some vitamin B for your breakfast."

Kirk expelled his breath in a faint sound that could have been a laugh, and sipped at the murky brew in the cup. "It should take that long for me to figure out what I'm going to report to the base commander," he said. Then, as the doctor turned to leave, he added, "Thank you, Bones."

McCoy paused in the doorway, studying him for a moment without speaking. All that he could have said had been said, by his own presence in the captain's quarters at a time when, by his own advice, he, too, should have been sleeping. So he turned and left, and Kirk prowled restlessly back to sit on the edge of the bunk, his mind worrying again at the problem of Spock's transmissions from the Klingon ore transport.

It was there that the half a grain of phylozine that McCoy had slipped into his coffee while his back was turned took hold, and he slid almost without knowing it back into a heavy sleep tortured by too-familiar dreams.

Spock's first transmission had come as the last of the *Enterprise* crew members were beaming aboard.

Kirk had returned early to the visiting officers' quarters on the base, and had paced the oddly shaped rooms like a tiger caged by time. Fourteen hundred hours had come and gone—fifteen hundred. Driven by restlessness, he had had the image of the ore transport piped into his quarters' viewscreen: an unwieldy black giant of a ship, a floating mountain. In the distance behind it Kirk could glimpse the deadly silver angularity of the Klingon battle cruiser *Rapache,* which had arrived at the base inexplicably early and was now in orbit, hanging like a hawk upon the winds of night.

Still Spock had not come.

At 1540 Kirk had tapped back into Base Control, to learn that the ore transport had just lumbered out of orbit, and was headed in the direction of the Tau Eridani Cloud.

At 1730 Kirk began canceling shore leaves, calling all personnel unobtrusively back to the *Enterprise.* After a final, cautious communicator scan of the base he returned to the ship himself and took his post on the bridge, preparing the ship to leave orbit, watching the gleaming shape of the *Rapache* still riding in its orbit, mentally weighing possibilities against inevitable consequences.

The *Rapache* was a heavily armed fighting ship, capable of mauling the *Enterprise* badly in a pitched battle. He had put himself and the Federation in the wrong by sending Spock aboard the transport to begin with. The Klingons didn't know that, of course, but if they found it out . . . what was their secret worth to them?

19

He did not want to think about how they might find it out.

"Mr. Sulu," he said quietly. "Lay in a course for Alpha Eridani III."

"Aye, sir." The helmsman's voice was impassive, but Kirk felt the flicker of those dark eyes. The tension that crackled under the bridge crew's usual calm efficiency was almost strong enough to pick up on a voltmeter. Instinct—or, as Spock would have insisted, subliminal clues—told them that there was something behind this sudden change of course other than new orders from the Fleet.

Kirk studied the wide-range readouts on the small screen on the arm of his chair. A course for Alpha Eridani III would parallel the transport's along the fringes of the disruptive field of the cloud, but was a perfectly legitimate bearing for a Federation ship. The Klingons might have their suspicions, but could hardly prove that the *Enterprise* had some reason to follow the transport. If the transport changed course, Kirk knew, and headed deeper into the cloud, he would have the choice of abandoning the pursuit or playing tag with some unknown weapon through that mazelike welter of shifting navigation points with the *Rapache* very likely on his back—neither of which course of action would help Spock any.

With a sudden harsh crack of static the *Enterprise* communicator came to life. Even through the distortion, Spock's voice was recognizable. The message was short.

"White dwarf, Khlaru, Tillman's Factor, Guardian." A flash of static, and silence. The whole had taken less than two seconds of transmit time.

"What—" Kirk began, and Uhura said, "It's a generalized subspace broadcast from the direction of the Tau Eridani Cloud, Captain." The dark wings of her brows pulled together. "Was that—"

"That was Mr. Spock, Lieutenant. He's aboard that Klingon ore transport. He had only a hand communicator. . . ."

"He could have wired it through their communications system via a centralized computer," said the communications officer thoughtfully. "Only—transports don't carry that type of sophisticated equipment."

"No," said Kirk grimly, "they don't. Did you get a tape?"

She touched a button, rose from her station to hand him a tiny spool.

"Yeoman Donnelly—take this down to Spock's pet whiz kids in Science. Get them to play it backwards, forwards, sideways if they have to: find out what he means and get it back to me. Lieutenant Uhura—was that message traceable to the *Enterprise?*"

"No, sir. It was a wide-band frequency. It could have been for anyone on the base."

"Could they have traced Spock's position on the transport from it?"

She was silent a moment, thinking, her long hands resting lightly on the complex patterns of her console. Then she said, "I don't think so, Captain. He could have wired through the computer at any point on the ship. But now they know that he's aboard, and they'll be watching. If he makes another transmission they'll be able to fix his position."

That had been the beginning of the nightmare. As Starbase Twelve dwindled on the rear viewscreens Kirk could see the *Rapache* peel out of orbit behind them, dogging them on the farthest limits of their scanners but lying between them and any Federation outpost. Kirk kept to the bridge through three consecutive watches, bullying McCoy for stimulants, checking and rechecking the position of the transport as its image flickered and shifted through the random variations of the cloud's ion fields. Through his skin he could feel the tension of the bridge crew as they moved with unwonted quiet about their duties, keeping the *Enterprise* on her noncommittal course for Alpha Eridani III, and waiting. . . .

Kirk knew—they all knew—that Spock's capture would only be a matter of time. The science section reported back that the transmission Spock had made was, as far as they could tell, totally ambiguous. Kirk suspected that Spock, wherever he was hiding in the mazes of air ducts and holding bays on that gigantic transport, knew it too. He would have to clarify with a second transmission.

And then—what?

Kirk wondered how important that weapon aboard the transport was to the Klingons. Important enough to risk breaking the Organian Peace Treaty by attempting to prevent the *Enterprise* from reporting back to base? Powerful enough to let them break the treaty with impunity? There was a disturbing thought. Or did they think they would be able to justify their action on the grounds of the *Enterprise*'s having started the trouble by sending a spy aboard in the first place?

If Spock did make another transmission he would be caught. If he was caught, the Klingons would use the Mind-Sifter, and then it would only be a matter of time before they knew who had sent him.

Spock's last transmission was less than a second long. Again on the generalized beam, wide-flung enough to be intended for anyone from here to Starbase Twelve. Short—no more than a quick burst of words and static. He gave three numbers, and signed off.

That was the last they heard of him.

An hour crawled by. Two. Kirk stared down at the dark glassy surface of the readout screen at the captain's station, watching the colored dots that swam there: the luminous green that marked the mass of the *Enterprise,* the blue-green fleck of the slightly smaller *Rapache* at the far edge, the yellow square of the transport, its color and shape shifting uneasily in the interference of the cloud.

Why the cloud? Kirk wondered. Had they suspected they would be followed, and taken refuge there for concealment? Or was there some other reason? Was what they had on board a weapon at all, or something else?

At the dark edge of the readout screen, the blue-green dot began to move.

At the same moment Sulu said, "Klingon battle cruiser accelerating to maximum sublight, Captain. Moving in."

Kirk touched a button on the arm of his chair. "Battle stations. Yellow alert."

Lights began to flash. Kirk felt the tautening of the atmosphere on the bridge like a subsonic note. Through his fingertips on the chair arms, through the deck below his feet, he could almost feel the controlled speed with which the crew readied the ship for battle. *A battle,* he thought, *that could end in any fashion, from destruction to Organian intervention to . . . anything.*

"Klingons decelerating, still coming on medium slow," reported Sulu. "Klingon shields raised."

"Raise shields," ordered Kirk. "Lieutenant Uhura, attempt to hail the Klingon bridge as soon as they're in range."

"Captain," said Chekov, glancing up from his post at Sulu's side. "The ore transport is moving into warp speeds. I think—I cannot get a clear reading—I think they are up to warp five, and accelerating."

"Track them," snapped Kirk. "Keep an eye on them, Chekov, cloud or no cloud. Mr. Sulu, hold course for Alpha Eridani III. Mr. Chekov, keep me informed if they change speed or direction."

"They are changing speed, Captain. I think it's warp seven but—but ore transports cannot make that kind of speed. And the reading is changing. . . ."

Kirk strode down to look over the navigator's shoulder, the deadly blinking of the battle-alert lights flickering over him as he moved. Not only was the transport—impossibly—still accelerating, but it seemed to be shifting its absolute mass.

"Recompute that," Kirk ordered, and glanced up at the rear screens where the angular shape of the *Rapache* was visible now, growing against the darkness. Above him Uhura, impassive as a bronze idol, was calmly readying an ejection pod with tapes and readouts of every ship function, standard procedure in the event of a battle. Automatically his glance shifted to the science console, and he was startled, almost shocked, to see a stranger there.

"Captain!"

His eyes snapped back to the sensor screens. The transport had vanished.

"Run a wide-band scan. Recalibrate the whole board if you have to."

The Russian's hands played across the console like a pianist's, rapid and sure. "Nothing, Captain. No debris, no antimatter residue, no disruption in the field—and no transport."

The intermittent scarlet glare of the alert lights played across the small screen like bloody dawn.

24

Chekov ran the sensor beams over that part of the cloud backwards, sideways, inside-out. But there was nothing—no sign of the ore transport, nor any indication of what had become of it. It had simply vanished, into the thinnest air in creation.

"A cloaking device?" He glanced up at Spock's replacement at the science console.

She shook her head. "Difficult to say, sir. In theory even a cloaked ship would leave an antimatter residue. Besides, a cloak would suck off so much power that they shouldn't even have been able to break light-speed, let alone make warp seven. But then, with the distortion effects from that thing . . ." She waved a rather bitten tentacle-end in the direction of the cloud. ". . . anything might have happened."

Kirk stood still for a moment, looking down past Chekov's shoulder at the increasingly confused readings within the cloud as they approached the outer fringes of the dwarf-star's wide-flung gravitational influence. Then he turned away, and stepped back to his chair, followed by every eye on the bridge. "Mr. Sulu," he said quietly, "hold course for Alpha Eridani III, at present speed."

The *Enterprise* had remained on battle alert all the way to Alpha Eridani III. The *Rapache* had followed them, never coming into hailing range, to the edge of that star system, then with a showy roll had fallen abruptly away and headed back in the general direction of the distant Klingon Empire.

And after that . . . nothing.

No sign of the ore transport, though the *Enterprise* had gone into the outer edge of the cloud at several points on its way back to Starbase Twelve and had taken readings as accurate as any could be there. No hint of what had been aboard. All clue to its nature gone—the transport itself gone—Spock gone.

Dead, Kirk hoped, lying in the gray lassitude that is the aftermath of heavy sleep. He glanced at the chronometer. It was a few minutes short of 1100. McCoy had doubtless not only slipped him a Mickey Finn, but had arranged for his replacement on the bridge as well.

But it Spock was dead, he thought, it would not have been an easy death.

It was typical of Spock, he thought, that he had died alone, stubbornly following the logic of his duty to its bitter conclusion. Typical that he had simply gone, without saying good-bye.

Typical that his last words to them had been numbers, the obscure key to some unguessable riddle.

But whatever that riddle was, Spock had considered the answer well worth his own life. And the Klingons had considered it worth the risk of the wrath of the Organians to protect.

And whatever had been aboard that transport, it was still at large, somewhere, in the galaxy.

Kirk rolled stiffly from his bunk, and began preparing to go ashore.

Chapter 2

FAINT AND CLEAR, THE TAPPING OF A HORSE'S hooves on the damp clay of the roadbed sounded through the misty opal colors of the morning. Aaron Stemple, returning from the settlement of Olympia to Seattle, rode wrapped in his own thoughts; almost, but not quite, oblivious to the wan white beauty of the foggy morning. He was aware of the salt-sweet sea smell of Puget Sound, and the headier tang of the pines that stood like a silent cathedral—clay red or black with damp—above and below the road that tacked its way along the steep hem of the sound; was aware of the sharp cold of the morning and the familiar taste of coming rain. But he was aware of them primarily as distractions. Not being an imaginative man, he pushed the awareness aside from long habit. As owner of the only sawmill in the backwoods lumber boomtown of Seattle, Stemple had enough to think about between his investments in land and shipping deals with the San Francisco companies without worrying over his own personal impulses to sloth.

Thus he was unprepared when his horse suddenly shied. Catching up the reins with a jerk, he wondered if he had even seen the light, or heard the sound, away between the trees downslope to his left. He turned the horse's head as he felt its muscles bunch for a bolting run, cursing alike the equine race and his own momentary distraction of mind. Stemple fought grimly for a moment as the horse backed and shifted and pulled wildly at the bit; then as it quieted again he sat still in the saddle, listening.

Around him, the woods were silent.

Too silent, thought Stemple, as he heard the distant sough of the waters of the sound. *Birds were starting a minute ago.*

He scanned the woods, but found no answer to the riddle in their columned depths. Nothing that would account for that uncanny silence, nor for the sound that he was almost certain he had heard, and the brief shimmer of silver light he could have sworn he'd seen between the trees.

Indians? Surely not.

The horse had stopped shivering. Experimentally, Stemple slacked the rein, and though the animal pulled a little on the bit it showed no further signs of bolting. Somewhere in the distance, a tentative lark began to sing.

The mist flattened the shapes of the trees, and blurred the three-foot-deep carpet of fern that blanketed the steep hillside above and below the road. The light could, Stemple supposed, have been the sun reflecting on standing water—for the sun was beginning to break the fog—and that was what had spooked his horse. If it was Indians—though what tribe would be this close to the settlement?

Outlaws, then? Stemple was uneasily aware of the emptiness of the road, and the evident wealth announced by his dark broadcloth suit and gold watch chain.

He clicked his tongue, urging his mount forward.

Down the hill to the left, the brush rustled once. The horse started, nostrils wide, but this time Stemple was ready and pulled the dithering animal in a tight circle. When they came to a halt, the woods were again filled with that listening silence.

There was definitely something down there.

Like all men in Washington Territory, Stemple didn't travel unarmed. But he'd never had call to use the carbine holstered before him on the saddletree and he wasn't sure he could hit anything with it if he tried. Though he was aware he'd put on flesh from the sedentary life of running the sawmill, he knew himself to be in good shape for a man of forty, broad-shouldered and strong, an ironic legacy of heaving bales on the Boston docks from the age of fifteen. But outrunning wild beasts or wilder men wasn't much in his line, and neither was taking them on hand-to-hand.

But, it could be that someone was hurt down there. Some earlier traveler on this road? He discarded the idea at once. The ferns that covered the ground all down the mountainside were netted over in a gauze of dew, unbroken by the passage of any body. A glance at the road told him that he was the first man to take this way in days.

Cautiously, he reined around, and urged the horse toward the slope. It took a few hesitant steps in that direction and balked, ears flattening and eyes showing white with fear.

Stemple sighed, annoyed and at the same time perversely curious. *What the hell,* he thought. *If it's an ambush they've had God's own sweet time to spring it.*

Common sense told him to ride on. But he knew that if he did, the itch of his own curiosity would only drive him back.

He stepped down from the saddle, tied the reins to a

stout sapling close by the path, unshipped the carbine and began picking his precarious way on foot down the fern-covered slope. The dew soaked his dark coat and squished wetly underfoot, but nothing in all that great silence threatened him.

When he found the man, his first thought was: *Indians.* And then, "Oh, my God." In the split second of unreasoning panic that followed, he considered shooting him—it—as he lay unconscious in the ferns.

For he was alien. Alien, foreign, not of Earth or of any sane place. The fluid that dripped from the slashed thigh and knee and oozed from the puckered and abraded flesh around the burns on the hands and face was clearly analogous to blood, but it was a thick, dark green in color. The skin, waxy with exhaustion, had a greenish cast to it, and the rubbed and blistered bruises ringing the bony wrists were colored like no human flesh.

Who, and what, and from where, Stemple did not know, nor could he imagine. But not human, for all the human shape.

He knelt beside him cautiously, and turned the unconscious man on his back. The face of an intellectual Satan, thought Stemple; pinched and sunken with the marks of the last extremities of pain. The dark eyebrows slanted inhumanly upwards; the ears were wrong, different. High cheekbones stabbed whitely through the taut and wasted skin. The dark clothing was of a texture Stemple had never encountered before, though he'd spent most of his childhood sewing garments in the sweatshops of the Boston slums—a strange and metallic texture.

Alien, he thought. *Nothing of the human Earth.*

And hurt. Dying, maybe. Stemple knew that sunken look from his slum childhood as well. He felt the man's face and hands, and found them clammy with shock.

Searching, he found the big vein in the wrist, and felt the slow, weak movement there.

At least he has a pulse. That implies a heart to move it.

Stemple leaned forward, and dragged the man up onto his shoulders. The man—creature—alien—was taller than he, but not so heavy. Still, it was a struggle to get him through the wet and slippery ferns up the slope to the road again. At the scent of unhuman blood the horse shied, and Stemple, cursing, laid his burden down and went to blindfold the beast with his handkerchief against any further trouble. Between the unaccustomed weight of a limp, unwieldy body and the frantic jittering of the horse, it took him a good fifteen minutes to get the alien slung over the saddle, secured like dead venison. By the time he was done Stemple's coat and shirt were soaked with dew and mud and dark green blood.

He had already decided what he must do.

His mind shied from the thought of taking the alien to Seattle. He knew what his own first reaction had been, to destroy the alien thing. There were those, among the half-educated loggers of the town, who'd have the same initial response, and others who would give the matter more mature consideration and come to the same conclusion. Indeed, Stemple was not entirely sure that this would not be the best course. The alien was an utterly unknowable quantity, and the implications of finding him here, on the Olympia road, were myriad and terrifying. It might be that some train of circumstances was starting that could be stopped now, and only now, by a single well-placed bullet.

But Stemple knew himself not the man to fire that bullet. He had foreclosed on widows and orphans in his time, but there were things he knew he could not do.

That left only the cabin on Eagle Head Point.

It belonged to Stemple, and had in fact been his home for two winters, before his town house by the mill was built in '62. He still stayed there occasionally, for it was within a half hour's walk to the town. It could be reached from here by back trails. Unless he ran into some of the Bolt brothers' men as he trespassed his way across the footslopes of Bridal Veil Mountain, he could get the alien there completely unseen.

And when I get him there, thought Stemple, wiping the muck of sweat from his brow with a kerchief that was scarcely cleaner than his sleeves, *there'll be time enough to figure out what to do with him.* Beyond that he did not permit himself to think—Stemple was a man who knew his own limitations.

It was raining.

It was always raining, in Seattle. Lottie Hatfield, laboring up the long pathway from town, listened to the slivery patter and trickle of water on pine needles and reflected that, since her coming to the young town eight years ago, she had seen an average of maybe a year's worth of sunny days.

Good for the trees, of course, and for her own trade of selling drinks to cold, wet men who'd been cutting trees in the rain all day. Tonight would see good business in the saloon. But there was something that had to be seen to first, if the old skinflint would let her see to it.

She hoped Aaron wasn't in any kind of trouble.

In the grayish light of the last of the afternoon the rain beat against the trunks of the trees like breakers, flinging back clouds of spray. Despite the hood of her oilskin cloak Lottie's frizzed blond bangs were wet and drooping, and water dripped into her eyes at every step. Puffing as she trudged, her corsets creaking and her taffeta petticoats weighted with damp, Lottie cursed Aaron Stemple for putting his hideout so far from town, and for—whatever it was.

She'd known for a week there was something wrong. It wasn't like Aaron to turn hermit like this. He wasn't anybody's idea of a gay blade, but he would usually drop around the saloon of an evening, to exchange gossip and hear the news if Captain Clancey happened to be in port. One of the men who worked for Stemple at the mill had said something last night about the "old man" being sick.

Not sick, thought Lottie, as the warm gold lights of the cabin glimmered ahead of her through the trees. She'd seen him yesterday, on his way back from the mill, though earlier than usual; had noted then how drawn he looked. For all he was a closefisted and shut-hearted man, she knew the look of trouble when she saw it. Twenty-five years and more of pouring drinks had taught her that.

He opened the door to her knock and stood for a moment, the light from the lamp behind him touching an edge of gold on the white of his shirtsleeves. "Lottie," he said, surprised. Perhaps he'd thought no one would notice his changed behavior, or maybe he'd just assumed that no one would care.

"Aaron," she greeted him, and pushed back the hood of her cape.

After a moment's hesitation he stepped aside to let her in, and took her cloak to hang in the shelter of the lean-to kitchen. "What brings you so far from town?"

He looked bad, she thought. His saturnine face had a harried look to it, and there was an upright line between his low black eyebrows that she hadn't seen before. As he preceded her into the small parlor and reached to turn up the lamp she saw on his wrist and hand livid purple-brown bruises, as though impossibly powerful fingers had all but crushed the bones.

"I was worried about you," she said simply. "You've been holed up here like a wintering bear since you came back from Olympia. I was afraid you might be in some kind of trouble."

Stemple was so touched by this that he didn't even make his usual sarcastic reply. "I—thank you, Lottie. But it's nothing. A man's got a need to be by himself now and then. . . ."

She brushed off the obvious lie. "Are you ill?"

He shook his head. "But thank you, truly, for your concern."

"Is it anything I can help with?"

"No. No, it's a—a personal problem."

In the softness of the lamplight that threw their magnified shadows across walls and ceiling, Lottie could see that Stemple had been reading. *Not reading, really*, she thought, looking around her at the books strewn over the desk among the accounts and financial papers of the mill and stacked on every piece of the cabin's simple furniture. *Searching for something through the pages of every volume he possessed.*

"I won't pry," she said softly. "But if there's anything I can do to help—anything any of us can do— you'll let me know?"

Stemple hesitated, torn between his desire for secrecy and his need for help. It occurred to him that Lottie could aid him, for she had doubtless done her share of pool-table first aid and backroom midwifery in a checkered career that spanned the Natchez riverboats and San Francisco's Barbary Coast. For all there had been a time he'd looked down on her as a common saloonkeeper, life on the frontier had changed things for him. He knew that this stout, handsome, competent woman, who could outcurse a

British sergeant of marines, had a good and gentle heart. Few things could shock or frighten her anymore, and he stood in desperate need of clearheaded advice.

"I don't know whether you can help," he sighed. "Or whether anyone can. In fact I don't really know what kind of help I need. Come here, Lottie."

He took her arm, and guided her to the small door that led into the tiny bedroom.

The lamp there was turned down dim. She saw the shape of a man beneath the quilts of the bed, the face a darker blur between the white of the pillows and the white of bandages. Bandaged hands lay on top of the cover. There were more books here, and the small litter of medical aid: the ends of bandages, stained dressings, scissors, the smell of sickness and herbs and tallow. She glanced quickly at Aaron, his heavy features obliquely lit by the glow of the fire in the other room.

"Who is it?"

He shook his head. "I don't know. I found him in the woods seven days ago, on my way back from Olympia."

She moved in a rustle of heavy petticoats to the bedside. "But why didn't you—"

Stemple reached to turn up the lamp. "That's why." He heard the woman's breath catch in something like horror.

The quickening light revealed the man's features, and the color of the blood that stained the discarded wrappings. Lottie whispered, "What on God's earth . . ."

"That, Lottie," said Stemple quietly, "was exactly my question." The lamplight stitched in brief gold the line of his watch chain as he leaned one shoulder against the doorpost, then left him as only a dark cutout of shadow. Behind him, rain drummed faintly on the curtained windows.

Hesitantly, she extended a hand to feel the man's face, and drew it back in alarm.

"He's been hotter than that," said Stemple's voice over her shoulder, "but never cooler, once he came out of the first shock. He seems to be sleeping easily now, so I'd say that's his normal temperature. If his blood's not like ours, why should the rest of his body be? But you can see why even if there was a doctor closer than San Francisco I couldn't send for one."

"No." Lottie had seen men lynched for the color of their skin before this, let alone the color of their blood. "Has he spoken?"

"No." Stemple shifted his weight against the frame of the door. "I've sat with him for seven nights now. He'll go into delirium sometimes, dreaming things— seeing things—reliving whatever experience brought him here." He held up his bruised hand. "He's tremendously strong. Whatever it is he dreams about, I have no desire to experience. Those injuries on his face and neck are laid out in a pattern, Lottie—they were deliberately inflicted. Yet in all his dreaming, he's never uttered one word, Lottie. He's never made so much as a sound."

He came into the room, to kneel beside her where she knelt next to the bed. He went on, "When I found him in the woods, the ferns on all sides were covered with dew, dew that hadn't been disturbed. But there was none on his clothing, except where it had been brushed off when he moved a little. But no trail—no track."

"But where—where had he come from?"

"It isn't where that bothers me so much, Lottie," said Stemple, "as why."

She glanced sharply aside at him. "Why?"

"Why is he here, Lottie?" He gestured to that still, strangely boned face in its frame of straight black hair. "Whoever he is, whatever he is, wherever he's from—he isn't on the Earth by accident. He can't be."

"On the Earth?" she repeated. "You think he's from—not on the Earth?"

Stemple shrugged. "I don't know what to think. But I do know that mankind has explored most of the corners of the globe by this time, and though they've found some fairly strange people, they're all human. From the Hottentots of Africa to the Laplanders to the Chinese, they all have red blood. Earth is a planet, like Mars or Venus. Is it inconceivable that, like Earth, those other worlds could be inhabited as well?"

Lottie made no reply for a time, gazing down at the face of the man on the bed, seeing him for the first time as a man, not an alien being. Saw that he was a man in his full prime, tall and spare and dark; that his supple, sensitive fingers had never been broken by manual labor. His nose had never been broken, either. *Not a fighting man,* she thought. Then she looked back at Aaron, struggling with thoughts long unexplored. "Not—inconceivable," she said slowly. "But—how would he get here? What would he be doing here?"

"We may learn that," said Aaron, "when he wakes up. But what I'm wondering is—what about the others? Others like him, healthy, unhurt, walking among us. His hair is almost long enough that if he combed it forward to cover the tips of his ears, who would know? How many of them are among us now, passing for human?"

The woman shivered, though the room was warm.

He got to his feet, prowled to the window where now only darkness lay beyond the rain-streaked glass.

"I don't even know if I did right by saving him. If he comes from somewhere—Mars, Venus, some other world entirely, since they tell us every star is really a sun—it would have taken him—them—a great deal of trouble to get here. They wouldn't have made the trip for no reason, Lottie. The deliberateness of those wounds tells us something about the people who inflicted them. What if they came with ill intent, toward us, toward the Earth?" He turned back to her, his dark face grave and lined with tiredness. "I don't even know whether he's human or not—what we would call human."

Lottie rested her arm among the blankets on the edge of the bed where the alien lay motionless. Seven nights, she thought. *He has sat here seven nights, beside that silent, tormented sleeper, with those thoughts his only company.*

"What is human, Aaron?"

"You tell me. I've met wealthy and educated gentlemen who didn't consider their own slaves human. I've looked . . ." He gestured toward the books that piled the room's wing chair and small table. "What makes us human and not beasts? He looks like us, Lottie, but he may have no more soul than a panther."

Aaron returned to her, and gave her his hand to help her up, her whalebone corsets creaking as she moved. They paused in the doorway to the parlor, and she looked back at the still face of the alien, the pity she felt for him as a man in desperate trouble struggling for a moment against her fear of the unknown. "You did save his life, Aaron."

"True enough," agreed Stemple cynically. "And if he isn't human, that might mean he won't turn on us, after all."

He took a lantern down from the parlor wall and lit it

with a long spill from the fire. Lottie took it, and vanished into the rainy darkness of the night.

As Lottie had foreseen, the saloon was thriving when she returned there. Wu Sin, the China boy who worked for her, gave her a solemn little bow as she came through the door and took her heavy oilskins as she shed them. Half a dozen loggers were bellied up to the rough planks of the bar, and a little knot of mill-hands was grouped around the larger of the room's two tables, playing monte with Joshua Bolt, who was cleaning them out with his usual quiet efficiency. Joshua's older brother, Jason, senior of the three brothers who jointly owned Bridal Veil Mountain, stood at one end of the bar. He nursed a whiskey and listened to Captain Clancey, just in from the San Francisco run, and holding forth about the possibilities of running a railroad from Independence, Missouri, through to California to replace the wagon and stage routes.

"It'll never work, Clancey," someone was saying. "The Indians'll kill off the crews. . . ."

"Ah! Listen, boy-o, if the United States Army could lick the Rebels, it'll sure be able to lick the Indians. . . ."

"But they'll never be able to get it across the Rocky Mountains. . . ."

Impromptu demonstrations of engineering were organized with whiskey glasses and twigs to prove the point all along the bar. The whole place was smoky and warm in the deep orange-gold of the kerosene lamplight, smelling of whiskey and damp wool and maleness.

Lottie smiled to herself.

Home.

"Hey, Lottie me lass." Clancey made a grab for her

ISHMAEL

which she ducked as lightly as if she'd been a girl of sixteen, and stepped behind the bar. "And how's the belle of the Pacific Slope?"

"Wet as a drowned rat," she replied with a twinkle. "How's the sound tonight?"

"Rough as the road to Heaven and cold as an Orangeman's heart," said Clancey, but the tone in his boozy voice was one of love for the sea and the wild rainy weather. Thick-built, red-faced, with a great ruff of fading red whiskers, Roland Francis Clancey had spent the better part of his life on the sea, and though he would never admit his love for that wild and terrible mistress, he would follow the sea till he died. "And how have things been mindin' themselves here?"

"Never better," said Lottie brightly, smiling away the disturbing shadow of the man who lay unconscious in the cabin at Eagle Head Point. "Miss Pruitt tells me that the New Bedford girls are planning a New Year's celebration already, to mark their first year here in the town."

"That's right," agreed the sea captain, smiling, "January first it was that we landed here, after all that way 'round the Horn." He gave Jason Bolt a wink. "And that'll be the day your bet with Mr. Stemple is up, will it not?"

Bolt shrugged, as if he had only just remembered.

Clancey gave him a sly dig in the ribs. "You think you'll be makin' your bargain?"

Jason smiled with expansive confidence. "No problem. They'll all be spoken for by the first of January, bank on it. Which you probably have, if I know you. Aaron Stemple may have blackmailed me into putting up Bridal Veil Mountain as collateral for bringing the girls out here, but half of them are married already, and more spoken for. I'll win that bet."

"And Miss Biddy Cloom?" asked Clancey slyly.

40

"Clancey," said Jason, "if it comes to January first and Miss Cloom hasn't found a husband yet, I'll marry her myself."

"Brave man," declared one of the mill-hands with a laugh, and Lottie, angry for that plain and loud-voiced girl's sake, shot him a look that silenced him.

"Speaking of the New Bedford ladies," said somebody else, "Tom Naismith tells me his wife looks to be presenting you with your first godson."

Jason beamed. Having arranged to bring the thirty New England girls around the Horn to wive the settlers in Seattle, he felt a paternal interest in them, quite apart from having a personal stake in seeing them all married or at least spoken for by January. He had stood up for every one of them who had so far had weddings, playing father of the bride with as much pride as if they really were his daughters. The thought of it made Lottie smile. Jason, big and strapping and a handsome and eligible thirty-two, was a sight to behold when he was being paternal.

Then the closing of the door against the night drew her attention across the room, and she caught her breath in a quick gasp of shock.

In her mind she heard Aaron Stemple's voice again: "How many of them are passing for human?"

Passing for human. Were these?

There was nothing markedly alien about them, not like the man in the cabin. Two men, strangers, swarthy and bearded and dark. An odd look about the tufted eyebrows, she thought, but perhaps it was only her imagination. She found herself looking covertly at the way their thick black hair hung down over their ears. But it was not this, so much as their eyes, that frightened her.

Even at this distance, through the wavering shadows of the kerosene lamps and the smoke that

41

hazed the room, she knew that they were alien. Alien and evil.

One of them stayed at the corner table, watching the room with an expression in his eyes that Lottie had last seen in the eyes of the buyers at the Natchez slave markets before the War. The other came to the bar, and paid silver for whiskey. Watch him though she would, she could see nothing different about him, except for the look in his eyes. But as he crossed back to his partner she shivered.

"You all right, Lottie?" She turned, startled, at the sound of Jason's voice.

"I'm fine—it's hot in here, that's all."

The tall man frowned, looking closely at her. She drew a deep breath and patted Jason's wrist. "Just a turn," she went on with forced brightness. "Maybe I'm sickening for a cold. Can I get you another whiskey?"

Bolt nodded, and took his drink to join the two strangers at their table. Lottie busied herself pouring a drink for one of the mill-hands whose week's owl-hoot money had just gone into Josh Bolt's pockets, and she found her fingers were trembling. *He's injured,* she told herself. *He's harmless. He can't hurt Aaron.*

Passing for human. A train of events that could be stopped now. Maybe I am sickening for a cold, she told herself firmly. *I'll be seeing boogies and burglars like Biddy Cloom does in another five minutes.*

But turning back to the room, she caught sight of them again, talking casually to Bolt. In their faces was an alien arrogance, a terrible assumption of superiority that has nothing to do with snobbery, but rather with the placement of the boundary line between who is accorded the rights of a human being, and who is not.

". . . humanitarian?" she heard Jason say in answer to some question, and laugh. "It takes leisure and civilization to be a humanitarian, and around here, mister, believe me we've got neither."

"It also takes money," said the shorter of the two strangers. "A luxury of the rich."

"Well, in these parts you don't get rich by loving your fellow man," responded Bolt, grinning. "And the richest man in the settlement's also the meanest, with a heart like a Pierce and Hamilton safe."

Lottie thought she saw a look pass between the two strangers, a look and a small shrug. The conversation turned to other matters—politics, the Reconstruction of the South, representation in Congress and when Washington would be accorded statehood. When they left, Jason made his way back to the bar, half his whiskey still in his hand—Jason would nurse a drink or two along all night—and stood leaning quietly on the elbow-smoothed planking for a time, watching the door that had shut behind them.

Lottie asked, "Just passing through?" as casually as she could.

He glanced at her, picking up the uneasiness in her voice. "They say."

"But you don't?"

He shrugged, and shook his head. "I got the feeling they were looking for someone."

The alien, thought Lottie. *Their partner—maybe their spy. I have to warn Aaron that the creature he's harboring is evil.*

Then someone opened the back door of the saloon, and boots thumped on the board floor. With the sound came the roaring of fresh rainstorms from outside. Jeremy, the youngest of the three Bolt brothers, came in, wet as though he'd just swum up out of the sound.

43

He'd been walking out, it seemed, with Miss Candy Pruitt. "Have you been out there?" he asked, shaking out his long wet hair. "It's p—pouring oceans."

Jason grunted with distaste. "Josh? Let's get going. In another hour the trails back to the cabin will be flooded out."

Joshua pocketed his monte winnings, and collected mackinaws from the pegs beside the door. The mill-hands and loggers had been thinning out for the last half hour or so—as the Bolt brothers left, the last customers to go, Captain Clancey was already helping Wu Sin to snuff the lamps.

Lottie stood for a moment in the doorway, watching the brothers make their way up the sodden black street; two tall shadows with Jeremy's short, sturdy one between them. The unpaved street was already several inches deep in water. The trails up to Eagle Head Point would be drowned.

Her warning to Aaron would have to wait.

Chapter 3

THE CABIN ON EAGLE HEAD POINT WAS FILLED WITH warm lamplight and the murmur of rain falling in the dusk outside. Aaron Stemple, sitting with a ledger and a bundle of financial reports in the wing chair in the small bedroom, listened to the plashing of rain and the moan of the wind and wasn't surprised that Lottie had not come up from town that day. Fresh storms were coming in, by the look of the sky that afternoon. It looked like a long siege.

He sighed, and turned back to his figuring, the rustle of papers a dry whisper in the small room. The mill was showing good profit, and would show more with the town building up as it was. There'd be more still in January, when he took over Bridal Veil Mountain from Jason Bolt.

Not that he didn't expect Bolt to put up a struggle over it. *Well,* he thought, *let him. I have the papers, signed and witnessed.* Because he knew for a fact that at least one of those girls would be unspoken for come January. Stemple couldn't imagine any man who would trade the joys of bachelorhood for matrimony with Biddy Cloom.

Biddy was Stemple's hole card. Five years older than the oldest of the other New Bedford girls and desperate for a man, Biddy had the coy predatoriness of one already treading the perilous line of old-maidhood that would drive away even the slightest expression of masculine interest.

It wasn't that she was a bad girl, really, thought Stemple. Just plain as a mud fence, and screechy-voiced and featherbrained into the bargain. A good heart coupled with an appalling lack of tact. Stemple chuckled to himself at the joke Fate had sprung on Jason Bolt. It might, he thought, just might, be worth it to see Bolt marry Biddy out of desperation. *He'll cheat me out of the mountain, but at what cost to himself!*

Stemple glanced up from his books, suddenly aware that the alien was watching him.

Their eyes met. The alien's were black, somber, intelligent, with the incurious calm of extreme weakness. Human eyes.

Stemple got to his feet, moving without haste, and came to the bedside. "You're among friends," he said quietly, knowing that the alien would not understand but knowing also that the sound of the voice alone can calm.

But the alien asked, "How did I come here?"

Stemple halted in his tracks. He did not know what he'd been expecting. But not that. Not English, and a deep, slightly rough-textured human voice. The host of implications of an English-speaking alien, with the ability somehow to have reached Earth from whatever planet he called home, crowded disturbingly to his mind. But he only replied, "I found you in the woods, eight days ago. You were unconscious, hurt badly. You're in the town of Seattle. My name is Aaron Stemple."

The stranger's gaze traveled slowly around the room, taking in the low, beamed ceiling; the fogged glass of the windowpanes with the dark tossing shapes of wet branches beyond; the clay-brick fireplace and faded oatmeal paper of the walls; the rag rug on the puncheon floor and the muted reds and blues of the quilt's kaleidoscope pattern. Then back, weary beyond curiosity or wonder, to Stemple's face. He said hesitantly, "Thank you."

"What happened?" asked Stemple. "How did you come to be hurt?"

The alien started to answer, then stopped, slanted brows pulling together into a frown. "I—I do not—recall," he said. "It is all—a silence." He stared into space for a moment, his breath suddenly coming quicker. Pain, or the memory of pain, lurked at the back of those haunted black eyes. "I have tried to remember why—what happened—where I was. . . ." He looked up at Stemple, fear and weariness and puzzlement clouding his face, making it more vulnerable and suddenly far more human. "I cannot. I do not even—remember—what I am called. I think . . ." The pain returned to the eyes, exhausted and baffled. "I'm so tired," he said quietly, and there was a break, like a hairline fracture, in the timbre of his voice.

"Don't worry about it," said Stemple encouragingly. "It'll come back to you when you're stronger." But he was shaken to the core. He had been prepared for any knowledge, but had not counted on continued ignorance. "You're safe here," he continued. "Do you feel strong enough to sit?"

The stranger nodded weakly and Stemple helped him to a sitting position, surprised again by the strength of the man's grip. Then he heard the alien's breath catch; followed his shocked gaze across the room to the mirror on the wall and the two faces, human and alien, reflected in the glass. He looked quickly back to the alien, and read shock in the dark eyes. "One of us," said the alien slowly, "is—different. Who are you and who am I?"

Stemple shook his head. "I'm very much afraid," he said, "that it is you who are different. You are—obviously—not of my people, not even of this world. I believe you are from some other world entirely, one that we have no knowledge of. Not even human, as we reckon human. I'm sorry," he added, watching the stricken horror on the man's face. "I was hoping you could tell me, but it doesn't matter."

The alien shook his head, numbly trying to gather what was left of mind and memories, to find something to hold to. "All of this"—his small gesture took in the room, the rain-light and trees beyond the window; his voice was hoarse with pain—"this is nothing that I remember—and now, nothing that I can be part of. It is all—emptiness, like a white hollow in my mind, as if I had never been. But if—if I am not even of this world—then there is nothing—nothing—" He paused, groping for the fragments of speech and thought that would let him go on accepting, not only isolation from his own world, his past, his self, but from his new world and his future as well. He sat for a long moment, lost in thought; then his hands began to shake, and a vast, sustained tremor took hold of him as he sank down, shuddering, his face buried in his hands. Stemple laid a compassionate hand on the quivering shoulders, but there was nothing that he could say to ease that terrible gulf of hurt. The stranger made no sound, but watching him, Stemple knew that Satan cast out of Heaven must have wept so.

For the next three days torrential rains turned the paths down the mountain to floods, and isolated the little cabin on the point. It was a silent world but for the roaring of the water. Stemple found that his fears regarding the alien had reversed themselves, for he saw the man as human now, human and far more vulnerable than the weakest of his race. Far from being without a soul, he saw in him a soul that was broken, and though the alien was able to be up and about now, Stemple had in the back of his mind the fear that he would not live long.

Something had broken in him. Whatever lifeline holds being to body had come loose, and the man was drifting. Stemple saw it in his eyes, haunted and frightened and puzzled; heard it in the enormous silence of the man's hesitant presence; felt it in the shaken, flinching movements as he limped around the cabin. He would listen politely to Stemple's endless coaching on the things of this world—what to do, what to say, what not to say—but there was no spark to him. Stemple felt he was only waiting his time to die.

On the third day of this Stemple had had enough. He was explaining something—the United States Government or tipping one's hat to ladies, it scarcely mattered which—the stranger listening and absorbing it all with the same quiet, commentless interest—when he glanced up, and saw the stranger's eyes. Something stopped his words in mid-sentence.

Exasperated, he snapped, "Talking to you is like talking to a wall. At least if I talked to a wall I'd get an echo."

"I am sorry," said the alien quietly, folding scarred and wasted hands on the table between them. "I have nothing to say. What you tell me is unfamiliar, and I have no comment."

"Well, say anything, dammit!" rasped Stemple. "Ask a question, give me an opinion, anything!"

The alien began to speak, stopped, fumbling for

words. Then, "Aaron—what purpose is served by telling me all this?"

Stemple was startled into momentary silence. Outside the light rain drummed on the cabin roof, puckered the reflections of the last evening light that grayed the sheeted water in the flooded dooryard. "When you leave here," he said at last, "you'll have to make your way in this world. People are mostly ignorant and vicious, and fear the unknown. If you're not going to be spotted as an alien, a misfit, and killed out of hand, you'll have to know enough of the ground rules to get by."

The alien regarded him in silence for a moment. By the lamplight Stemple noticed uneasily that he'd lost flesh, that he looked drawn and wasted, worse instead of better. He asked, "What makes you think that I shall live long enough to put your advice into practice?"

It was Stemple's turn to fish for words, and find none. "What?"

"Aaron—has it not occurred to you that my only logical course of action is to die?"

"*What?*" He had known the alien ate next to nothing—it had not occurred to him before this that he might be deliberately starving himself. "What in hell does logic have to do with it?"

"It is logical," insisted the alien quietly. "I am less than nothing in this world. A stranger in a strange land, with every man's hand turned against me. I am neither myself nor anything else. Death is my only alternative."

"The hell it is!" roared Aaron.

The alien only regarded him with those sterile dark eyes, registering the display of emotion without feeling any in return. "I am sorry, Aaron," he said, quite sincerely. "I appreciate your motives in giving me the choice, but—how much do you think I can learn? With no experience, I shall be identified very quickly, and, if your estimate of human conduct is correct, very likely killed in short order. As is logical, for if your civilization has no space-flight capability, my position here is an anomaly which it would be easier to eliminate than to let stand. And even were I not killed, what would it be worth to me to continue the masquerade? I will always be different. I will always be alone. What is life worth to me on those terms?"

Stemple regarded him for a moment, seeing, and wishing he did not see, the sharp cant of the eyebrows, the strange ears half-concealed under the long black hair, the black eyes empty of everything save pain.

Oddly enough, Stemple remembered a time when he himself had been trapped and alone. Ten years old, sewing in the blazing heat of a Boston sweatshop, with no place to stay but that single crowded room and nothing to eat but what they chose to give him for his labor. No money, no way to escape and nowhere to go if he did. The despair came back to him like the taste of the watery soup and the stink of stale sweat. No way out, and no one caring.

"Life is life," he said quietly. "You're alive and you hope."

"Hope?" The black gaze shifted from him to the mirror and back again, with calm irony.

"Hope you can get away with it another day," said Stemple wryly. "Hell, hope you may meet one of your own people here on this planet one day."

"I would not recognize them if I did," pointed out the alien reasonably.

"Maybe not. But they'd recognize you."

The alien considered this, expressionless. Stemple pushed his point. "You came here for a purpose," he said, "you have to have. Whoever sent you, whyever they sent you, they wouldn't have sent just one man. I don't think you came alone and I don't think your memory will be gone forever. And if you don't remember—you will have a different life than you had before, that's all."

Still the alien remained silent, and Stemple could feel him retreating, drawing back into that polite, wary shell. Suddenly weary of the whole business, Stemple got to his feet and made his way back to the lean-to kitchen, leaving his strange visitor to puzzle that one out for himself. He had said all he could say.

Maybe too much, he reflected, digging around in the cupboard for bread and salt beef and cheese. Maybe death was his only way out, though it chilled him to hear the alien refer to it as a logical alternative. But that was like this man—precise, well-reasoned, intellectually considering even the most appalling of alternatives with that chill calm. He dumped a handful of coffee into the pot and set it on the back of the stove, cursing as the steam burned his fingers.

Still—memory was a strange thing. He'd forgotten his own days without hope, until tonight. Well, not forgotten. He'd remembered being hungry, being cold, being scared—being scared all the time. From a vast distance he contemplated that skinny, hook-nosed little boy in his shabby, cut-down knee pants and man's shirt, sleeves rolled up over bony wrists. He'd always remembered that. But not until tonight had he recalled how it had felt, to know that no one cared. If he had died then, of cold or hunger or whatever it is that children die of in the slums of Boston, no one would have cared. He remembered how it had felt to know that.

He was sorry he had lashed out at the alien.

Quietly, he went back into the parlor. It was empty, as was the tiny bedroom. Listening in the silence for

52

the familiar dragging limp, he realized that the rain had stopped.

The alien was sitting outside on the stump in the dooryard, a slim dark figure in his borrowed shirt and jeans. The wind soughed in the dark pines, making a noise like the roaring of the sea, breaking the black cover of the clouds.

The alien was looking at the stars.

They spread in fierce glory behind the shadow of his head, the Milky Way unfurled like a banner of light, the Hunter of the Heavens coursing his jewel-eyed hound. Aaron paused in the doorway, awed by that great beauty; the alien heard his step, and turned his head.

"It seems," he said in his quiet voice, "that although I do not remember, I recognize things that I have seen before. This . . ." The movement of his hand took in all the turning firmament. "I . . . I know. I have seen it before, know the names and magnitudes and distances from one star to the other, and the navigation of the darkness between. I feel that I know things about the stars that I would remember at once, if only I could be reminded. But I know them." In the star shadow his face was unreadable, but there was life, and a kind of mild amusement, in his voice. "If this much is possible, perhaps it is within the bounds of possibility that I can—pass for human."

Stemple had been going to say something else, but he smiled, though the cold wind bit into his shirtsleeved arms. "If that much is possible, maybe you can answer me a question."

The alien considered. "So far my success in that field has been limited. Yet unlikeliness of an answer places no stricture upon the asking of a question."

There was absolutely no jest in his tone, but Stemple detected some note in it that told him that the alien was not without humor. And that in turn implied both humanity and acceptance of life. "I think you can answer this," he said. "How are you at accounting?"

A quick, startled turn of the head, recognizing the offer, and touched by the welcome and all that it implied. In the starlight, one slanted eyebrow lifted.

Chapter 4

SPOCK'S VOICE CRACKLED, HARSH AND STRAINED BUT perfectly level, into the silence of that small room.

"White dwarf, Khlaru, Tillman's Factor, Guardian." There was a long pause. Then, as calmly as if the words had not been his death sentence, "Eighteen sixty seven." Then again that riddling silence, broken only by the faint hiss of the recording machinery until Kirk touched the button that stilled even that.

After a long pause McCoy said, "The Guardian." He folded his hands around his glass of bourbon, stared down into its clear gold depths for a time, going back for a moment to memories that were largely a nightmare blur of madness. Kirk remained unmoving at the small console that contained both recorder and terminal to tap into the Starbase Twelve central computer. "He knew you'd understand."

From the depths of a very old-fashioned overstuffed armchair, Base Commander Kellogg asked, "What was the Guardian?"

Kirk started to speak, then let his breath out unused. He sat silent for a time, wondering how he could best explain the Guardian that stands in the ruins of the City on the Edge of Forever.

The official part of his report to Base Commander Kellogg was over. Kirk had detailed for the record his own minor infringement of the Organian Peace Treaty, the disappearance of the Klingon ore transport and with it that of his science officer, now listed MIA. The recording machines were off now, and Kellogg had returned with him to the visiting officers' quarters for the unofficial part of the interview, for bourbon and supposition and thought.

Like the rest of the visitors' quarters of the base, this sitting room between Kirk's room and McCoy's was essentially Karsid in appearance, part of the far older hive of tunnels that base funds had been too limited to refurbish. It was a sort of bubble in the rock of the planetoid itself, slightly larger than humans would consider comfortable, with a little round fireplace set halfway up one wall. The massive table beside the fireplace was Karsid, too, of the last decadent period, fluid and overly serpentine-looking, especially in contrast to the rest of the furnishings, which were of a style Lieutenant Uhura generally referred to as Star Fleet Ugly. The small terminal/video unit and the overstuffed armchair in which Kellogg now sat had the appearance of lost travelers from separate galaxies who had wandered in by mistake.

"The incident of the Guardian," said Kirk finally, "dealt with the retroactive alteration of history. The Guardian itself is a gateway—a gateway to Time."*

He kept his voice neutral as he spoke of the events leading to the death of a woman whose voice he still occasionally heard in dreams. McCoy's gaze flickered sharply to him, then away.

*Star Trek episode, "City on the Edge of Forever," by Harlan Ellison.

"That section of the *Enterprise* Log is classified, for obvious reasons. Spock, McCoy and I are the only ones who know the full story."

"Could the Klingons have found out?" asked Kellogg worriedly, folding her long fingers like a pile of ivory spindles on her bony knee. "Could they have discovered it for themselves, for instance?"

"They could have," said Kirk. "But it's a great distance from here. They'd have to pass through huge tracts of Federation space to reach it, or else travel sectors out of their way. And the Federation does keep an eye on the planet. Always supposing they knew where and what it was, I don't think they'd be able to get down to the surface."

"If they had some kind of new weapon they might not have been worried about the Federation guards."

"Might they have been on their way there," asked McCoy somberly, "and they entered the Tau Eridani Cloud simply as an evasive maneuver, to lose us? For that matter, they could have been destroyed in the cloud itself. With the gravitational effects of the white dwarf star it must be twice as difficult to navigate— they could have been blown to ions."

"They could have." Kellogg leaned back in her armchair and slung a casual knee over its arm. The dim colors of the lamplight and fire gleamed on the gold of her tunic. "I'll bet you Metebelis crystals to little green apples that they didn't, though. The Klingon imperial representative on this base never reported that transport missing, in spite of the fact that the *Rapache* passed within hailing distance on its way back to its home turf."

Kirk's eyebrows went up. "Oh, really?"

A wry smile flicked at the corner of her lips. "The imp rep here might not like dealing with a woman BC, but he follows the regs like they were his hope of

Heaven. It's standing orders that any ship, even drones, that disappears anywhere near that cloud gets reported. That thing . . ." She gestured, a casual motion of the hand to indicate the unplumbed hole in the cosmos at the heart of the Tau Eridani Cloud. ". . . seems to be variable. Nobody's ever really figured out what it is—not even the Karsids, and it was smack in the middle of their space. I think they put this base here for the same reason we did—to keep an eye on it. It—changes. It does funny things sometimes. And it's a damn sight too close for comfort. So anything strange that goes on in or near the cloud has *got* to be reported, to the Science Section and to me, personally. And the imp rep hasn't said dicky bird." She shrugged, and reached for her bourbon glass again. "So your friends might still be headed for the planet of the Guardian."

"They might." Kirk stared for a long time at the reflection of the firelight in the liquor, as though, like a seer, he could call images in it of things far away. "But on the other hand, Spock had only a second or two to work with, and he was picking his words very carefully. He knew the transmission might be intercepted. He might have been speaking metaphorically—that the Klingons' goal was not to tamper with the Guardian per se, but to accomplish the same thing in another fashion—the retroactive readjustment of history."

There was silence, broken by Kellogg's uncomfortable murmur, "They can't really do that, can they?"

"I damn near managed it," retorted McCoy bitterly.

"They can," said Kirk, his voice almost inaudible, as if he spoke to himself. "Believe me, they can. But if they're in the past now, it means they already have."

"There is no *past now,*" pointed out Kellogg. "And anyway, what would they change? And where and when? Even if they could create a time warp."

"That's just it," said Kirk, glancing up at them in the restive flickering of the shadows. "Time warps can be created—generally accidentally, but I've heard rumors of civilizations that deal in them as a matter of course. What made the incident of the Guardian so nearly disastrous was that we were operating at random. We had no idea what would be changed, what kinds of ripples of events we would set up. If that could be predicted . . ."

"Could it?" McCoy demanded.

Kirk and Kellogg exchanged a glance. "If you had a big enough computer," Kellogg said finally, "you could narrow it down pretty close."

There was another uneasy pause. McCoy rose from his chair with a kind of explosive restlessness. "Great. Just great, Jim. They've narrowed it down pretty close, but the rest of us are left with an eternity of time and every possible point in the galaxy to choose from."

"Not every possible point," Kellogg corrected him, and glanced over at Kirk again. "What's Tillman's Factor?"

"According to the mathematicians in the Science Section, it's a mathematical constant dealing with acceleration past light-speed. I suspect there's some relationship between that and the white dwarf star that the Klingons might have used to create a temporary time slip."

"And the numbers?" asked Kellogg. "Could they be a triangulation?"

Kirk shook his head. "We thought of that. Navigationally they're meaningless, either as eighteen, sixty and seven, or as eighteen and sixty-seven."

"Time, then? Though that would have been 19:07," she answered herself. The way she said it, nineteen-oh-seven, triggered something in Kirk's memory.

"Time in another sense, maybe?" he said. "An Earthdate?"

"No," she said disbelievingly.

"Old Reckoning," said Kirk. "Without the B.C. or A.D. or O.R. We're so used to thinking in Stardates and Standard—but it could be an O.R. Earthdate."

"Yeah, but even in O.R. they'd still use B.C. or A.D.," protested Kellogg.

"Not necessarily," said McCoy suddenly. "Edith . . ." His voice barely paused over the name of the woman whose life Kirk had prevented him from saving. "Edith Keeler didn't."

"No," said Kirk softly. "I remember her saying, 'Nineteen-thirty,' not 'A.D. nineteen-thirty.' And besides," he added, "Spock had to keep it short."

"It would tie in," said McCoy. "What's Khlaru?"

"I fed that into the *Enterprise* computer," said Kirk. "There were several possible spellings and pronunciations, though I tried to stay as close to Spock's inflection as I could on vocal. Khlaru is a place, a province on Klinzhai itself."

McCoy's eyebrows went up. "Klinzhai?" he said. "That's going to be tough if we're going to try to second-guess them, Jim. My Klingon history is about nil."

Kirk nodded glumly. "So's mine, I'm afraid. All I know is that they were taken over by the Karsids about six hundred years ago, and went from a feudal society to a space-flight one—albeit as mercenaries of the Karsid Empire—without any interim development. In a way they're a sort of object lesson in the non-interference directive. It was their rebellions that hastened the downfall of the Karsids. Their own empire is founded directly on Karsid technology and Karsid ruling systems. They simply stepped into the power vacuum when the Karsid Empire crumbled. But about individual events of Klingon history, particularly before the takeover, I'm afraid I'm as ignorant as you are, Bones."

"And I thought you majored in history," McCoy grumbled.

"I did." Kirk's grin was rueful. "But space flight put the oar into generalized history of any kind. Commander?"

Kellogg's eyebrows shot upwards. "Don't look at me, Jamie, I'm only an engineer. But I'll tell you one thing—Khlaru isn't just a place on Klinzhai."

She rolled to her feet, and set her glass down on the dark, shining surface of the room's big table. "About ten years ago they dug a cache of old Karsid records out of the rock here, the only ones they've found outside the Klingon Empire. There's been a couple of research teams going through them for years. One of them's funded through the Vulcan Academy of Archives—the other one's Klingon. The head of the Klingon team is a man named Khlaru."

"An interesting supposition." Trae of Vulcanis tented his thin fingers and regarded Kirk, McCoy and Kellogg over them with wise, ancient black eyes. He was old, even for a Vulcan, his hair turned snow white and his faced seamed with marks of an age more awesome, in its experience and intelligence, than any human can survive to achieve. He was well into his third century and, if he did not choose to die before that time, looked good to make it into his fourth.

The sense about him of the limitless piling of ages, of wisdom garnered and unforgotten, melded the old man with his rooms, making him one with them as a dragon is one with his hoard. Beyond the small cleared space that surrounded the semicircle of padded couch, the place was an archive, piled high with boxes of microfilm runouts, crates of discs and tapes, photocopies of original records curled together like ancient scrolls and pages of jotted notes scattered like leaves after autumn winds. There were books there, too, massive and leatherbound, and Kirk's whole bibliophile soul so yearned to touch that he had to put his hands behind his back. In the midst of it all rose two computer terminals, like islands in the shifting seas of time. They hummed and blinked at one another as if conversing in their operator's temporary absence.

Kirk turned away from surveying this enchanted sanctum at the sound of Kellogg's voice. She asked, "Is it scientifically feasible?"

"A time warp?" The Vulcan considered, with the relaxed immobility that humans never attain—no shrug, no gesture, no motion whatsoever, still and quiet as air. "I am not a scientist, Commander. But as a historian I have come to believe that any scientific achievement is not only feasible, but at some time, on some planet, has been commonplace.

"Nevertheless," he went on, regarding them from those old, wrinkled eyes, "this—retroactive readjustment of history. Writers of speculative fiction revel in it. Scientists, theoretical physicists, examine the mechanical constructs and fear dreadful consequences. But how much could one do, by simple means? Contemporaries dabble in it all the time, optimistically attempting to change the course of history, but what does it bring them? To use the paradigm of your own planet, Commander Kellogg, the death of Julius Caesar did not prevent the imperialization of an already politically moribund Roman Republic."

"You may be right," agreed Kirk, turning from the stacks of books to face the three who stood between couches and computer terminals, restless in the shadows like some black-and-gold, scholarly tiger.

"But the incident of the Guardian proved that change can be affected, at certain times and under certain conditions. It doesn't have to be a big change. It could—in fact it would almost have to be—a very small one, analogous to the rerouting of a single synapse in brain tissue."

"Which," added McCoy quietly, "they'll be able to do in a very few years."

"The fact that the Klingons are attempting it at all— have taken as much trouble as it appears they have— indicates to me that they are working to gain some specific end by a specific act." He came back to stand before the Vulcan, the faintly blinking lights of the larger of the two terminals alternating in red and green patterns over them like a water reflection. "What was your colleague Khlaru working on?"

"Nothing so melodramatic as you seem to believe," replied Trae steadily. "Like myself, Khin Khlaru was engaged in the cataloging of Karsid records for this sector covering the last fifty years of the Karsid Empire's occupancy of this asteroid. Copies of official correspondence, technical readouts from the base, reports regarding the shifts within the Tau Eridani Cloud, shipping cost indexes. That is the true stuff of history, Captain, and the reason that history is more difficult to rewrite than it seems. The information is only valuable to those with an interest in the final days of the empire's hegemony, and in the effect of the first Orion revolts upon outpost stations. There is nothing in it that would save the galaxy, or alter the course of the empire's inevitable decay."

His deep voice was still expressionless, but Kirk thought he saw a faint flicker of something at the back of those dark eyes. "Moreover, my colleague Khin Khlaru is, like myself, first and foremost a historian, and a man of honor and intelligence. As a military man, Captain Kirk, you have become accustomed to regarding all Klingons as unquestioning servants of their emperor. I assure you that in Khlaru's case this is an error on your part."

He folded his narrow hands upon the sable of his sleeves. "To tamper at all with time is almost unfeasible because of the veritable mountain of random factors involved, factors which could be neither foreseen nor controlled. If the tampering were done in a pre-space-flight society, anything that far away from us in time would be subject to a Doppler effect of cumulative events. In a space-flight contact society the exponential progression of the ripple effect would be totally unmanageable. Khlaru is not a fool, Captain, nor is he any man's puppet. I sincerely doubt that even were such a project afoot within the Klingon Intelligence and Security circles he would have anything to do with an act so appallingly irresponsible."

"Very well," Kirk said quietly after a moment. "Could Spock have been referring to the old realm of Khlaru? Could 1867 be a pre-Karsid Klingon date?"

Trae considered for a moment, eyes thinned to slits of thought as he fished in the awesome darkness of his memory. "As I recall, the planet Klinzhai had no standard system of dates before Karsid takeover," he replied finally. "Most areas used reign-dating by the name of the local ruler, sometimes in conjunction with two or even three simultaneous cycles of identifying years. Khlaru—if indeed Spock was referring to the old realm of Khlaru on Klinzhai and not to my colleague—I believe was one of them."

He crossed to the larger of the two terminals in a slurring rustle of black robes. Skeleton-fragile fingers played over the input board for a moment, paused, then tapped in something else.

Watching the play of the green light over those

sharp-angled features, Kirk wondered if Spock would have become like that in time, when his Vulcan body had outlived those of his few human friends. Would he have settled into that distant and terrifying calm, coming at last to terms with the buried human side of his nature? Or would its stresses have grown instead of lessened, and eventually destroyed him? How human, Kirk wondered, had Spock been? How much of that occasionally maddening calm had been his true nature—the nature he was born with—and how much the result of his Vulcan conditioning?

Hard to tell, thought Kirk, with sudden wryness. *How much of my own stubbornness was inborn, and how much acquired in self-defense against a stubborn father? Who can pick apart the knots of the human soul, or trace the chains of circumstances to their first roots? Any event, as Trae said, causes its ripples. Spock had been what he had been: an enigma to his death.*

With a faint whirring noise the terminal extruded a half meter of hard copy. Trae tore off the pale green flimsiplast and returned to his guests. "Dating system in the realm of Khlaru just prior to Karsid first contact was a triple cycle of reign dates: the Arastphrid System common to the Gharhuil Continent in that era, and a longer cycle based on the variable star Algol. Thus the first Karsid contacts—which, of course, were in the Karsid's usual form of 'traders from another land,' as they never disclosed the fact that they were alien until their hold on the economy was virtually unbreakable—was recorded as 'In the Year of the Gashkrith in the reign of Khorad son of N'gar in the five-hundredth cycle of Algol'—or Shem, as they sometimes called that star. After the Karsids had established economic influence over the entire planet—not difficult to do, considering that Klinzhai was just entering into the early phases of industrialization and there was constant rivalry between the semi-industrial cloth-manufacturing towns and the land-based patriarchate—to the point where the Klingons could not do without them, the Karsids imposed cultural unity, wiped out recalcitrant minorities, dissidents and splinter-groups and adopted Klinzhai into full tributary status in Karsid Imperial Year 930."

He lowered the flimsiplast and looked at his guests.

Kellogg murmured, "And not an 1867 in sight."

A little despairingly, Kirk said, "And what was the Earth date when all this was happening on Klinzhai?"

Spock would have elevated one eyebrow. Trae had seemingly outgrown such extravagant emotional displays. He turned back to his computer terminal without a word. After a moment he replied, "Karsid first contact with the rulers of Thersach—the most warlike and socially flexible of the industrial federations— correlates to Earthdate O.R.-1486-A.D. Induction to full tributary status O.R. 1540-A.D."

McCoy frowned. " They didn't waste any time."

"It is surprising," remarked Trae, making a handwritten note at the top corner of the readout and placing it unerringly in one of the myriad of completely unmarked pigeonholes that formed a sort of wine rack of cubbyholes along the rear wall of the study, "how quickly a senior technology can acquire a stranglehold over a junior one—particularly if it knows how to play on inner rivalries within the junior culture. Basically, the Karsids took over in a single generation, as soon as the majority of the population had never known a time without these new weapons, new luxury goods. . . . "

"New drugs?" put in Kellogg cynically. She had seen Klingon methods of takeover.

The historian lowered his wrinkled eyelids a fraction

of a centimeter. "Not generally. The Karsids were neither savages nor fools. They wanted intact, semi-industrial economies that they could develop and exploit, not herds of opiated slaves. Civilizations under their rule tended to be physically healthier and more puritanical than their self-governing forebears. The Karsids used drugs in specific incidents—a technique which the Klingons have adapted to their own use—but in most cases they operated on the simple theory that no nation will willingly forgo its source of machine guns to return to the use of the bow and arrow."

His dark gaze returned to Kirk again. "Do you wish to question my colleague Khlaru himself on this subject?" he asked.

Kirk hesitated for a long moment, weighing factors in his mind. His instincts told him to trust the ancient Vulcan's evaluation of his Klingon colleague. Vulcans seldom declare any feeling of their own, and when they do, it is not without careful thought.

Kellogg broke in with, "You want the whole thing to get relayed to the imp rep? Whether Khlaru himself is a man of honor or not, he's obliged to report questions to his superiors. If the Klingons even get the hint that we're onto them, God knows what could happen."

Trae's eyes moved from Kirk to Kellogg and back again. It was the tiniest of gestures, but Kirk could feel Kellogg bristle under the implied dismissal of the military mind.

After a moment's thought he said, "No. Not yet. But what we have spoken of, we have spoken of in confidence."

"This I understand," said Trae quietly. "The matter is none of my affair."

"If you hear of anything . . ." he began, and the Vulcan, who had turned away, glanced back at him.

"I have said that it is none of my affair," he reiterated. "You can scarcely speak ill of Khin Khlaru for reporting to his superiors what he hears, and then require me to do the same. I am a historian, Captain. I am not engaged in your temporary conflict with the Klingon Empire."

Kirk inclined his head, accepting the rebuke. "My apologies," he said. "But if it happens that you do find yourself engaged in that conflict in the future, come to one of us."

With that he led the way from the room, and the transition from the age-piled gloom of the rock chamber to the bright aluminum and plastic of the halls of the starbase was like emerging from dreams into the cold brightness of an eternal and artificial day.

Chapter 5

"LOTTIE." CANDY PRUITT LOOKED UP IN SURPRISE AS the saloonkeeper emerged onto the gallery above the main barroom. "Where are you off to? It'll be raining again before noon."

Lottie came down the stairs, pulling her gloves on as she moved. She paused for a moment to look down at the saloon, and smiled. The place was closed, as it always was this time of the morning, and filled with girls.

They were turning the place into a rope walk with stretched clothesline, stringing it from the rough banisters back and forth across the big room; chattering, giggling, talking as they worked. The place smelled of wet laundry and soap and the cool wintry smell of the rain, that had fallen steadily, drearily, on Seattle for the last four days now. The saloon itself was warm, and the wet clothes and the girls' damp skirts steamed faintly in the cool filtered daylight.

Lottie loved the girls. They were young, most of them, but above the age when girls back East would be married. Some of them had lost sweethearts in the War; others, only the chance to have them. New

Bedford had been a town bereft of three-quarters of a generation of young men when those unlikely Pied Pipers, Roland Francis Clancey and Jeremy Bolt, had arrived, with the promise of a brave new world out beyond the frontier. Whether the girls had sought a woman's destiny of marriage and children, or only forgetfulness of what had been, they were the ones who had turned their backs on their old lives and old memories, and that itself gave them a kind of beauty.

Lottie smiled down at them, listening to their treble babble. Candy Pruitt turned her head to give some instruction to the girls stretching a clothes-rope, her mahogany red hair gleaming in the pale light like wet autumn leaves. She was the unofficial spokeswoman and captain of the New Bedford girls, twenty years old, her face less pretty than strongly beautiful, with its close, secretive mouth. She was slim and strong as oak, and Lottie had often considered Candy as a good match for Jason Bolt. It would need her kind of stubbornness and temper to keep that big, bold bastard in line. And so it might have been, had Candy not met Jeremy Bolt first.

Candy came over to Lottie as the saloonkeeper finished her descent. "Thank you for letting us use the saloon to dry in, Lottie. I think we were down to the last of the clean towels, and there's simply no room in that dormitory to get anything properly dried."

"And besides, it's baking day," Biddy Cloom put in, shaking out white cotton petticoats briskly and hunting in her apron pockets for clothespins. "*And* Sheila's meeting her beau in the parlor this afternoon, and she said she'd *kill* us if she had to do it with everyone's *unmentionables* dripping on the floor."

"And who's Sheila's beau this week?" asked Lottie, smiling.

"*Well,*" Biddy said archly, fluttering her straight, thin eyelashes, "*I'm* certainly not one to spread tales, *but* . . ."

"Jules Horne." Candy stepped equably into Biddy's dramatics. "And you haven't said where you're off to yet, Lottie. Look, it's already starting to rain again. You'd better take my cloak."

She made a move toward the piled cloaks that the girls had left heaped on the end of the bar. Their mothers would die if they knew their daughters came and went in a public saloon as freely as if it were their own living room. Never during open hours, never familiarizing with the men who came to drink, but still, their mothers would have said, it was the principle of the thing. Ladies didn't frequent saloons, and they certainly didn't lend their cloaks to the type of woman who ran them.

Someone knocked on the front door, and through the pebbly glass of the windows Lottie could make out two gray, silhouetted figures. She yelled, "We're closed!"

A voice called back, "It's Aaron, Lottie!"

Her heart jumped, and she hurried to let him in.

"Aaron," she said quickly, as she opened the door, "I have something important to . . ." She stopped, looking past over his shoulder.

"Lottie," introduced Aaron formally, "this is my nephew, Ishmael Marx. Ish—Lottie Hatfield."

Lottie's blue eyes met Aaron's dark ones, wide and warning, frightened at the memory of those two other aliens. Then they went past, and met the black, oddly wise gaze of the alien.

Softly, Aaron said, "He's lost his memory. We thought it was best this way."

"I—I'm sorry," said Lottie, confused, not knowing what else to say. She held out her hand, and Ishmael bowed very properly over it.

His eyes met hers again, and he said for her ears alone, "Aaron tells me that you know."

"I—yes. I saw you."

"Then I thank you for your silence." He had an odd mouth, strangely shaped, thin but sensual. The slant of the eyebrows and the tips of the strange ears were hidden under Indian-straight black hair, which had been suffered to grow long, after the custom of a country where barbers are few. For the rest, she had an impression of catlike slimness and darkness; faded trousers, a dark sweater, a dark plaid jacket. When he moved past her into the saloon she saw that he was lame.

Then she became aware of the loud silence in the room behind them. She turned, to meet the watching, curious eyes of the girls. Seattle was a small town, and any stranger worthy of mark; particularly, thought Lottie suddenly, this one. She glanced up at the hawk profile, then back at the girls.

Stemple broke the silence. He stepped into the room, said, "Ladies, permit me to introduce my nephew, Ishmael Marx. He's come to Seattle from the East; he'll be doing the accounting at the mill. Ishmael—Jason Bolt's seraglio."

Those who didn't know what a seraglio was only studied Ish with frank and lively interest, but Stemple caught a glimpse of warning fire in Candy Pruitt's eye. Under cover of the chatter of introductions, he took Lottie aside, and asked her, "What was it you wanted to tell me, when we came in? Something important, you said?"

Past him, Ishmael was listening to the soft soprano confusion of the girls' voices; deferential, attentive—

not out of flattery, as Lottie knew some men would listen, but out of grave and genuine interest in this crowd of very young strangers. She said, "What do you mean, he's lost his memory?"

Stemple shook his head. "He was injured, I don't know how. But he can't remember how he got here, what brought him to Earth. He remembers nothing of where he came from, what happened to him, not even his own name."

He glanced over his shoulder. Candy was gently, patiently drawing this stranger out of his reserve; Ishmael picking his way cautiously through the morass of this first test of his disguises. "He's very adaptive," Stemple went on. "He learns fast. But I thought I'd better break him in here, before he meets anyone more suspicious than the girls."

Typical of Stemple, thought Lottie, not sure whether to be amused or admiring. The man had manipulated people and situations for his own ends so long that he could use that talent to serve someone else's needs. She knew, as he'd known, that the girls would be too fascinated by this dark stranger to notice or question the little lapses that must occur, and that would give Ishmael time to find his feet.

"Then he's starting out clean," she said. "Like a child."

"No," replied Stemple. "Like every man who comes West with something in his past he'd rather forget, and have forgotten." His dark eyes rested on hers for a moment with ironic amusement. "I imagine there are men who'd pay gold for what Ish seems to have gotten at the cost of a sprung knee and a couple of burns."

Lottie sighed, remembering some of the past, and her own reasons for coming West. "Ladies, too, Aaron," she murmured. "Ladies too."

"What was it you wanted to tell me?"

She shook her head. "It wasn't important."

"All of these young ladies belong to Jason Bolt?" asked Ishmael, bending his head under the light rain as they moved along the soupy mess of what was optimistically called Madison Street. Stemple heard the light irony in Ish's voice, and thought, *You've come far, fast, my friend.*

He grinned wryly. "In a sense."

"Fascinating."

The rain barely ruffled at the puddles that sheeted the muddy thoroughfare—the two men kept to the rim of tussocks that bordered the straggling buildings. Behind them, Seattle spread itself in a brave display of clapboard, canvas and mud over its hills—a handful of stores, a land office, two liveries, a laundry operated by some stout and smiling relative of Lottie's barboy Wu Sin and the half-erected plank walls of some larger building with delusions of grandeur. Like a wall behind the town, the mountains rose, a looming blue-green bulk of mist-shawled trees, diminishing down into lesser mountains as they approached the town and finally to the hills on which Seattle itself was built. The street sloped down to the harbor, where the masts of the San Francisco lumber boats and the coast-running sloops bobbed at anchor, a second forest. The wind made tracks of white on Elliott Bay, and blew the salt smell of the sound over the shabby town. Laundry hung on more than one covered porch, and smoke poured in white billows from tin chimneys, caught and whipping like thin clouds into the mist gray sky.

Just above the harbor, where First Street branched off toward the mill, Aaron and Ishmael passed a large pine barn of a building, two stories high and narrow, surrounded by a white picket fence and a border of dripping autumn flowers. "That's the dormitory," said Stemple. "And that . . ." He gestured toward the eye-piercingly rich green of the slopes that rose nearest above the town to the south, its trees thrusting into the soft shroud of mist that hid its towering head. ". . . is Bridal Veil Mountain. And Bridal Veil, and Seattle, and that dormitory, make the three strangest bedfellows since—well, never mind."

Overhead, gulls wheeled, crying. From here the turmoil around the docks could be seen and heard, a milling of men and horses hauling logs and cut timber, the strident arguing of voices.

"As you may have noticed," Aaron continued expansively, "Seattle isn't what you'd call much of a town. It's at the back end of nowhere, the wettest, coldest, unpleasantest piece of real estate you're going to find in this end of the Territories. But it does grow good trees, and it's got the best harbor to ship them out of on this coast. The town's going to be big one day, but right at the moment it doesn't have a whole lot to recommend it.

"Now," he continued, as they descended the deteriorating First Street toward the trees that screened the mill from town, "I can hire transients, men passing through. You'll find out all about that once you try doing the payroll accounts. If there's a bit of flux—well, it gets made up, and I've got the capital to see me through times when the output's slack because we haven't got enough men. But Jason, he needs a full crew if he's going to make his contracts. And although he owns the mountain, he doesn't have the capital to pay week by week. He needs a settled town, and settled men."

Aaron shrugged. "But why's a man going to settle out here in the wet back end of the world just to cut trees? It got to a point where Jason's men threatened to quit him, if he didn't get them some ladies—not San Francisco fancy ladies, but real ladies, wives and mothers for the new town. The land's a land of promise, but at thirty men for every woman, there wasn't much reason to settle here.

"So Jason came up with the scheme of sending Captain Clancey around Cape Horn to the East, to bring out girls to marry the settlers."

"I see." Ishmael turned back to look at the dormitory again, small as a pine cracker carton on its long, narrow lot, its bright calico curtains only vague blurs inside the heat-misted windows, smoke billowing from its kitchen chimney.

"I told you about the War," Stemple went on. "It left the East short of men, and left a lot of girls without any prospect of marriage. Clancey and Jeremy Bolt got back there—oh, late in '66. They got thirty girls to make the trip back with them."

Ish nodded. "A practical, if somewhat insensitive, scheme," he agreed. "And where does Bridal Veil Mountain fit into this tale?"

Stemple chuckled. "Well, Jason Bolt, for all he owns it, isn't a man of means. Wiving the settlers wasn't altruism on his part; his men would have walked out on him. But it costs money to bring those girls out here, and costs money to keep them till they choose the men they'll marry. His back was to the wall, and he had to have financial backing."

He grinned at the memory of it. "Now, Jason Bolt and I have never gotten along. He's as arrogant a son of a bitch as you're likely to meet, but he can charm the little birds out of the trees. The month I came here I bought title to Bridal Veil Mountain, at the sale of old John Bolt's estate, only to find he'd deeded the mountain in gift to his three sons jointly the night before he died. Jason won the case, and kept the mountain, and since then we've done each other a dirty turn or two.

"So the long and the short of it was: Jason bet me title to Bridal Veil Mountain, and got his two brothers to sign the papers, in exchange for my paying the expense of bringing those girls out to Seattle and providing them board and keep for a year. And if every one of those girls isn't married or spoken for in a year—Bridal Veil is mine."

"And do the girls know this?" inquired Ishmael.

Stemple shook his head. "I think Candy Pruitt suspects. They know there's some kind of bet going about their getting married in the first year, but they don't know Jason Bolt's going to lose his mountain over it."

They passed through a patch of the woods that hemmed Seattle so thickly on three sides, climbed a short, steep hill in the slaty shadows of the trees. The roar of the creek was deafening from here, and they could hear the incessant, high-pitched buzzing of the saws. As if through a gateway they stepped into daylight again, and paused at the head of the sloppy pathway that drenched its way down to the mill. Ahead of them to their left stood the small, whitewashed box of the mill offices, and behind that, where the ground rose again by the fall of the creek, the long buildings of the mill itself. Stump-scarred and trashy with shavings, the hillslope around Stemple's Mill looked like a badly shaved chin. Men could be seen there, moving about among the tall stacks of lumber. Soupy with mud and rain, a narrow path wound away past a screen of trees to where Aaron's four-room town house stood. Beyond, the dark bulk of tree-cloaked mountains reared into the obscuring mists.

"And will Jason Bolt lose his mountain?" inquired Ishmael curiously.

"Oh, yes," said Stemple. "The wager's up January first. He has—three and a half months. Of the thirty, ten girls are married already, and half the rest are spoken for. If I know Jason he'll be working like a beaver in a bad autumn to get the rest off his hands by Christmas." Stemple grinned. "But he won't get them all."

"Is this the law of averages, or a certainty?"

Stemple laughed. "A little of both. Come on, I'll show you the mill offices. God knows taking you on as my accountant isn't doing you any favors. The work's months behind." He pointed away down the path. "That's home," he added, and strode off toward the small, shabby offices.

Limping in his wake, Ishmael instinctively checked out the lay of the land, then spared a glance toward the pie-shaped segment of ridgepole and clapboard visible through the trees. In spite of the loss of his memory, he wondered why he had the impression that he had never called anywhere "home" in his life.

Chapter 6

"SO WHAT DO YOU THINK OF HIM?" ASKED CANDY Pruitt, coming back from the sideboard with coffee and seating herself between Jeremy and Joshua at the long oak table in the Bolt kitchen.

Jason, at the table's head, paused in the act of slopping sorghum into his coffee, and glanced over at her. "Ish Marx? He's an odd duck."

Candy's eyebrows went up. "In what way?"

Jason smiled at her defensive tone. He knew Candy liked the stranger, just as he knew several of the New Bedford girls were in love with Stemple's nephew; as, indeed, several of them were in love with Jason himself.

Dinner was over. Night had settled on the big clearing where the Bolts had their logging camp. Through the dark glass of the windows a glimmer of lamplight shone from the bunkhouse windows across the yard. Somewhere an owl hooted; far off on the wind, the voice of a distant coyote answered it, unutterably lonely in the icy dark.

From her position halfway down the table Candy watched the steam rising off her coffee, and surveyed the plainly furnished room, and the three bachelors who inhabited it, with affection.

Jeremy had cooked dinner with his customary skill—Jason's dinners tended to be spartanly plain and Joshua's absentmindedly burnt. Though she'd dined at the cabin numerous times before, Candy could detect that for this occasion the place had been given a thorough and much-needed cleaning. Only Joshua, she thought, would have taken the trouble for that.

Her eyes went to him, the changeling of the Bolt family, fair-haired and fine as whalebone in contrast to the bronzed, broad-shouldered strength of his older and younger brothers. Then she glanced back at Jeremy, reading in his half-turned profile the reflection of her own inner peace, and of his quiet, easygoing nature. As if he felt her gaze his eyes met hers, then dropped again in sudden shyness.

Jason was still considering her question, seeking to put his finger on what he felt about Stemple's nephew. Finally he said, "He—feels wrong."

"You mean because of the dogs?" asked Joshua, glancing down the table at him. No dog in Seattle took to Ish at first meeting. Reactions had ranged from hackling snarls to yelping flight, but even the friendliest curs gave him wide berth. Cats, on the other hand, found him as fascinating as the New Bedford girls did.

"Not exactly," said Jason. "It's just that I get the feeling that he's lying about something, and I wonder what it is."

"It's his b—business," said Jeremy, and held out his hand for the sorghum pitcher, which Jason slid expertly down the length of the tabletop to him. "If you distrust any man with something in his p—past, you'll end up with mighty few friends, especially here in Seattle."

"He's one hell of a mathematician," added Josh suddenly, as if this were a point in Marx's defense. "You know what he showed me? Look . . ."

Jeremy leaned closer, for he enjoyed Josh's fascination with numbers though he was unable to share his genius for them. "You pick any number," Josh explained, "multiply the ones just before and just after it, and they'll come out to one less than the square of the number. Always. Any number."

"Hunh?" said Jeremy.

"Look—you have five. Six times four is twenty-four. That's one less than five times five is twenty-five."

"Yeah, but that c—can't work all the time," Jeremy argued. "Uh—ten times twelve is—uh—"

"Hundred and twenty," prompted Joshua. "And eleven elevens are a hundred and twenty-one. And do you know what he told me about prime numbers?"

"Something incomprehensible, I'm sure," said a smiling Jason, who had put up with the lonely overflow of Joshua's fascination for numbers for many long years. Joshua laughed, albeit a little self-consciously, at that. He was aware that no one else shared his appreciation for those cool and abstract beauties, and did his best to keep from boring his brothers to death with them.

A pity, thought Jason, watching as Candy, Josh and Jeremy went into the further ramifications of testing Ishmael's mathematical principle ("A hundred and fifty-seven times a hundred and fifty-seven is carry the one—three hundred and eighty-five—no, that's seven hundred and eighty-five—carry the two . . ."), that Josh hadn't been able to get a better education than he had. The years that he himself had found so rewarding, the years of work, first with his father and then with his brothers, to make something of himself and of Seattle as well, had been years taken from something else that Josh might have had.

Well, he told himself, *we never had the money to send Josh to college anyway.* But he had seen his brother's hunger for knowledge of these things, things that no one else had any comprehension of. In all the years in Seattle, Ish Marx was the only kindred spirit Joshua had ever found.

Candy put down her chalk and grocery slate and announced, "Twenty-four thousand, six hundred and forty-nine," and Jeremy protested, "That c—can't be true *all* the time! What about—what about eighteen hundred and sixty-seven?" He pulled the year's date out of the air, and everybody showed signs of plunging back into the numerical fray.

Jason broke into their enthusiasm with, "Before you return to the contemplation of higher mathematical theory I think we'd better get settled which of the pair of you is going to San Francisco with Aaron and Ish on Monday. I'd like to have one of you go, just to make sure we hear the *real* figures on that tea-clipper deal they're doing with Struan and Sons."

Josh and Jeremy traded glances, each knowing his own strengths and his brother's. It was universally accepted that Josh was better with figures, but Jeremy dealt better with people—possibly because, being the youngest of the three and five-feet-four, he'd been forced to develop this skill at an early age. Jeremy said, "I'll g—go," and Josh nodded, satisfied.

"Now," said Candy, "1,867 times 1,867 is . . ."

Later that evening, as he walked her toward the head of the trail that led back to town, Jeremy asked her, "When I'm in San Francisco, is there anything you want me to get?"

Candy adjusted her cloak over her shoulders. "You

could buy me some yarn. Lottie's birthday's in No-
vember—she won't say what birthday—and I'd like to
crochet a shawl for her. Biddy's teaching me how to
crochet. I never had the patience to learn it before, but
I seem to be getting the hang of it now."

"All right." There was a small pause. The air was
changing again, the watery moonlight paled and died
as thicker darkness rolled in from the sound. Candy's
cloak stirred a little in the cold turning of the rain-
smelling wind. Then he asked, "C—can I get you a
ring?"

Jeremy heard Candy's breath catch, but in the dimness he caught the narrowed glimpse of her tip-tilted
green eyes, and the sudden tightening of that wood-
sprite mouth. "Did Jason put you up to ask that?"

"No!" burst out Jeremy. It wasn't a lie, but it wasn't
the entire truth, either. Jason had been urging him to
get at least that marriage out of the way for days now.
In the vehemence of his denial Candy caught the
partial affirmation.

"Because I won't marry—you or anybody else—
just so that Jason Bolt can win his stupid bet." She
whirled and started down the path at a quick walk.
Jeremy hurried to catch her.

"C—Candy, I wouldn't ask you to and it wasn't a
stupid bet. It's . . ."

"But you just did ask me!" she flared, all her
comfort in Jeremy's presence in the earlier part of the
evening forgotten in her sudden rage at Jason for
meddling in what should have been hers alone.

"I did not! I asked you because I love you and why
the hell did you c—come to Seattle in the first place if
it wasn't to get married?"

Candy rounded on him, her eyes blazing and her lips
white. "That's none of your damn business, Jeremy
Bolt! And if you don't think I had second thoughts

about being shipped out here like a lot of cows, you're stupider even than your brother! And then to have him make some kind of stupid bet on it . . ."

"It is not a stupid bet!" yelled Jeremy, trying to make his voice carry over hers but in doing so failing in his hope of calming the discussion.

"Did he make one?" she demanded hotly. And when Jeremy, torn between his loyalty to Jason and the terrible combination of his love and desire for her, didn't reply, she turned in furious silence and strode toward the path back to town. Jeremy ran to overtake her, and she pulled her arm violently from his staying grip. "Don't you speak to me," she said through gritted teeth.

"C—Candy, the bet doesn't matter."

"It matters to me," she flung at him, "because it's your mountain, too, isn't it? You have just as much personal stake in marrying me as Jason does. What did you do, draw straws? The short one gets to marry Biddy? Was that it?"

Jeremy said nothing, wondering if he should tell her the truth, tangled as it was, or finagle his way out of admitting to the bet, as Jason had commanded. And, fatally, he was silent too long.

"You—men!" She stormed past him, and down the path in the freezing rain. When Jeremy ran after her she added furiously, "And don't you follow me!"

Jeremy stood in the rain for some minutes, watching long after she had disappeared down the trail into the darkness. The rain soaked his long hair and trickled down the collar of his mackinaw. The world, sodden with two consecutive weeks of monotonous rain, was suddenly bleak and very cold.

Then he sighed, and started down the path after her. Jeremy was far too good a woodsman, and far too much a gentlemen, to let her walk the three miles back to Seattle alone.

From the kitchen windows, fogged with the steam of washing up, Joshua and Jason watched their brother's dark form vanish into the woods.

With a tired little wheeze, the camelback clock on the parlor mantel coughed out the three-quarter hour. Coming downstairs in pitchy darkness, Ishmael Marx subliminally identified it as quarter to four. He knew, though he had been asleep at the time, that the rain had ceased two and a half hours ago. Some of the clouds had cleared, enough to bathe the hillside in front of Stemple's house by the mill in leaky white moonlight and show him the faces of the two women whose knocking had brought him to the door.

"Mrs. Hatfield, Miss Cloom," he greeted them doubtfully. "Is there something wrong?"

"Well, we don't know," said Lottie, following him into the parlor.

Biddy added, "It's just that Candy was up to the Bolt brothers' this evening, and still hasn't got back. We wondered if something had happened to her. I waited and waited for her, but the rain's been over for just *hours,* and there's still no sign of her."

"Might she have spent the night there?" inquired Ish, going to the embers of the fire to light a spill with which he kindled one of the kerosene lamps.

"Oh, *no,*" Biddy protested. "That wouldn't be proper."

"But perhaps more sensible than a long walk back to town at midnight."

"As I said, we don't know," said Lottie, her round pink face puckered with worry. "But I think Candy would have waited the rain out and walked back, no matter how late it was. I realize it's an imposition, but I was wondering if you or Aaron would walk with us as far as Bridal Veil Mountain, just to be sure."

"What's this?" Aaron came down the stairs, sleepy and rumpled in his shirtsleeves and pants that, like Ish, he'd hastily pulled on at the sound of voices downstairs. "What the hell time is it, anyway?"

"Three fifty-two," replied Ishmael, with his customary precision. "Allowing for the error of the clock. Lottie and Miss Cloom would like one of us to go with them to Bridal Veil Mountain, to make sure that no ill has befallen Miss Pruitt on her way home."

"At this hour? She'd have stayed over, surely?"

"I don't think so," insisted Lottie. "The girls are all pretty strict about that, and Candy especially. And it wouldn't hurt to check."

"I will go," Ishmael offered, and vanished upstairs to get his boots. Stemple grumbled, but fished around in the corner by the fireplace for his own.

Almost an hour later the four of them were climbing the last hill to the Bolt brothers' logging camp on Bridal Veil Mountain. There was already a light on in the cook shack in the big clearing, and small movements in the shambling log barracks were the men slept. As they came toward the darkened cabin that old John Bolt had built when he'd first claimed the mountain, they saw a light go up in the lean-to kitchen. A drift of white smoke snuffled out of the tin chimney.

Joshua answered the door, barefooted in jeans and long-handles, his blond hair falling in his eyes. He took one look at them and asked, "What happened?"

"Did Candy Pruitt spend the night here?" asked Stemple bluntly.

Josh's eyes went quickly over Lottie and Biddy, reading in their mere presence that Jeremy had not, as he and Jason had supposed, spent the night on the parlor sofa in the Seattle dormitory. He shook his head. "I'll get Jason. Come in." He padded swiftly back through the long front room, adding as he went, "There's coffee in the kitchen."

"I knew she wouldn't have stayed," wailed Biddy. "I *knew* it. Oh—" She flustered away into the kitchen, competently locating several cups and bringing them out to the table strung on her fingers like rings. "Oh, Aaron, what are we going to *do?* Oh, Jason . . ."

"Calm down, Biddy." Jason was pulling on his buckskin shirt as he came down from the loft that the three brothers shared.

"But *anything* could have happened to them!" she moaned. "They could have been captured by *Indians,* or eaten by a *bear,* or washed away by a *flooding river. . . .*"

"There is no river between here and Seattle," Joshua reminded her.

"But anything . . ." she began again, disregarding this obvious fact.

"Miss Cloom," said Ishmael severely, "your speculations are alarmist, illogical and exaggerated. 'Anything' could not have happened to them. They could neither have been run over by a railway train nor devoured by dinosaurs, and if you are not silent, I will put my hand over your mouth."

Biddy shut up, round-eyed. Jason turned away to hide a snort of laughter behind his coffee cup. Ishmael went on, "As the rain will have washed out any tracks that they might have left, we can only follow the route they would have taken, and make casts in the woods on both sides for clues."

"But you did follow the path they'd have taken," pointed out Joshua. "There *is* only one path back to town."

"But we half expected to find them safe here,"

Stemple said. "It'll be daylight in an hour—we can begin the search then."

The hunt started as soon as it was light enough to see clearly. Stemple noticed with a stab of his old uneasiness that Ishmael was able to distinguish finer details in the dim gray light of the rainy morning far sooner than any of the Bolts or their men. Biddy, rather typically, had refused to be escorted back to town, insisting upon joining the searchers herself. In this, Ish unexpectedly seconded her.

"But it's no job for a woman," protested Stemple indignantly.

It was the first time he'd seen the alien nonplussed by anything he had said. An eyebrow tipped up in the closest thing to surprise he'd ever seen out of Ish. "What is the logic of that statement?" asked Ish after a moment.

It was Stemple's turn to be stumped. "Er—that is— she'd only be in the way!"

The other eyebrow went up. "As I would, Aaron. Miss Cloom has nearly eight months' more experience with these woods than I have, and moreover is not lame."

Aaron struggled for a moment, then fell back on the age-old clinching argument, "But she's a woman!"

"An astute observation, Aaron," replied Ishmael. "Perhaps you would care to enlighten me as to what her gender has to do with her ability to locate missing persons?"

"Dammit, Ishmael . . ."

Ishmael waited politely for a continuation of the sentence. When none seemed forthcoming, he said, " 'Dammit, Ishmael' does not seem to be an argument remarkable for its cogency, Aaron."

Aaron watched him in exasperation as he turned back toward Biddy, and reflected that perhaps where

Ishmael came from the standards of ladylike conduct were less rigidly drawn. *Well, of course,* he thought, a little disgusted with himself for his own automatic assumptions. It didn't make it any easier to put up with Biddy, but it did make him pause to think.

That was, Aaron had found, one of the curious things about Ishmael. Aaron had accepted him as an alien, a stranger trying to blend into his surroundings, to the point where he found himself forgetting that Ish was not of this world. But there were times when Ishmael would not and did not blend, and his calmly critical observations had a way of making Aaron wonder about those surroundings which he had always taken for granted.

Ishmael might have lost all memory of the world that gave him birth, thought Aaron, as they pushed through the misty silence of the dawn woods, but that world had left its mark on him, almost visible, like a reversed image in an empty mold.

Biddy's voice broke into his thoughts as they turned from the main path to follow yet another obscure trail. "But *why* would they have come this way?" she wailed, hoisting her clammy skirts clear of the wet ferns that blanketed the ground. "There isn't *anything* out this way!"

"If they had become lost in the woods in the rain," replied Ishmael back over his shoulder, "they could have wandered anywhere. And if, as you say, 'anything' could have befallen them, logically there is no telling where they would finish up."

They halted, for the dozenth time, to let Biddy catch up, and Ish stood looking around him at the cathedral depths of the woods, now thick with curtains of drifting gray mists through which the voices of the other searchers drifted faintly, increasingly far away as the search widened.

Quietly, Aaron said, "Jeremy's a good woodsman. It isn't likely he'd have gotten lost between here and town no matter how hard it was raining."

"Precisely my thought." Ishmael glanced around him again, and his slanted eyebrows moved slightly downwards in annoyance.

"What is it?"

Ish gestured. "Nothing. It is just that I know there is an easier way to conduct this search. A way to scan large tracts of territory for life-form readings." His hand moved again, as though to conjure the familiar weight and shape of some instrument in his hand.

There it was again, thought Aaron, looking doubtfully up into the younger man's Mephistophelian face. A turn of phrase, a way of putting words together—a speech pattern emptied of its context but springing unconsciously to Ishmael's unguarded tongue. The phrase "life-form readings"—whatever that meant— was like his assumption that a woman could join into a man's task of searching the woods or would even want to, a spar thrown up out of the dark sargasso sea of lost memory.

Ishmael went on, "Was there somewhere that they might have taken refuge when the rain was at its worst? It was very bad toward midnight."

Aaron didn't inquire how he had deduced that. As far as he knew, they had both been in their respective beds and asleep long before that time. He only said, "There used to be an old mineshaft hereabouts, that somebody dug back in '53 hoping they'd find gold. The main tunnel fell in years ago, but there were half a dozen smaller entrances, plus a couple of airshafts."

"It doesn't make *sense* for them to come out here." Biddy stumbled through the ferns to join them, holding up handfuls of skirts to reveal stoutly laced shoes and quantities of dew-soaked cotton petticoats.

Ishmael turned to give her a hand up the trail. "Nor does it make sense to me for Miss Pruitt to have walked three miles in the pouring rain to preserve some obscure propriety about spending the night under the same roof as an unmarried man."

She slipped on the wet ferns, and Ishmael steadied her with an effortless strength that made Stemple remember the crushing power of the man's grip during his delirium at the cabin. In the weak, rainy daylight Ishmael's face looked harsh and strange, alien in spite of the dark hair that hid its odder angles. For a moment Biddy, looking up as Ish caught her arm, seemed to see it, but his remark distracted her and she said, "Oh, but she *would!* Candy would. You see, for her to stay there would be all the worse, because she and Jeremy . . . Well, there might be talk."

"And talk, I suppose, is more to be dreaded than pneumonia?"

"Oh, *yes!*"

Ishmael turned, and led the way into the deeper woods. As he brushed past him, Stemple thought he heard him mutter, "Humans!" to himself in disgust.

"It's true," pointed out Biddy, holding Stemple's arm for support as they started off after him. "You can always get over pneumonia."

The wind came up, slashing at the black branches of the pines that surrounded them and roaring with a sound like the sea. Laboring along the rising trail in Ishmael's wake with Biddy Cloom hanging for support onto his arm, Stemple wondered how someone with a bad leg could move as quickly as Ishmael did. Black clouds were moving in off the sound, darkening the gray daylight. In another hour the search would have to be abandoned.

They broke through the deepening shadows of the trees. Ahead of them, on the open ground of the rocky mountainside, Aaron could see Ismael standing alone, the wind billowing his oilskin cloak around him and catching in his long black hair. For a moment, silhouetted against the violence of the cloud-wracked sky, he looked wholly uncanny, alien and unhuman, and Stemple heard Biddy gasp with a kind of uncomprehending shock. Then the gust of wind died, and in the resulting silence Ish stood head bowed, listening for some sound that only he could hear.

Stemple made a move to go to him, but Biddy's hand tightened over his arm, as if for a moment she feared to go forward.

Ish raised his head. "Do you hear it?"

"Hear what?"

Ish raised his hand for silence. A gust of wind shook the branches overhead, threw rain on Stemple and Biddy as they stood listening.

"Voices," said Ish quietly. "Voices in the ground."

Stemple and Biddy looked confusedly at one another, but Ish was already moving, swift as a cougar, his head still bent to catch some unheard sound. After a puzzled shrug and a traded glance of bafflement, they followed.

They caught up with him where the woods grew thicker again, on the other side of the rise of land. He was standing near a collapsed wooden structure, like a smashed outhouse half-buried under a wild tangle of vines.

"Why, it's one of the airshafts of the old mine," said Biddy. "They put these buildings over them to keep animals and things from falling in. . . ."

"Be silent for once in your life," snapped Ish, "and listen."

Biddy obeyed. Stemple said after a moment, "I don't hear anything."

Impatiently, Ishmael laid hands to the fallen mass of

struts and lumber, ripping them aside with a strength that was suddenly frightening. The shaft, a narrow hole down into the darkness of the rock, was almost completely choked with weeds. Ish knelt on one knee beside it, his head bent. Hesitantly Stemple followed suit, and finally faintly heard something—voices in the caved-in galleries of the old mine, a man's and a woman's, singing in the darkness.

"I'd taken refuge in one of the old shaft entrances from the rain," said Candy, many hours later, when she sat wrapped in blankets in the dormitory parlor, her long hair still streaked with filth and water from the mine. She accepted a cup of cocoa from the solicitous Biddy, and choked a little on the brandy Jason had stirred into it. Outside, the renewed rain hammered viciously against roof and walls. "Jeremy followed me. I suppose it was foolish, because the whole hillside was so wet it was a wonder it hadn't caved in before that."

Jason shook his head. "It's not something you usually think of happening." He rubbed his damp, mud-splattered hair with a towel. Most of the men who had participated in the wet, laborious task of digging out the airshaft had gone home by this time. Only Jason and Joshua were left in the dormitory parlor with Ishmael, Stemple, Biddy and Candy. The rescue, once it came down to a matter of digging, had taken most of the day, and the light was fading now, the glow of the fire and of the few lamps that had been lit making deep patterns of apricot gold against the charcoal gray of the parlor's long shadows.

Joshua asked, "Why were you singing?"

Candy hesitated before answering, turning the china mug slowly between hands that were still red and stiff with cold.

"Did you expect to be heard?"

She shook her head. "We found a draft of air that Jeremy said he thought was a shaft—it was pitch-dark, we couldn't see and the roof was too high for either of us to reach. We'd been calling for hours. We knew no one would hear." She glanced up, the firelight picking the green flecks in her hazel eyes. "I suppose you could say that was why we were singing. Because we were afraid. Because we knew we'd never be found." Her eyes went to Ishmael, standing silently in the shadows beside the chimney breast. "Thank you."

Biddy said, "I *still* don't see how Ish could hear . . ."

The kitchen door opened, and Lottie came through, rolling down her pushed-back sleeves. "Jeremy will be fine," she said, in answer to Jason and Joshua's inquiring looks. "Just a bump on the head, and chilled through. Keep an eye on him for a few days—if the pain gets worse or he starts seeing double . . ." She broke off. If there were complications beyond her rough-and-ready skills, there was nothing to be done about them. There was no doctor closer than San Francisco.

Jason sighed, and some of the harsh lines that the last twelve hours had seemed to carve into his face relaxed. After a moment he said, "I guess that elects you to go to San Francisco with Ish and Aaron after all, Josh. Can you be ready to sail in the morning?"

Biddy, never one to release a promising topic, reiterated, "But I still don't see how Ishmael could have heard you. . . ."

"Well," broke in Stemple, with slightly exaggerated cheeriness as he gathered up his and Ishmael's mackinaws, "if we're going to sail in the morning, Ish, we'd better get the last of our packing done. We'll see you tomorrow, Joshua." He threw open the door, and

Ishmael followed him obediently out into the rainy afternoon. They walked back toward the mill in silence.

Only when they were passing through the woods that divided the mill and the house from the rest of Seattle did Aaron speak. "You'll have to be careful about that. Human hearing isn't that good. If you have any other abilities that are different from ours . . ."

"I have no way of knowing that, Aaron, until the occasion arises," replied Ish. Their boots brushed through the wet weeds that fringed the path; all around them, the dark woods murmured with pattering rain. Ahead the rushing of the millstream was a faint thunder in the murky semidark. "By what means could I have convinced Jason that I had located them? A forked stick?"

Stemple's head whipped around. "What?" He frowned. "Do your people have water diviners, too?"

An eyebrow went up slightly. "Wholly aside from the illogic of that method, there is no free groundwater on . . ." He stumbled to a halt, putting his hand instinctively to his head. Aaron, who had been walking a little ahead, came swiftly back to where he stood.

"What is it?"

Ish shook his head. His breath was harsh in the darkness of the tree shadows. "I—I do not know." He pressed his other hand to the place where, Stemple knew, the square greenish burn scars still marked his forehead. "A memory . . ."

"Of what?"

There was a long silence, Ishmael staring with unseeing eyes into the distance, seeking that place, Aaron thought, that had no free groundwater. Then he lowered his hands, and sighed. "It's gone," he said simply. "I thought for a moment—the place that I came from—but it is gone." Subconsciously he rubbed the scars that circled his wrists, an absentminded gesture, and began walking again.

"Well, whatever the reasons," sighed Aaron, falling into step with him once again, "if it hadn't been for you being whatever you are, Candy and Jeremy would have died in that mine before they were ever found. So maybe it's best that you did come here—for whatever reasons you came, and from wherever it is that you came. It hasn't been a wasted trip."

"No," said Ishmael suddenly, stopping once again. Before them, the open stretch of ground that surrounded the mill lay in desolation, scaled with the gleam of rain puddles. Ishmael's voice was hoarse with strain. "No. I came here to do something, Aaron."

"Here?" said Aaron quietly. "To Seattle?"

Ish pressed his hands to his forehead again, and Aaron could see the sudden beading of sweat on that curious, alien face. Ishmael's breath had grown swift and harsh again, as though with an inner struggle.

"I don't know," Ishmael whispered. "I don't remember. But there was something I had to do—something vital—yet when I try to recall there is only the memory of pain. I must . . ."

A memory of pain, thought Aaron, watching him worriedly, *that seemed to amount almost to pain itself.* He touched the alien's shoulder, and felt the shivering of his flesh. There was active torment in those dark eyes.

"Ish," he said quietly. "You say that you do not remember, but that you recognize things which you saw before. Isn't it—logical—that when the time comes you will recognize what it is that you came here to do?"

For a time Ishmael made no reply, but Aaron could feel him relax, and his shivering stopped. He had drawn back from trying to pierce that inner wall that cut him off from all that he had been. At length he said, "Perhaps."

"Who knows?" said Aaron, trying to break him out of that strange mood of desperation that was so close to his earlier despair in the cabin at Eagle Head. "It may be something you've already done, unawares."

"True," agreed Ishmael, turning back to the path toward the mill. "And it is equally possible that I have, unawares, done something to prevent it ever being accomplished."

Chapter 7

"OH, HELL, JAMIE, THE BASE IS CRAWLING WITH scientists." Kellogg strode ahead of Kirk through the steel and con-bast corridors with her familiar, long-legged stride. "Half the galaxy showed up to watch the fireworks caused by that damn dwarf star. We've been tripping over them for months. We might as well get some use out of them."

She turned and passed through a double door marked LAB DOME VII, her boots rattling briskly on the punched aluminum steps. Kirk followed. "And you think Dr. Steiner might help us?"

"I know she can."

They emerged into the lab dome. After the claustro-phobic rock of the older hive of tunnels, the newer part of the base felt weirdly airy for an enclosed space. This dome was half-unfinished, the aluminum floors still untouched by plastic patina and wads of insulating material visible through the con-bast shells of the inner walls. The place smelled of ozone and echoed eerily with the voices of people—human or otherwise—mov-ing about in lab smocks or their equivalent with pur-poseful (if varied) motion.

"Aurelia's one of the finest practical astrophysicists I've ever met," went on Kellogg, leading the way down another corridor, this time with no ceiling but the far-off roof of the dome itself. "She trained in the engineering section of the *Potemkin,* so she has a better practical base than most of the neutrino-splitters you'll find around this place. If the Klingons did figure out how to create a time warp of some kind, she'll be able to deduce how they did it and probably how you can do the same. If they didn't she might be able to extrapolate from the data you collected when the transport disappeared and tell you what the hell they *did* do."

Kirk nodded, impressed. Kellogg, he knew, had been chief engineering officer on the Starship *Republic,* a circumstance curious for several reasons, among them that she had been one of six humans in the crew. He cast back in his mind, reviewing the women engineers he had met, for an Aurelia Steiner.

Then Kellogg said, her hand hovering over the opening plate of the doors of Astrophysics Lab 14, "Oh, by the way, do Drelbs make you nervous? Aurelia's a Drelb. She just took that name for administrative purposes." And she preceded him into the lab.

Like Maria, thought Kirk, following her with a wry grin, to have forgotten to mention it. She seldom thought of aliens as aliens—one of the qualities that made her such an excellent BC. For all her claims to be a simple engineer, Kellogg displayed an uncanny knack for intuitive xenopsychology that had more than once saved her life.

She had certainly needed it, he thought, as engineering officer on a starship crewed primarily by Orions, Kzinti and Trisk.

The Drelb astrophysicist was working alone in her lab amid a wild litter of computer printouts. She was standing at a tall corner desk, but when the doors opened she turned her enormous blue eyes with their long, realistic, but purely ornamental lashes toward Kirk and Kellogg. She did not speak, but the gelatinous cone of her body mass turned a soft rose color with pleasure, and a faint, pervasive odor akin to that of vanilla or baking bread drifted momentarily on the sterile air of the lab.

Taking the welcome as she would have a verbal one, Kellogg said warmly, "I'm glad to be with you, too, Aurelia. This is Jim Kirk, captain of the *Enterprise.* We have a problem, and I thought you might be able to help us if you have time."

The Drelb's glutinous bulk faded from rose to yellow, and developed bright kelly green stripes. The long eyelashes blinked, and somewhere in the protoplasm there was a shifting and a round, knobbly-tongued mouth formed. A soft voice inquired, "Is the problem theoretical?"

"In a sense." Kellogg drew up a stool to perch on.

The blue eyes turned toward Kirk again, studying him. Then suddenly a deep blue suffused the entire tall cone, and that soft voice said, "Deep sorrow with you in your grief, Jim Kirk."

She said nothing further for a moment, but Kirk knew that her empathy was deep and genuine—the shift in color and smell were not polite fakes. Drelbs are among the politest species in the galaxy, but also among the most honest, a point not always in their favor. The few Drelbs that trouble to leave their home world know how revolting their appearance is to creatures of less free-form identity, and, since they are photosynthetic and practically indestructible, their first concern is generally to make those around them as comfortable as possible. Kirk was aware that the Drelb had produced those large, human blue eyes simply because she knew that humans are more comfortable if eye contact is made—even so, the gesture touched him.

"Thank you," he said. "It is in connection with that incident that we need your help."

The Drelb shifted a little, settling into a comfortable blob of gelid protoplasm and retracting her white, delicate-fingered hands back into her body mass. The eyes remained, and he could see every variation of thought and feeling in them as he spoke of the ore transport, the events of the Tau Eridani Cloud, the Klingons and his interview with Trae.

Aurelia did not speak, but the colors that moved through the viscous mass mirrored her feelings. When he quoted Spock's first transmission from the Klingon vessel she turned a bright red-violet, and her eyes grew more intent and far less human. If she had been a Vulcan, reflected Kirk wryly, she would have remarked, "Fascinating." As it was, she merely exuded an odor of cinnamon.

"Trae of Vulcanis tells us that no alteration of a single event in history—either Earth's or Klinzhai's would have a predictable result. What I want to know is: Could the Klingons have gotten back in time to make that alteration?"

"Ninety-eight percent affirmative, Jim Kirk," she replied, after a moment's mental calculation. "Temporary ignorance of precise method, but whiplash effect between gravitational fields of cloud and of white dwarf relating to Tillman's constant offers high degree of probability."

A tentacle emerged from the body, snaked across the room, and plucked a slab of soft plastic calculating material from the far end of the table. Another tentacle snagged a calculator, and other limbs extruded to manipulate both items—the equivalent of a human

ISHMAEL

operating a calculator with one hand and taking manual notes with the other. The Drelb's body mass was vivid yellow now, with occasional throbs of red or violet as equations momentarily stumped her. After a time the calculating activity ceased. The Drelb seemed to settle a little, and her color went to a deep, contemplative violet and stayed there.

"What about it?" asked Kellogg, speaking for the first time. "Can we do it?"

The eyes, which had almost disappeared in the effort of Aurelia's concentration, returned, and opened wide. "Temporary ignorance," replied the Drelb again. "Presently calculating program to discover ways and means. Starship readouts at point of transport vanishment would help."

Kirk held out to her the plastic carrier with all the spools of data, recordings taken of all readout screens throughout that hellish journey from Starbase Twelve to Alpha Eridani III. A tentacle extruded to take them, hesitated, then turned into a dainty little white hand complete with pink-painted fingernails to remove the box from his palm. An area around the squashy top of the cone of the Drelb's body turned warm gold with thanks, but she remained largely violet, preoccupied with the greater problems of astrophysics.

After a moment the violet melted to a more businesslike red, and Aurelia turned away, oozing toward the computer terminal in a thick trail of silver snail-track. Kellogg hopped down from her stool, and walked to where Kirk stood.

"End of interview," she said in a low voice. "Drelbs aren't much at long good-byes." She raised her voice slightly, " Do you need us for anything else, Aurelia?"

The mouth materialized on the opposite side of the cone from the eyes this time, the side facing Kirk and the base commander. "Negative," it replied. "I will expedite all solutions and reports. I am deeply glad for the challenge of this problem, and for the opportunity to meet you, Jim Kirk."

"And I for the chance to meet you, Aurelia," replied Kirk. Like the Drelb, he spoke the truth. She flushed momentarily rose again with the pleasure at his sincerity, but was back in her violet study by the time Kirk and Kellogg were out the door. For all their empathy, Drelbs are businesslike creatures at what passes in them for heart.

Kirk and Kellogg met McCoy in the base's main cafeteria. Like messes the galaxy over, it was a vast room filled with half-occupied trestle tables of metal and plastic, the walls a neutral shade not violent enough to be actively displeasing to anyone or anything, with a close-woven floor-covering in orange and green patterns vaguely reminiscent of spilled food. At this point in the shift the huge room was largely untenanted. A couple of Gwirinthans were clumped together at a corner table, nibbling daintily on porridge made of peas and cheese. As Kirk and Kellogg entered, one of them extended its neck over the head-level of the others and gave the BC a warm smile. Elsewhere, a tight-knit group of Klingons huddled standoffishly over megacaffeinated coffee, looking like they were discussing studied trivialities and each privately wondering who in the group would report their words back to the imperial representative.

"That's him," said Kellogg quietly, as she and Kirk crossed back to McCoy's table with their coffee. Kirk followed her glance, to observe the tall Klingon who had just joined that group. He was a man in his middle sixties, his thickly curling black hair and beard shot with white. His face had a closed, uncompromising look to it; a craggy face, like something put together from odd slabs of cement and mortar. A faded tattoo, like a caste-mark, was visible on his forehead, and the cut of his clothing was noticeably less military than those of the scientists at the table.

"Khlaru?" Kirk asked softly, and the base commander nodded.

"You don't see many Klingon scholastics around," she said informationally, sliding into the chair beside McCoy. "They're a sub-caste of Klingon society and they're not allowed off the home world much. But I guess Khlaru's some kind of big noise in Klingon historical circles."

"Such as those are," remarked Kirk with distaste. "Klingons subscribing to the loose-leaf textbook school of history."

"Give them a break," said Kellogg cheerfully. "How many people in the Federation know the truth about the Ellison trials?"

Kirk sighed, and had to admit that she had a point— the Federation's hands had been far from clean in that case, and the cover-up had had to be very thorough indeed. His eyes returned to rest on the Klingons.

McCoy mused, "That's the trouble with Klingons, you know. Even when they're on R and R, they never look like they're having any real fun."

"Would you, if you knew everything you said was likely to end up on file somewhere?" replied Kirk.

"Maybe," agreed McCoy. "So what's the verdict? Can it be done?"

"Steiner seems to think that it can." He sipped his coffee, which, like cafeteria coffee on any planet in the bounds of Federated Space, tasted like it had been dredged from the bottom of a particularly badly polluted swamp. It was said to be much worse in the Klingon Empire.

"If," Kirk went on, "that was what Spock meant in the first place."

"If?" McCoy's thick brows quirked upwards. "Spock mentioned the Guardian. . . ."

"Spock said the word *guardian*," Kirk corrected him. "Is there anything else he could have meant? A guardian of what? Or who or where?" He glanced across at Kellogg, who was stirring cream into her coffee and unobtrusively keeping an eye on the room with the absentminded watchfulness of a Wild West sheriff. "Could *guardian* be a file-code in the central computer? Or 1867, for that matter?"

"I thought of that," said the commander. She leaned forward on her bony elbows, and the harsh overhead lighting twinkled on her gold sleeve braid. "Nothing in Base Central, and all the computers on the base tap through that, even the Klingon ones. Log entry 0001867 is about twelve years old and has to do with air-recycling regulations. I also checked dome-numbers and room numbers on the base, and no combination of them comes up to 1867. Peoples' serial numbers—invoice numbers—I keep being reminded of my Uncle Franklin who became convinced he was the reincarnation of Franklin Delano Roosevelt because the numerological permutation of Franklin Delano Roosevelt came up to a number that was the square root of my uncle's numerological computation. I suppose that kind of thing is easier to do if you've got a computer. I think the cafeteria staff mixes their coffee grounds with shredded political prisoners." She set the cup down. "I think your first guess was right, Jamie. I think 1867 is a date."

"So do I," said Kirk quietly. "And my instinct tells me it's an Earthdate. But that instinct isn't enough to justify the dangers of trying to take the *Enterprise* through a time slip in the TE Cloud."

"Would it be that dangerous?" asked McCoy.

"Hell, yes." Kellogg and Kirk spoke in approximate

unison—it was Kellogg who continued solo. "Christ, Bones, I'm astounded the imp rep didn't report that ore freighter torn to pieces in the cloud. Even if they knew what they were trying to do with that white dwarf and Tillman's Factor or whatever the hell it was, there are high odds that all that came out the other end of the time warp was a bucketful of components. The stresses involved in that kind of messing around are incredible, even if the energy drain didn't blow the engines or kill the life-support systems on the way through."

"Well, if that's the case," said McCoy, "it's more than likely that the Klingon mission—whatever it might have been—was ended right then and there, and we don't have to worry about it."

Kirk glanced sideways at him, and grinned at the note of doubt that had crept into the surgeon's voice even as he spoke. "And what are you willing to bet on that?"

"Not a rubber nickel."

Chapter 8

FOG HAD LIFTED LIKE A GREAT GRAY WING FROM SAN Francisco when Aaron, Joshua and Ishmael left the offices of Struan and Sons, and made their way along the precarious board sidewalks of East Street through the primordial mud and chaos of the San Francisco yards. Above them, the city was emerging from pewter mist; the freshening wind carried to them the bite of sawdust and salt, the banging of hammers and men's curses and laughter in every language of Earth, the din of the sea and the endless mewing of gulls.

Sea wind tangled in Joshua's straight fair hair as he walked on ahead up the steep slope of Union Street. Ish and Aaron followed, talking of lumber and money as they climbed the board sidewalks between the narrow, iron-shuttered fronts of the modern brick warehouses and the hulls of old ships hauled aground and converted into buildings when the press of the city's trade left no time for construction; past the saloons and crimping-houses that infested the waterfront along with the offices of shipping and trade. They were jostled by British seamen in striped jerseys and pea-coats, dour Scots shipmasters and Yankee captains in tall hats and jawline beards, Chinese coolies in black pajamas, gesticulating Italian fishermen, whores painted to within an inch of their lives.

Seeing Ishmael's fascinated gaze, Aaron laughed and said, "I'll bet you never believed this much variety was possible."

Ish shook his head. "They are all human."

They climbed the hill of Union Street, rising above the din and squalor of the docks, and the city spread out below them like a carpet of trash to the east and south. Solidly palatial brick buildings that housed the banks, stock exchanges, gambling palaces and whorehouses clustered near the scrollwork mansions of the rich away south of Market Street; clapboard boardinghouses and stores huddled in the shadows of the hills and a dense, rickety congestion of color and dirt marked where Chinatown lay off to the south. The streets here on Telegraph Hill were paved with boards, broken and so smeared with mud as to be nearly invisible—the sidewalks, board also, transmuted themselves into stairways through which the long, thin, brown California grass waved in the salt breeze.

They rounded the shoulder of the hill as the last mists faded. North across the bay, the tall brown hills of the Golden Gate emerged, tawny in the morning's golden light.

Aaron heard the quick take of Ishmael's breath. Turning, he saw his nephew had stopped short, staring out across the bay with surprise and shock and something very close to pain in his eyes.

Ishmael's hand groped for and found the splintery wood of the rail of the sidewalk stair; he did not take his eyes from the hills. He whispered, "Aaron . . ."

"I'm here, Ish. What is it, what's wrong?"

His gesture took in the hills, the lay of that tumbled

land. His voice was bewildered. "Aaron, I have been here."

"What?"

"All this . . ." His hand seemed to touch the bay, the great headland of the Gates and the blue-black Pacific beyond. "I have been here, but it was not like this. The city is different. There is something—missing—from the hills, but I know those hills. I have seen them in the wintertime, all green with new grass. I know their shape."

"That's impossible," said Aaron, stunned. "You only think that because . . ."

"No," whispered Ishmael desperately. "No." He looked down across the shipyards, then shut his eyes, his face tense with effort and beaded with sweat. "Aaron, I see—things—remember things—but they make no sense. I see ships that they built here—metal ships, huge ones—so big they have to build them in sections and—and—" His hand moved again, but what was done with the sections was lost, as if in a drift of the mists that blew across the bay. "I can see rooms, I know how they look inside, I can remember—see inside the walls, even, know the tiniest wire and microcircuit. I know what they're for, what they do, how to put them together. But it all means nothing."

His eyes opened again, staring bleakly out over the yards. "I remember, but I do not understand."

"It could be that you're remembering two different things," said Stemple quietly, coming to stand close beside him. A couple of dark lascar sailors and cat-footed Chinese crowded past them on the narrow stair, headed down toward the docks, and took no more notice of them than if they'd been standing admiring the view. "Juxtaposing them, as you do in dreams."

"Maybe." Ish turned his gaze back to him, and his eyes were terrifyingly distant, wholly unhuman. "But where would I have seen the hills?"

"You coming, Ish?"

Ishmael looked up from his newspaper, which was spread out across the big table in the dim vastness of the dining room of Mrs. O'Shaughnessy's boardinghouse. Most of the other tenants, regulars and transients like himself, Aaron and Joshua, had gone out for the evening. It was Saturday, which he knew held some sort of significance that he did not grasp. Aaron was decked out in his best gray broadcloth and a ruffled shirt, an impeccable homburg in his hand and a cane tucked beneath his arm.

"I see no logic," Ish stated mildly, "in 'relaxing' by staying out late, in the rain, drinking alcohol and losing money at games of chance. To relax is—to relax. To rest. To do nothing."

Aaron laughed, and vanished into the shadows. Other footsteps thumped in the big parlor, doors opened and shut, but gradually the tall house on Filbert Street grew quiet, save for the soft patter of the rain. Ish settled himself in the dim circle of the kerosene lamp's glow, letting the silence pervade his soul.

Humans, he had found, habitually talked too much, and seldom had a great deal of importance to say. He wondered briefly how he would be able to endure living among them, and dismissed the thought as redundant and unprofitable. He searched in his mind for the fleeting memories of what he had thought he had seen on the hills that afternoon, but even that was fading. It had been blindingly vivid at the time, but was pale and unreal as watercolor to him now.

What had happened to him? he wondered. Something—some sense of something left undone nagged at him, and he shivered as the fresh scars on his temples and wrists ached anew, like the faint echo of a pain that had seared through his entire body.

He put the thoughts aside as Joshua Bolt came into the dining room, nodded a greeting to him and silently borrowed part of the newspaper and settled down on the other side of the table. They read in companionable silence, Ishmael picking his way cautiously through the overwritten fastnesses of pulp journalism and town politics and wondering why the humorous account of two Irishmen caught roasting a Chinese in the boiler of his own laundry should shock him so. It evidently hadn't shocked the reporter who had written the article.

Presently another boarder joined them, one of the regulars who had rooms on the third floor, a slim, dark girl with big gray eyes behind thick-lensed round spectacles. Without a word Joshua slid a section of the paper across the table to her, and she, too, relapsed into quiet perusal. Here was another, thought Ishmael, who prized silence.

Three-quarters of an hour later the girl rose, and padded softly into the kitchen. There was the clank of a tin pot on the stove, and the soft slurp of water from the bucket. A stove-lid rattled and ashes were stirred to life with a silken slurring.

Josh raised his head. "Are you making tea?"

"Do you want some?" called back the girl's voice from the semidarkness of the kitchen.

"If it wouldn't be any trouble."

Beyond the doorway a light moved around a little, then she came back, blowing out a kitchen candle. "It should be ready soon," she promised. "You're—"

"Joshua Bolt. This is Ishmael Marx. We're from Seattle."

"Ah." She smiled, and her thin, somewhat stern

face flashed into brief brightness. "Sarah Gay. Thank you," she added, as Ish handed her another section of the newspaper. A comfortable time of quiet again, as they wordlessly traded pieces of the newspaper back and forth, until the kettle in the kitchen bubbled, and she disappeared again, to return with three tin mugs on a cheap japanned tray. "It's my tea, by the way; I keep my own canister in my room, so don't let Mrs. O. charge you for it afterwards."

"Would she?" asked Josh, raising his head.

Sarah Gay chuckled. "She'd charge you for the mud on your boots. She's a good sort, but as she'll tell you, life ain't cheap. We will, however, wickedly steal her sugar, and not tell her about using her spoons and mugs." She handed Josh a sugar bowl, with white squares of lump sugar glistening like snow, and a couple of round-backed, almost S-shaped little tea-spoons.

"Why not?" Ishmael wanted to know.

"You want to be charged rental for the spoons?" She widened her gray eyes at him in mock dismay. Ish raised one eyebrow in reply, and cautiously tasted the sugar. He flinched in surprise from the sweetness, and the alien thought flashed through his mind, *Don't they know refined sugar is a poison?*

Evidently not. Joshua was happily putting three lumps of it into his tea. So was Sarah Gay, but neither commented when Ishmael did not. Food preferences, he had noted, were loose within certain strictly defined limits. No one had commented more than once upon his vegetarianism, the result of a vague sense of disgust at the thought of eating flesh. They seemed to take it as one with Aaron's unobtrusive avoidance of pork. Not putting refined sugar in one's tea seemed to come under the same heading. There were so many things to be careful of, so many traps that did not even appear to be traps.

Joshua stirred his tea, and set the spoon down beside his section of the newspaper. Then, with a glint of mischief lurking in the back of his eye, he hit the lip of the deep-curved bowl of the spoon, flipping the implement end over end and landing it precisely between Ish's hands.

Ishmael looked up in surprise. Josh was innocently reading the paper. Idly, Ish positioned the spoon, calculated the angle of the curve and amount of force necessary, and tapped the end, and the spoon landed with a neat "plop" in Joshua's tea.

Josh looked up, startled, and Ish was leafing through the editorial page without a sign of having moved. Sarah, her head bent over the advertisements, gave no indication of having seen the interchange at all.

Joshua regarded Ishmael narrowly for a moment. Then, with that same air of innocent doodling, he idled a lump of sugar onto the end of the spoon-handle, calculated distance and angles and vectors and force, and launched it, like a stone from a miniscule catapult, to drop smack in the middle of Ish's newspaper.

Ishmael considered. The game was absolutely illogical. Yet if he remembered correctly the principles of gravitational-vector gunnery—and he did, though where and how he had learned them in the first place eluded him—he could easily top Joshua's simple trajectory acrobatics. And besides, he had no intention of allowing a human to win at this game. . . .

Far-off city clocks were chiming midnight. Fog had settled once more upon San Francisco, muffling the steps of the man who trudged up the hill toward the tall clapboard house on Filbert Street. There were no lights in the windows that Aaron could see. Humming the rags of a gaudy tune to himself, he fished in his waistcoat pocket for his latchkey, then stopped at some sound in the fog. The sidewalk at this point turned into steps up the side of Telegraph Hill—surely he had heard other footfalls than his own?

But there were none now.

He climbed a few more steps, and heard them again, just enough out of sync not to be an echo. He paused—they paused. He wished he had Ish's acuteness of hearing, and then modified the wish to a desire for Ish's company at the moment. Very little of the moonlight was able to penetrate the fog, and his world was limited to a few feet in any direction.

Cautiously, he looked at the hillslope where it dropped away past the edge of the board steps. Rough, weedy and very steep; but if worse came to worst he could circle over the open ground and up toward the boardinghouse that way.

That thought was foolish, he told himself. If he were being pursued by robbers it made better sense to stick to the path than to scramble around vacant lots where they could slug him and relieve him of his money in peace.

Besides, they might not be robbers at all.

He called out, "Is anybody there?"

In the dining room of Mrs. O'Shaughnessy's, Joshua and Ishmael completed their precariously-balanced chevaux-de-frise of saltshakers, forks, and a folded section of the newspaper, and were now angling two spoons and a much-battered sugarlump into position to create an elaborate double flip that would throw the sugar into Josh's mug of now cold tea. It had taken them dozens of unsuccessful tries. Sarah, sitting on the sidelines, had refrained from comment, but as she finished each section of the newspaper she carefully exchanged it for one of the others in the barrier, making the substitutions with a mathematical neatness and timing that spoke well, in Joshua's eyes, for her appreciation of the importance of the experiment.

Just as Joshua was raising his finger to trigger the first spoon into flight Ish held up a hand, and said, "What was that?"

Josh froze in mid-motion. "I didn't hear anything."

"That was Aaron's voice."

Josh intercepted Sarah Gay's glance of surprise, and realized the impossibility of Ishmael recognizing, or even hearing, voices in the street. But then, according to Biddy Cloom, it was only due to this man's abnormally acute hearing that his brother was alive today. He started to speak, just as a shot cracked from somewhere outside, very close to the building. Josh snatched the lamp from the table and headed through the parlor toward the outer door at a run, Sarah and Ishmael in his wake.

The raw cold of the inky night smote him in the face as he flung open the outer door. Holding the lamp high he yelled "Aaron?" and thought he saw two forms bulking through the foggy darkness. They seemed to have been looking out across the dark, uneven steepness of the hillside beyond the sidewalk, but as he appeared in the lighted doorway they swung around. The lamplight gleamed on a long cylinder of metal. For a split instant Joshua realized what a fool he was, to show himself up as a target, and wondered if that realization was to be his last.

But the men plunged away into the fog. He heard the retreating thunder of their footsteps on the board stairs. Then silence, all sound muffled by the clammy mist that walled them in and ate like cold sickness into his bones. For a moment all he heard was the faint hissing of the lamp in his hand, as the cold damp of the night contacted the heated glass.

Then, quite close, he heard the dragging limp of Ish's footsteps in the thin dirt of the field. The dark, narrow shape appeared on the edge of the lamplight's glowing circle. He realized Ish must have kept low and ducked out the door around and past him while he was stupidly making a target of himself, and it crossed his mind to wonder if Stemple's nephew had ever been an Indian scout. That kind of instinctive strategy wasn't something you'd expect of an accountant.

But his thoughts were broken by Ish's quiet voice. "He's down here. Carefully—the ground is very rough."

"I haven't the faintest idea what it was all about." Aaron Stemple looked up, still a little groggily, as Ishmael shut the bedroom door on the last of the inquisitive boarders and the strident questions of Mrs. O'Shaughnessy and came back to the bed. In the hallway the boardinghouse-keeper's voice could still be heard.

"Whist, and I've run a good house all me life . . ." retreated away amid a rustling of cheap chintz and curling-papers.

"What happened?" asked Josh, holding a china wash bowl filled with cold water from which Sarah occasionally fished a cloth to add to the compresses on Stemple's ankle.

The mill owner shrugged. "I assume I was followed up from the gambling hall. I'd won a little—about fifty-five dollars—nothing to kill over."

"Mr. Stemple," said Sarah Gay, her head still bent over his wrenched ankle and her dark hair half-unraveled from its restraining hairpins, "in this town there are men who will kill for fifty-five cents. Does that hurt?''

Aaron's gasp of pain made a reply unnecessary.

"Excellent," she said heartlessly. "Hand me another cloth, Mr. Bolt." She pushed her specs further up her nose, and went on wrapping.

"You think they might have been crimps?" asked Joshua doubtfully.

"Crimps?" asked Ishmael, uncomprehending.

"Out to shanghai him?" said Sarah thoughtfully.

Aaron opened his mouth to explain these somewhat arcane terms, which he knew must mean nothing to the alien, but Ishmael said, "But if they were attempting to kidnap him to press him into service on a ship, why would they shoot at him? Dead he would be of no value to anyone."

Stemple was still trying to assilimate the realization that his nephew understood that very colloquial expression when Sarah asked, "Could it have been because you resisted them?"

"No," said Aaron. "In fact I never even saw them. I heard them behind me as I came up the hill. When one of them fired at me I took a dive into the field, and of course your"—he visibly cut off the word *damn* out of respect for a lady's presence—"your San Francisco fields are more like taking a dive over a cliff. Maybe it was just as well, since by the time I'd rolled to the bottom they couldn't have shot me in the fog." He reached up gingerly to touch the cut on his forehead, under its neat bandage of torn sheet and sticking plaster.

Standing beside the lace-curtained window, Ishmael glanced back at them with a sudden flicker of surprise. Why, he wondered, had he simply assumed that weapons could still be aimed in the zero visibility of a foggy night? These people didn't have . . . didn't have . . .

He put his hand to his forehead, struggling to remember. Something you clipped to the barrel of a
weapon, a sighting device that didn't need light. Like
the microcircuitry that operated automatic doors and
the faint, characteristic hum of air conditioning, it
hovered momentarily within touching distance of his
mind, then retreated again into the cloudy memory of
white pain.

He shook his head, and returned to Stemple's bedside. Aaron's mud-smeared coat hung over the back of
the room's single wooden chair; his shirtsleeves
looked very white against the mingled colors of the
faded quilt upon which he lay. Sarah Gay finished
tying up her work with deft fingers. Ish made a note of
the treatment she had used, and asked, "It is a sprain,
then, rather than a break?"

She nodded, and pushed aside the tendrils of her
hair that had fallen around her face, one hand going to
the bun at the nape of her neck to locate more hairpins.
"Although a bad sprain can be worse than a break.
You'll have to be off that for a week at least, Mr.
Stemple."

"Are you a doctor?"

Joshua and Aaron both looked up at Ishmael, startled and a little taken aback by the suggestion. Ish
realized he had walked into yet another unmarked
trap.

Their surprise wasn't lost on Miss Gay. A trace of a
wry smile flicked the corner of her mouth and vanished. "I do nursing at St. Brendan's Charity Hospital," she replied in her low voice. She got to her feet,
shaking out her black skirts. "And as I begin work
there at six in the morning, I had best get a little sleep
if I'm to be worth anything. Goodnight, gentlemen."

Joshua walked with her to the door. When Ishmael

slipped from the room a few minutes later the pair of them were still standing in the narrow, ill-lit hall, talking in quiet voices; neither of them looked up as he made his way down the stairs. He crossed the parlor in darkness, soundlessly unbolted the front door and stepped out into the night.

The fog was thicker now, the last of the feeble traces of moonlight gone. Around him, the city was utterly silent, wrapped in its cotton-wool wadding of mists, like something set adrift, cut off from all space and all time. Ishmael scouted for a distance down the board sidewalk and steps, and into the field along the side. He was not certain what he was seeking, if anything. In any case he found nothing that meant anything to him. Yet he could not rid himself of that sense of something vital that he must do, of the feeling that there was something here that he ought to know. The feeling persisted as he returned to the boardinghouse, and followed him into his uneasy, unhuman dreams.

Chapter 9

IT WAS NOT CAPTAIN KIRK WHO FOUND THE FIRST loose end of the knot of time and space whose center was Starbase Twelve, but Lieutenants Uhura and Sulu, returning to the transporter section disgracefully late from the Wonder Bar, with eight minutes to go of a twelve-hour shore leave on the base.

"So here I am," Sulu was saying, "completely unable to find a room for the night because everything in walking distance of the terminal is rented out to the local streetwalkers and their clients. . . ."

"Poor Sulu," commiserated Uhura, giggling. "If you hadn't been so virtuous . . ."

"Virtuous hell"—Sulu laughed—"I was *tired*. So the only thing I could do was get back on the train again. . . ."

"Oh, *no* . . ." And she leaned against his shoulder, chuckling helplessly over the picture of a seventeen-year-old Sulu wandering through half the countries of Southeast Asia, armed only with his OmniRail Pass, vainly seeking a room for the night. "So where did you finally spend the night?"

Sulu laughed again at the memory. "Well, that was

pretty funny, too. I got *back* into Saigon, it is now six-thirty in the morning, I haven't had any sleep and . . . What's that?'' He raised his head, as if the scent of trouble had hit his veins like a sobriety drug. Uhura was silent, turning her head to listen.

But the sound was not repeated, nor was any other. The corridors of the private sector of the base were never very well-lighted, no matter what the hour. Power was too expensive for private operators to waste on mere corridor-space. Even the main hallways, like this, were generally pretty dingy, and this close to the end of the third shift it was not uncommon for them to be completely deserted.

About ten feet in front of Sulu and Uhura was a junction where one of the smaller hallways crossed the wider one in which they stood, leading away toward what Sulu presumed to be barracks or semiprivate residences of those who in another era would have been termed camp-followers—not necessarily prosti-tutes, but that secondary army of merchants, enter-tainers and purveyors of alternate food sources that attaches itself to any military establishment. Soundlessly, Sulu indicated that he would backtrack the forty or fifty feet to the last crossing and circle the block that contained Sexy Sadie's Literature Empo-rium and Haircutting Establishment, and flank what-ever the trouble was.

Uhura nodded. Starbases on the whole are among the safest places in the galaxy because the control of the environment is, of necessity, so strict. Even civil-ians walk a little more carefully, knowing how easily they could be tracked down if need arose. Thus any danger that does break out on a starbase is seldom petty.

Mentally Uhura counted steps, giving Sulu time to move down the corridors, around those blind aluminum corners. She listened for any further repetition of the sound she wasn't even certain she'd heard, a kind of thump and slur, as of suppressed struggle. She thought she heard something else—the mutter of voices, and a guttural curse. The click of metal touching the corridor wall.

She moved forward, her sense of danger heightened by the vast quantity of alcohol she had imbibed in the course of the evening. But no troopers, even on their own ship, will get so drunk they can't react to danger, and Uhura was no exception. A glance around the corner showed her two dark forms supporting a third, half-dragging and half-carrying it down the hallway, the dim yellowish light of cheap lumenpanels gleaming wetly on the streak of green blood in the unconscious man's white hair.

Uhura called out, "Halt!" and braced herself to duck back behind the corner if the people on either side turned out to be armed. No military personnel carried phasers on leave, but there was no real way of making sure the stricture was obeyed by civilians.

The men turned. She had a confused glimpse of swarthy, bearded faces—Klingons, she thought, before they turned away again and started to run as fast as their burden would let them.

Sulu stepped out from the next junction of corridor. "That's far enough!" he yelled, though he hadn't a weapon to back himself up with any more than Uhura did.

But as he'd half-expected, his mere appearance was enough to unsettle the kidnappers. The Klingons—if they were Klingons, because out of uniform and in the bad lighting they could have been any of the mid-range brown-pigmented variants of the humanoid races—dropped their burden and ran, heading back toward

Uhura under the mistaken impression that she presented the lesser threat.

She knew she couldn't get both of them, but she sprang at the nearer one as they split to pass on either side of her. Her hands closed around his arm, hard muscle under the slippery jersey, and she turned and levered to stop him. He whirled, hand raised to strike her, and she caught his descending wrist and flipped him in a small, neat circle that ended with him slapping like a wet towel into the hard composite of the floor.

She saw the second man's kick coming at her head in time to roll with it but not in time to duck or block. It caught her across the cheekbone instead of the temple, knocking her staggering. The man scooped up his partner, who seemed to have recovered a little of his breath, and the two went pelting away down the hall.

Uhura pushed herself to her feet off the wall where she'd fallen, but didn't see much point in pursuit. She turned, her head stinging from the blow, and went back to where Sulu was bent over the body of the fallen victim.

"How is he?" she asked, kneeling beside him.

Sulu had turned him over; the thin Vulcan features looked sunken and drawn in the gray, shadowless light, reminding her with sudden poignance of Spock. "Bad. You think McCoy's still at the bar?"

She unhooked the communicator from her belt, touched the code-keys with that unthinking flicker of her thumb that becomes second nature to any trooper. "Dr. McCoy?"

By the faint tinkling of the piano background she knew he was still where they'd seen him earlier that evening, quietly absorbing brandy alone at the corner table. Spock's death, Uhura suspected, had hit McCoy far harder than he would admit.

"McCoy here." His accent had increased, as it always did when he'd been drinking.

"Doctor, this is Lieutenant Uhura. We've got an injury on corridor ten, junction of 145. We're calling Base Medical but I think you'd better get over here."

There was a moment's pause, then a laconic, "Right," and the click of the doctor's communicator shutting off.

Sulu glanced up from the unconscious Vulcan. "Are *you* all right?"

Uhura grinned wryly, and touched the rapidly swelling lump on her cheekbone. " 'I got your footprints on my heart,' " she quoted a line from a currently popular song in the singer's well-known drawl, which made Sulu laugh, and added in a normal tone of voice, "but I think I'll live." She tucked back the rumpled ends of her disheveled black hair, and touched the code buttons for contact with the *Enterprise*. "Uhura and Sulu here. Reporting in and requesting emergency extension of shore leave until 0500 hours. . . ."

"Zedrox." McCoy tossed the half-empty plastic capsule down on the small bedside table. "The modern equivalent of the poisoned bodkin."

Kirk looked from it—an inch-long oval of soft plastic with a single thornlike needle projecting from one side—to the still face of Trae. The purplish color around the old man's wrinkled lips was fading to the normal slightly greenish tinge, and his breathing seemed stronger. On the monitors above the bed, all indicators were rising to Vulcan normal. Still, he thought, looking down at that delicate profile against its frame of snow-white hair, the old man looked very fragile.

McCoy went on, "Illegal as hell, of course—but also damn easy to smuggle in, especially if you have official connnections." Two heavy shots of trepidol had neutralized the effects of the alcohol in his system, but the Southern accent was still a little stronger than usual in his voice.

"Like the Klingon imperial representative?" Kirk glanced across the bed at Kellogg, who had joined them a few minutes ago, her dark hair hanging in a loose, sloppy braid between her hatchet-sharp shoulder blades but otherwise not evidently worse for being wakened at 0430 by an emergency call. Irregular sleeping hours are the occupational hazard of being a base commander.

She shrugged. "The imp rep says there's some seventy-five Klingon male civilians in the private sector of the base, over whom he has jurisdiction but no direct control. He says he'll inquire."

McCoy made a remark generally written as "Huh," and went back to studying his feinberger readings of Trae's metabolism. He loaded an ampoule into his injector and pushed up the sleeve of the dark, close-fitting garment that the old Vulcan wore under his flowing robes. There was the soft *spang* of the medigun, and the fluctuating green indicators on the monitors rose a fraction of an inch, then stabilized.

Kellogg came around the bed to stand beside him. "What I wonder is why they'd have tried to kill him in the corridors?" she asked. "They could have gotten into either his quarters or his study just as easily."

"Could they?" said Kirk.

She thought about it. "Well, maybe not his quarters, but certainly his study."

"Do you really think you could be sure of overpowering and killing someone—particularly a Vulcan—in that study without disturbing something? Something that might be noticed by someone who knew the way things in that room are ordered?" Kirk touched the

zedrox capsule gingerly with the back of one fingernail. "My guess is that they wanted to find out what he
might have known about Khlaru's work—whatever
Khlaru's work had uncovered—and that the men who
were sent to bring him for questioning only panicked
and tried to kill him when Sulu and Uhura caught
them. Have you notified Khlaru that his colleague has
been injured, by the way?"

"If Khlaru didn't know it already," remarked Mc-
Coy sourly.

"I don't think he did," Kellogg said. "He was
recalled to Klinzhai at 1500 hours yesterday. That was
just about an hour after you put through your request,
Captain, for a forty-eight-hour extension of base leave
for the *Enterprise*. He was kept incommunicado in the
Klingon sector of the base and left on the shuttle when
the Klingon cruiser *Schin'char* came through at 0300."

"Interesting."

Kirk looked down, startled at the murmur of the old
Vulcan's voice. Trae was looking up at him, the dark
eyes beneath their wrinkled lids weary-looking but
perfectly clear.

"What's interesting?" Kirk asked.

"The timing," said Trae. "Historians are always
interested in timing, Captain, even that of their own
murder. Khlaru told me that he had been assigned here
for five years—that all of his obligations upon his
homeworld were nullified for that time. There was no
time for a message to go from this base back to
Klinzhai itself, of course; so the recall must be on the
authority of the imperial representative himself." He
sat up, with the slow care of one who doubts that his
body will obey him.

"It seems that I was incorrect in my assessment of
my position vis-à-vis the conflict between the Federa-

126

tion and the Klingon Empire," he remarked softly. "Let us go."

Kirk regarded in some surprise the fragile, blue-veined hand extended to him.

"Go where?"

The wrinkled lips tightened momentarily at this slowness of wit. "To my study, of course," Trae said thinly. "There are matters to discuss."

Chapter 10

"AARON." ISHMAEL CAME BACK INTO THE HOUSE, three nights after their return from San Francisco, and took off his heavy jacket and shook the rain from his long hair. He had just gotten back from walking Biddy Cloom home to the dormitory, as he had these last two nights.

Biddy, never one to let well alone, had taken it upon herself to come up to the house by the mill and do the cooking for the two bachelors as soon as she'd heard that Stemple was laid up with a sprained ankle. Aaron had to admit to himself that the girl could cook—and, later on the first evening, had realized that her scatter-brained fluttering concealed an ability to remember a thousand tiny details of a conversation and a cutthroat knack for cribbage. At first he had only suffered her to be around him because of Ish's kindness for the girl, but he had to admit to himself that on closer acquaintance, she wasn't nearly as bad as he'd thought. He even found himself thinking, as Ish had escorted her out that first evening, that she probably wouldn't make a half-bad wife for Jason Bolt, if only Bolt would have the wits to see it.

Ishmael came over to the fire where Aaron still sat with his swollen foot up on a hassock, the cribbage board laid out before him like the picked-at remains of an abandoned meal. "May I ask you a favor, Aaron?"

"Sure," he said equably. "What . . . ?"

"Do not press Jason Bolt on your bet."

Aaron looked up at him, shocked. "What? Now, Ish, I know you're a friend of Josh Bolt's, but . . ."

"My—friendship"—he spoke the word as if it stuck in his throat—"with Joshua has nothing to do with it." He paused, marshalling his thoughts. Finally he said, "The bet should never have been made, Aaron. You have no right to do what you are doing."

"Nonsense, Ish," Stemple said briskly. "Bridal Veil Mountain will double our profits. And it was a fair bet. I put up capital, money I couldn't well afford, to pay Captain Clancey for his trip around the Horn with those girls. You know what that cost me, and what it costs me every week to feed and house the lot of them. I'm supporting a—a harem of twenty young women in that dormitory. That's what the profits from the mountain, when I get them, are going to pay for. Bolt knew what he was doing when he made that bet."

The firelight rippled in an uneasy dance of shadow over the angular, alien face, and repeated itself, infinitesimally tiny, in Ish's dark eyes. "I did not mean that you are being unfair to Jason Bolt," said Ishmael quietly. "You, and Bolt, have no right to do what you are doing to the girls themselves."

Stemple looked away.

In that dry, logical voice, Ishmael continued, "You know the kind of man Jason Bolt is, Aaron. You knew that when you signed the papers legalizing the bet. You know his charm, his single-mindedness, and the force of his character, and you know that he uses them to achieve his ends. Few of those girls have the maturity or experience to resist when he pressures them to accept some proposal or other of marriage, from one or another of his men. They, too, are strangers in a strange land, dependent upon him, and some of them are very young. He will push marriage at them, and they will marry."

Aaron shrugged uncomfortably. "All women want to get married." There was neither conviction nor innocence in his tones.

"Do they?" Ish said drily. "I have been talking to Biddy. . . ."

"Oh, *Biddy*."

"Do not judge her, Aaron. For myself I cannot understand the prejudice against her, perhaps because I understand neither beauty nor desire. But I know that very little passes among the girls that she does not know. They confide in her. I do know that at least Candy Pruitt is uncertain about marriage—does not, in fact, know whether she wishes to wed or not. You know she loves Jeremy Bolt, but she does not trust her own heart."

"That's no concern of mine," grumbled Stemple.

"Perhaps not. But logically, you know, and she knows, that she will marry him. She must, in the end, to save the mountain. But she will always wonder, if she does not act freely. No amount of love can eradicate the seeds of bitterness. You have no right to do that to her, no right to do that to Jeremy, who never harmed you, nor to their children."

Stemple was silent, understanding what Ish meant and unwilling to admit the truth of it, even to himself. The sense returned to him again, that he had felt after the rescue of Jeremy and Candy from the flooded mine and had felt even more strongly when he first had found this strange man, unconscious in the unmarked dew of the ferns—a sense of standing at the beginning of a long chain of circumstance that reached out long years past the time when the deed to Bridal Veil Mountain had any importance to anyone. He muttered defensively, "Bolt signed the papers. We need the money to recoup our losses."

"There is always money, Aaron," said Ishmael quietly. "What you are taking from these girls is time, and choice, and with those you have no right to tamper, for they are irrecoverable."

Stemple sighed, and pushed at the cribbage board discontentedly. Biddy had beaten him last game, too, which hadn't improved his temper any. But he knew Ishmael was right. Did every action, every person, stand at the beginning of such a chain of circumstance? His own decision to save Ishmael, to let the alien into the life of Seattle—what would the final repercussions of that single choice be? The marriage of some young New England girl to a man who loved her, instead of to the first man who asked? A child born of love instead of resentment?

Mushy sentimental consideration, he told himself bleakly. *It wasn't eyewash like that which got you where you are today.* But the words rang false in his mind. What would he himself have been, he wondered, if his parents had loved instead of resented one another?

"Well, I won't back down in front of Jason Bolt," he grumbled at last. "But I tell you what I will do. I'll offer to let him buy his way out of the bet, for a fair price. Will that satisfy you?"

"Indeed," replied Ishmael. He felt a curious, naggling sliver of shame somewhere within him, not so much for having taken the girls' part against his uncle, but for having understood their feelings—for having understood anyone's feelings. Why shame? he wondered.

131

Aaron settled back into his chair, and winced at the movement of his hurt ankle. He growled, "All I have to say is, for a mathematician who's always talking about logic, you're getting damn sentimental in your old age."

Ishmael raised an eyebrow at him. "Perhaps I am."

Sunday tea at the dormitory, the gray light of the afternoon already fading behind the curtain lace, firelight and lamplight warming the faces of the men and girls gathered there. Candy, cheeks pink with steam, was pouring tea; the soft murmur of talk formed a muted background as some of the girls worked at their mending and others crowded around Dulcie Wainright, planning yet another simple marriage ceremony in the white pine-box chapel on the edge of the woods.

Jeremy Bolt, seated on a hassock, was playing his old guitar, and the voices of men and girls joined his in the blending of old tunes:

> *And it's three-score and ten boys and men*
> *were lost from Grimsby town,*
> *From Yarmouth down to Scarborough*
> *many hundreds more were drowned . . .*

Lottie and Clancey shared the room's worn plush love seat, Aaron Stemple sitting, his injured foot still enthroned on a small footstool and a pile of pillows, nearby. Joshua and Ishmael flanked the chimney breast like bookends, watching and listening to the run of the voices, the smooth flow of the guitar and the light glitter of Biddy's hammer-dulcimer dancing like a child around the main flow of the melody.

From his seat in the wing chair Aaron surveyed the room, and smiled a little to himself at the homeliness of the place. The dormitory was a barnlike building, long and narrow, thrown together more or less at random after Clancey's ship had sailed away for New England to fetch the brides. He had to admit that the lumber he'd donated to the project was stuff he couldn't have sold elsewhere—the men from the mill and Jason's loggers, in an excess of sentiment, hope and frustrated desire, had knocked the place together with amazing speed.

Still, it was built with care and enthusiasm, and the simple decorations the girls had contrived gave it a kind of beauty; that elusive quality known as "a woman's touch" that comes of caring and comfort. There wasn't a girl who hadn't brought something from New Bedford: some knickknack, lace curtains, a braided rug. Clancey had run in some old furniture from San Francisco—a couple of battered wing chairs and the love seat—Biddy, bless her inventive heart, had framed prints from *Godey's Lady's Book* to hang on the walls. Since last January, it was all the home these girls had known.

They'd done well, he thought. Less than half the original thirty were left. Sheila Meyers had married last week, and was sitting across the room with her new husband, talking with her former roommates, teasing the stolid Miss Wainright to unaccustomed giggles and blushes. Katy Hoyt, Robin Manderly, Elizabeth Darrow were engaged this week. Jason was encouraging them to marry before Christmas—not, thought Stemple, looking at the shy Miss Hoyt holding hands with her equally shy beau, an enormous, silent Norwegian logger, that they needed much in the way of encouragement.

Yes, thought Aaron, the girls have done well. *Well for themselves, and well for the men they'd wed.* And having spoken to Jason, he himself felt better in their presence than he had before.

Jeremy's voice shifted into an old defiant tune, the girls' joining his in sweet, rising chorus:

> *One word more, a signal token,*
> *Whistle of the marchin' tune,*
> *For the pikes must be together*
> *At the rising of the moon . . .*

Captain Clancey's voice joined in, a buzzing bass rumble from a true son of the Rebellion. Aaron looked across at him, holding Lottie in the circle of one brawny tattooed arm. They were like an old husband and wife, content with one another, lovers of long standing and faithful as married; happier, Aaron knew, than many licit couples he'd seen. When Jeremy finished Clancey raised his teacup, and asked, "And will you be knowin' 'The Minstrel Boy,' buck-o?"

Jeremy shook his head, and leaned one arm over the slim waist of the guitar.

Clancey hummed a tune, rumbling but recognizable through his faded whiskers.

"Oh!" Jeremy began to pick the notes, a wild, soaring, archaic tune, like an old hymn.

"Aye, that's the song."

"Isn't that something about the crimson blood of the Lamb?" inquired Biddy doubtfully, tapping at the strings of her dulcimer.

"Bah! An Orangeman's puling hymn they made of it, that was a song for warriors and bards."

Guitar and dulcimer blended, and Clancey picked up the tune, his voice graveling over the climbing surge of the notes:

> *The Minstrel Boy to the war is gone,*
> *In the ranks of death you'll find him.*

His father's sword he has girded on,
His wild harp slung behind him . . .

His voice faltered, uncertain, as he forgot the words, which he could generally be counted upon to do. Ishmael's deep voice rose to support him:

"Land of song," sang the warrior bard,
'Tho all the world betrays ye,
One sword at least thy rights shall guard,
One faithful harp shall praise thee.

Clancey hesitated in silence; stronger, surer now, Jeremy and Biddy swung into the second verse, with Ishmael singing alone.

The minstrel fell, but the foeman's chains
could not keep his proud soul under.
The harp he bore ne'er spoke again
for he tore its cords asunder . . .

And Clancey revived, joining his whiskeyed voice to the deep baritone,

And said, "No chain shall sully thee,
Thou soul of love and bravery,
Thy songs were made for the pure and free,
They ne'er shall sound in slavery."

Aaron sighed, and glanced sideways to catch Lottie's troubled eyes. He leaned across to her, and under cover of the blending of those diverse voices he said softly, "Why, Lottie? If he were entirely alien, I would understand. You saw him. You know what he is. But this—this half-ness. How can he speak English, let alone understand things like shanghai-ing and water-witches? Why does he recognize things that he couldn't possibly know? The land around San Francisco Bay—the words to an Irish song? That's what troubles me. Not that he's alien, Lottie—but that he's not."

Chapter 11

"IT WAS A MISTAKE," SAID TRAE OF VULCANIS thoughtfully, resting his thin hands on the faintly glowing console of the larger of the two computer terminals in his study, "for the Klingon imperial representative to panic. Offhand I can think of no clearer way in which he could have told anyone who was interested that they were on the right track." He looked out at the three humans who sat in a semicircle on the small island of white couches in the midst of the cluttered and shadowy sanctum.

"All right," said McCoy. "So what was Khlaru working on?"

Trae's glance shifted to the doctor, an inflectionless query as to why Kirk had seen fit to saddle them with the retarded.

"It isn't that simple, Bones," said Kirk quietly. "It might not be a single event. And it might not have been told about directly. We'd need . . ."

"Well, it would have to be a simple event, wouldn't it?" McCoy said impatiently, a little tired of dealing with that maddening Vulcan superiority. "If the Klingons are tampering with time, it would have to be something very simple, and very small, because you said yourself, Trae, that we'd be dealing with an exponential progression of random factors. Every incident they tampered with, they'd run the risk of compounding the problem—every alteration of an event would put them in greater and greater danger of getting in their own way later on down the line. If it's predictable, it has to be simple, and it just about has to be single. Doesn't it?" He looked defiantly from Trae to Kirk, then back to the ancient Vulcan again.

"I agree," said the historian unexpectedly. "Yet such an incident as we seek might not have appeared to its contemporaries as important, and would not be recorded as such. To answer your question, Doctor— Khlaru, like myself, was working on translating and cataloging the Karsid outpost records discovered here ten years ago. The data had not been put in order even by its original compilers. It is a random assortment of intelligence reports, captains' logs, scientific studies of the Tau Eridani Cloud, trade invoices and data readouts from the base computers, information much as you collect today, Commander Kellogg. Khlaru and I both filed periodic reports on our findings. I can only assume that the information from which the Klingons began their plan was taken from one of Khlaru's reports."

"And where would those be?" asked Kirk.

"Copies of the reports are logged in data retrieval." Trae turned back to the terminal, long fingers poised over the console. "Logically, we can rule out reports filed within the last two years, as it would have taken the Klingons at least that long to evolve the mathematical theory and the hardware to implement their plans."

"Two years?" said Kellogg, aghast. "How many reports are we talking about?"

"Seven years' worth. Each report is approximately sixty thousand words, a total of roughly twenty reports to be read through for clues as to the Klingons' intentions." He tapped in a line of commands; from where he sat next to Kellogg and McCoy on the couch, Kirk could see the Vulcan's thin face lit by the reflected green glow of the readout screen.

"You're kidding," moaned McCoy.

Trae glanced up. "No logical purpose would be served in my 'kidding' you, Doctor McCoy." He returned his concentration to the screen before him as it flickered and changed.

"There'll be four of us working on it," said Kirk comfortingly. "Six, if we can get Sulu and Uhura to help. They already know some of what's going on—I don't want to spread the circle any wider than that because we can't risk letting word that we know what's going on get back to the imperial representative. It won't take more than a couple of . . ."

There was a sound from the console, a faint, sharp hiss of intaken breath that drew Kirk's eyes as though it had been a cry of raw rage. Trae was standing, gazing at the screen before him, the green flicker of its lights playing across the eroded lines of his face. Even in the stillness he seemed to smoke with wrath. His voice was perfectly uninflected.

"I fear not, Captain." The dark folds of his garments caught the sheen of the lights as he moved down toward them again. "It seems that the imperial representative is not so foolish as we had thought. He has wiped all of the reports."

Only Kirk, a historian himself, understood the extent of the Vulcan calm and control behind those expressionless words. He knew himself to be only a dabbler on the fringes of the field, a dilettante—a history major rather than a historian. Yet he still felt a hot blaze of anger that anyone would destroy a historical record. In his days at the Academy he had met mousy and mild-mannered members of the history faculty who would savage anyone who laid a hand on their notes, and for the most part they had only been involved in the love of history for forty or fifty years. The Vulcan had been steeped in records of the past for six times that long—were he any other man he would have been in a killing rage. As it was, the silence that surrounded him and emanated from him was as cold and weighty as the slag of a dead star.

Kirk said quietly, "We can come back later."

Trae's dark eyes flicked to him, and for a split second he glimpsed the molten anger in their depths. "No," said the Vulcan softly. "Delay would solve nothing. My—anger"—he almost could not pronounce the word—"is illogical, and I hope that I am sufficiently disciplined to think past it. Delay would only give the Klingons time—and of that, they already have more than a sufficiency."

His own attempted murder, thought Kirk, with wry amusement, *had not angered the Vulcan nearly so much.*

"Logically," Trae continued, "our best course now would be to re-extrapolate the data from the original sources."

"But that could take years!" protested Kellogg, aghast. "Hell, it took *you* years!"

Trae's glance touched her briefly, and moved away, dismissing the consideration as frivolous.

"Let's look at this another way," said Kirk. "Spock had only a second or so of transmission time—anything he said *had* to be vital. We've ruled out 1867 as navigation points or computer codes or dates of anything else—I'm virtually certain it *has* to be an Old Reckoning Earthdate."

"If it was 1867 it would have to be Earth," remarked McCoy, "because the Klingons couldn't go anywhere *but* Earth in this part of the galaxy without running into the Karsids and getting tangled up in their own history."

"Your argument is circular," said Trae crushingly, and turned his calm gaze back to Kirk. "But your point is well taken. I concede it conditionally."

"Thank you," said Kirk.

"Well then," McCoy said, "what happened in O.R.-1867-A.D.?"

"The forcible opening of Japan to Western trade, which precipitated the Meiji Restoration the following year," replied Trae unhesitatingly. "Unrest in the Southern portions of the United States following an abortive revolt. The beginnings of the American policy of systematic genocide against the original inhabitants of the North American continent and the Pacific Islands. Opium wars in China. Victoria I was queen of England and Tzu Hsi *de facto* empress of China. Early attempts at agricultural reform and the freeing of the serfs in Russia. All things that would have come about without the presence or absence of any single man or woman."

Kirk folded his arms, and gazed for a moment into the dimness of that age-cluttered room. His mind told him that the old Vulcan was right. No single event could displace Earth's history radically enough, predictably enough, to warrant the enormous expense and effort of going back to change it. And yet . . .

The memory of the Guardian returned to him, the cold in the bones as he had stepped through the stone circle of that icy gate. The stink of carbon monoxide and rain in the air and the sound of Edith Keeler's voice. The knowledge of what he had to do, to undo what had been changed . . .

Only Spock knew. Only Spock and McCoy had been with him. Spock's voice came back to him, haloed in static. . . . "White dwarf, Khlaru, Tillman's Factor, Guardian . . ."

Abruptly, he asked, "If you were a Klingon, what event would you choose to disrupt?"

The Vulcan replied, "I would have placed a single low-scale nuclear warhead on Washington, D.C. in October of O.R.-1963-A.D."

"Why?" asked McCoy, startled at the selection. Like most people he tended to think of Washington, D.C. as a somewhat down-at-the-heels tourist trap notable chiefly for overpriced fried chicken and tours of crumbling monuments.

"At the time it was the capital of the United States," said the Vulcan. "At that date tensions between the Allies and the so-called Communist bloc had reached maximum levels. A bombing would have precipitated instant and destructive war. Five hundred years later, Klingon takeover would have been easy, as soon as radiation levels had gone down. The result predictable, but the event itself marginally before any other space-flight civilization had contacted Earth."

"I see," said Kirk softly. "Then we aren't really talking about Earth history at all."

"But if A.D. 1867 is an Earthdate . . ." protested McCoy.

"Might I remind you, Doctor," said Trae dryly, "that to fully a third of Earth's population at the time, the date was not 1867 A.D. but the Year of the Snake in the reign of T'ung Chih." He turned back to Kirk. "Whether the date is of Earth's history or not, all history is governed, in a large part, by economics. I fail to see how the Klingons could alter the course of world political and economic history to the point where it could be of any possible benefit to them."

"I agree," said Kirk quietly. "I think we're looking in the wrong league."

"Hunh?" said McCoy.

"Clarify," requested Trae.

"I think you're right," said Kellogg.

"I'm not sure how to put this," said Kirk, moving restlessly away from the edge of the console where he had been standing and pacing the narrow length of the couch. "Earth history before we made contact with other space-flight civilizations is too limited for what we want. If the Klingons are taking the trouble to create a time warp and send someone back on a retrohistorical mission, they're going to be damn certain that it will benefit them. It is simply too expensive and too risky to be experimental. Now if, as you say, history is a history of forces, of economics, what single event that early *could* have changed it to their benefit? What event could have had intergalactic, rather than simply Earth, repercussions?"

"In 1867," commented Maria, "not many."

After a moment of thought Trae nodded. "I understand your argument," he said. "For that reason I doubt that Spock's second transmission was genuine. The date is too early to be feasible."

"You mean," said McCoy, "that the second transmission could have been faked by the Klingons to mislead us?"

Kellogg broke in, "But we checked that. It's Spock's voice, all right. The voiceprints are identical."

"A trap." The Vulcan shrugged. "The Klingons have a store of convincing arguments."

"No," Kirk insisted. "They could have cut Spock to pieces before he'd lead us into a trap."

"He was half-human," Trae commented, "and—weak—for a Vulcan. But if we accept the transmission as genuine, with what are we left? A date from which he assumed we would extrapolate both the place and the nature of the event—an event, as Dr. McCoy has deduced, necessarily small, but with intergalactic repercussions. There was a remarkable paucity of intergalactic incidents taking place on Earth in 1867 A.D."

"An event?" asked Kirk softly. "Or the absence of an event? Maybe it's a paucity we're talking about."

"I give up," sighed Kellogg. "If we're going to get into things *not* happening . . ."

"Something that should have happened but didn't?" Kirk went on. "What *didn't* happen on Earth in 1867?"

"Klingon intervention, presumably," said McCoy, a little snidely.

"No," said Trae suddenly. "Not Klingon intervention—Karsid intervention."

The three humans stared at him.

"There were intelligence reports here regarding a Karsid attempt to initiate an infiltration of Earth. It was scheduled to follow their usual pattern of trade concessions, followed by increasing interference and then enslavement. But it was delayed by stiff resistance from the first Terran government they contacted. The delay was evidently critical, because word reached them in the interim of the revolts in the Orion systems. The project was shelved, and, as those revolts turned into full-scale revolution, scrapped along with all new infiltration projects."

With smooth swiftness he rose, and crossed to the maze of shelves that filled the entire rear wall of the study. The pigeonholes were unmarked, each containing a pile of faded flimsiplast scrolls and the newer fiches of translations. After a moment's study Trae withdrew a photocopied translation, a stack of computer floppies and a yellowed original; his long fingers flicked through them, checking the one against the others. Then he turned back to Kirk. There was, as before, no sign of anger about him; only a sense of condensed rage that even his own attempted murder had not aroused within him.

His voice was steady and quiet. "The originals are still here," he said quietly. "They are intact. The imperial representative could destroy the reports by tapping through Base Central Computer, but without knowing which original documents to destroy, he would have had to destroy them all. Only Khlaru and I knew which of these was the original from which the reports were made."

He held up the roll of flimsiplast translation. "The next time you speak of the subservience of the Klingons to their imperial masters, Captain, and their lack of personal honor and integrity, please remember that it is inconceivable that Khlaru was not asked to identify this document."

Evidently, thought Kirk, Trae wasn't the only stubborn historian upon the base. It must have been at that point that Khlaru had been sent back to his homeworld, to what fate Kirk could only guess. He looked back at the Vulcan, and understood suddenly why Vulcans place the strictest possible bounds upon the expression of anger. The rage in Trae's eyes was like a silent and contained explosion; the implacable quality of it reduced the hatreds of lesser races like humans, Klingons, or Kzinti, to mere short-term pyrotechnics.

From his own seldom-spoken-of friendship with Spock, Kirk understood how rarely a Vulcan will admit to friendship and how deep that friendship must be before it is articulated. Yet Trae had spoken of Khlaru as his friend. There was nothing any of them could do for the Klingon historian, now that he had been called back to his home to face the consequences of his stubbornness. Spock's death at the hands of the Klingons was uppermost in his mind as he said, "I am sorry."

"Indeed," whispered Trae. "And one hopes that the Klingons will become a great deal sorrier."

He returned to them, the flimsiplast of the translation falling in a long wave down from his narrow fingers, like some arcane proclamation of a world's doom.

"Khlaru was the one who did most of the work on Karsid intelligence documents. He worked on this particular report, but as I recall . . . ah." He tapped a place in the middle of the report with a light finger. "At the time I attributed the resistance to native xenophobia—though it was curious that it was highly developed enough to prevent the acceptance of new technology. But according to the reports the resistance to the Karsid offers was largely the doing of one man—a minor government official who led an almost fanatical campaign against them. It is doubly curious considering the stage of economic development at which the Karsids attempted to intervene—a time of industrial expansion and the putting-aside of old taboos and fears. Here." He looked up from his scroll.

"What year was it in?" demanded McCoy, perching on the back of the couch.

"Karsid Imperial 1056.3, which correlates . . ." He leaned across to his keyboard, and tapped out a rapid sequence of letters. The tilt of his eyebrow was the most violent display of outer emotion Kirk had seen from him. "Earthdate O.R.-1873-A.D."

"Eighteen seventy-three?" McCoy traded a swift glance with Kirk. "That's . . ."

Trae straightened up from his console again. "The Karsids habitually monitored a prospective planet by means of automated drones for at least three Karsid Imperial years before first contact. That would place the first appearance of their drones in o.r.-1868-a.d."

"That's close," whispered Kellogg, into the silence that followed the Vulcan's pronouncement. "That's damn close."

"So it had to be 1867," said Kirk. "Any later, they would run into the drones. What was the name of the man they'd be looking for—this minor government official who managed to save the planet?"

Trae consulted his scroll again. "The United States representative from the old Washington Territory," he said. "A man named Aaron Stemple."

Chapter 12

IT WAS CLOSE ON TO SIX O'CLOCK, AND THE WINTER darkness had long since settled on the land. Up the hill the whine of the sawmill continued, as it would far into the night. Beyond the black glass of the office windows, the white boil of the tailrace fluttered like star-shot silk in the distant gloom. Peace and silence seemed to concentrate themselves in the lamplight of the small mill office; in the warmth of the stove, the aromatic steam of coffee, the soft scratching of the pen as Ishmael worked over columns of figures long neglected. The stillness, the silence, brought him a deep sense of peace, like something he half remembered but which he could not quite recall. Like so many other things, that feeling of an inner calming of the soul lay on the opposite side of the barrier in his mind. Trying to reach through that barrier was like trying to put your hand through a fluctuating geon field . . .

Ishmael paused for a moment, remembering very clearly what a fluctuating geon field was and how one set up the circuitry to make one, yet how or where he had acquired this knowledge he did not recall. Every path that his mind probed seemed to be cloaked in a poisonous white fog of pain. Only those things which he saw did he remember—the stars, and the green shape of the San Francisco hills.

He leaned his forehead for a moment on his fingers. It was growing late. Biddy would doubtless be at the house already, and she and Aaron would be waiting for him with supper. He returned to his figuring, wanting to finish the payroll accounts and irked by that now-familiar feeling that there should be some far easier way to do them.

Footsteps thumped on the steps outside, and voices lifted in raucous violation of the peace of the night. "Ishmael!" "Hey, Ish!" "Hey, in there!"

Resignedly, he laid aside his quietude as the Bolt brothers came trooping into the office.

Jason peered around the corner of the desk at Ish's booted ankles. "Where's the chains, Ish? Jeremy, get that key down from the nail on the wall and unshackle this poor serf."

Jeremy hunted for the fictional key to the imaginary spancels. "I can't find it, Jason. I think Aaron swallowed it."

"The fiend!" declared Jason, and Joshua, dropping into Aaron's swivel chair, hissed in shocked disapproval. Grinning, Jeremy swung a leg over the seat of the office's one "company" chair, and Jason perched himself on the corner of Ishmael's desk.

Carefully, Ishmael closed the ledger and folded his hands on top of it. He regarded the brothers for a moment with polite curiosity. "Can I help you gentlemen?"

"I'm glad you asked that," said Jason expansively. "As a matter of fact, you can."

"I feared so."

"Ishmael," said Jason, leaning across the desk toward him, "how would you like to go to San Francisco?"

"I have been to San Francisco."

"Not for business," said Jason in a mysterious voice. "For pleasure."

Ish started back, alarmed.

"Listen." Jason leaned his hands flat on the surface of the desk, his brown eyes bright with the dream of conquest. His voice was low and coaxing, the great love of life, of adventure, of new and wonderful things, expressed in every line of his big, graceful body. "You know Aaron's giving us the option to buy out of the bet. He wants $50,000, flat cash, no strings."

"I am aware of this."

"Well," said Jason, "that's mighty big of him, and I appreciate his generosity, because in five years Bridal Veil Mountain will be worth ten times that, with me working it and Seattle growing as it is. But," he went on, "you also probably know we haven't got that kind of money nor anywheres near it. Not now."

"But listen to me, Ishmael. In this land, a man can make what he wants of his life, twist Fate to do his bidding. All it takes is courage, and initiative—and money."

"And," Ishmael concluded for him, "lacking courage and initiative, money will suffice."

"Well, of course," admitted Jason. "But to get money, big money, you need to have big money—or else have luck."

"Or commit a crime," chipped in Joshua, producing a tin flask from his pocket and taking a swig, then passing it on to Jeremy. Ishmael had already concluded that the Bolt brothers had begun the evening at Lottie's and were fairly well flown before they set out for the mill.

150

"If you are going to ask me to hold the reins of your horses while you rob the San Francisco bank . . ."

"Nah." Josh dismissed the idea with a wave. "Jason'd lock himself in the vault in all the excitement and Jeremy'd shoot himself in the foot."

"Hey!" objected the youngest brother.

"But"—Jason's voice overrode this byplay effortlessly—"the big money's in San Francisco. All the wealth of the Comstock lode finds its way there. Fortunes are won and lost every night at the gambling tables on Montgomery Street. Hundreds of thousands of dollars, sometimes, on the turn of a single card. Think of it, Ishmael. . . ."

"I am," replied Ish in a dry voice. "And I believe that I will hold your horses, after all."

"Ish." Jason's gesture conjured all the gold in San Francisco between his palms. "Think about it. I've seen you and Joshua play your games with mathematics. I don't know how or why you do it, but I know you can make numbers sing songs and dance dances for you. And I know those gambling games aren't games of chance. Josh has told me that a hundred times. They're only games of odds."

His voice dropped low, like that of a prophet speaking his visions. "Run me a system, Ish. Joshua knows every card game in the book. The two of you could figure out a system—hell, you can do it, you've got a brain like a ledger—and Jeremy and I would play them. It's all numbers—fifty-two variables, Ish, that's all. We need you. We need your help. We can do it with you, Ish—but we can't do it without you."

Ishmael regarded him severely, exasperated, thinking that it was very like Jason Bolt to gamble what funds he had in an attempt such as this. But then, what had he to lose? If the mountain went, Jason would be forced to start from scratch again in any case.

"This is insanity," he stated, looking up at Jason.

"We need you," Jason replied.

Ish was silent.

"G—God damn it, Ish, we need your help," added Jeremy quietly. "You've g—got to break us free of this, at least g—give us the chance."

Ishmael's gaze moved from Jason to Jeremy. In his mind he heard Jeremy's voice again, twined with Candy's, echoing up out of the mine; and against it was the vague memory of what love felt like when it was tainted with expectations. Joshua had taught him to play some card games, and it would be ridiculously simple to calculate the odds—he did it semiautomatically already when he played with Biddy at home. Absently, he remarked, "I would need advice upon the rules of the games. . . ."

Jason let out a whoop you could hear in Portland.

"You'll do it! Ish, I could kiss you!"

Ish stared forbiddingly at him. "I trust you will restrain yourself."

The Bolt brothers were laughing and slapping one another on the back; Jason pressed the tin flask into his hand, and though Ishmael had never seen any point in deliberately imbibing alcohol he took a drink out of politeness. It seemed to be a ritual pact-sealing gesture, and obliquely it crossed his mind that the brothers must indeed trust him, to ask his help in thwarting his uncle's schemes. For some reason he found this both curious and gratifying.

Ten days later they were in San Francisco. A different San Francisco, thought Ishmael, as he made his fastidious way through the mob in the crystal gambling palace on Montgomery Street. A San Francisco of diamonds and silk, of brilliant ladies and smooth gentlemen, of gamblers laying cards on the green tables, and the black and red of the wheels turning, blinding to the eyes.

The dark uniform of evening dress suited Ish, the black broadcloth and white ruffled shirt setting off his dark spareness, whereas it only gave Jason a bull-in-a-china-shop air of having wandered into the wrong place in the wrong clothes. The mathematical and theoretical side of the combine, fair and dark, looked sober and professional; Jason and Jeremy, in their stickpins and fancy weskits, seemed bright and a little dudish standing next to them in the flickering atmosphere of gaslight and crystal. A piano tinkled—somewhere a woman was singing. From the gaming rooms in whose fancy-scrolled doorway they stood came a hushed and purposeful buzz of voices punctuated now and then by a woman's shrill laughter or a man's hoarse guffaw of triumph. On the other side of the archway was the barroom, noisier and rowdier. Over by the bar a good-looking boy in the dusty clothes of a trailhand just in from Virginia City and his oxlike older brother had gotten into a vociferous argument over a girl with a dark-haired gambler, their voices rising higher and higher over Ishmael's quiet instructions to Jason.

"There are only two things to remember," he was saying softly. "Do not under any circumstances get drunk, and follow the system exactly. When it is time to play, play. When it is not, hold your hand no matter what is in it."

Bolt wasn't looking at him; his eyes were on the kaleidoscope sparkle and color of the gambling room beyond. "Ish," he said over his shoulder, "I know what's riding on this. It's everything going for everything—you don't need to warn me."

"Nevertheless, redundant warnings are infinitely preferable to errors."

Jason looked at him then, and laughed. "Don't worry, Mother; your boy will be good. Josh, take Ish over to the billiard room and teach him how to play pool. Come on, Jeremy, let's go win some money."

They started toward the blackjack tables, armed with all the coaching, all the numbers, all the systems that Ishmael and Joshua had been able to din into their heads in the last week and a half. Josh watched them go, anxious but unable to help now, like a mother watching her children off to their first day of school.

Jason paused, and turned back with a teasing grin. "Aren't you going to wish us luck?"

"Luck," replied Ishmael in arctic tones, "is the last thing that you need."

Across the barroom the two trailhands and the gambler had worked themselves into an argumentative pitch impossible in sober men. The girl calmly finished her drink and departed on the arm of an untidy little man with a flute sticking out of one pocket of his threadbare velvet frock-coat. The combatants continued their quarrel unabated. Ishmael frowned, his memory teased; then Joshua called out, "Are you coming, Ish?" and he shrugged and followed him to the billiard room.

On the whole, Ishmael enjoyed the evening. He found the gambling palace fascinating, and, once grounded in the basics, billiards ridiculously easy. It was simple geometry and vectors, like—like something he almost remembered that was not a game. A couple of the local Cyprians made a try at him, gave him up in disgust as a cold fish, and returned much later in the evening simply to watch him play. When Jason came back to the billiard room much later to report he found Stemple's prim nephew in his shirtsleeves, his ruffled shirt open at the collar, making a complicated bank shot while a gaily dressed girl in green held his coat and another one guarded his winnings.

Ish made his shot; the girl in green handed him the chalk, and he thanked her with his usual grave courtesy, oblivious to the splendid display of bosom and calf, his mind clearly on the game. Jason came over to him, chuckling. "Oh, Ishmael, we'll make a gambler of you yet."

Ish bent over the table, and put a kiss of English on the seven-ball to carom it off three cushions to meet its ultimate destiny. "I trust not," he said, but Jason had the momentary impression that he was pleased.

Daytimes, San Francisco had other treasures to offer. Jason spent his days following up business connections, dabbling a little on the stock exchange, meeting in their offices and hotels men he had met in the gambling palaces to make links with the web of finance that connected the state of California with the banking and commercial East. It was good to have access to newspapers, and to shops. He and Jeremy spent time wandering up and down the steep streets of downtown, finding those things that Seattle lacked and would lack for a long time yet. In a store on Mission Street Jeremy found what he wanted, a red-gold ring with a diamond and two small emeralds, and bought it out of his share of the winnings. He also found a guitar that it wrenched his heart to pass by, and, walking away from the shop window and up the long stairway of Columbus Avenue, Jason knew in his heart that his brother would find a way to go back for it if it cost him every penny of his dinner money for the rest of their stay and he had to live on hard-boiled eggs in the hotel-room.

Well, what the hell, thought Jason with a grin. *We can all afford a little slack.* "The system's slow," he said, pursuing his thought as they walked down Sansome Street toward the Palace Hotel, "but it's working. All we have to do is hang on and wait for it to come in."

"That's what surprises me," said Jeremy, hurrying a little to keep pace with his brother's long-legged stride. "It feels like we win some, and lose some, p—pretty evenly all night. But we always c—come out with a little more than we start with. I don't see how they know it, how they can do it, just with numbers, but it c—can't be just luck."

Jason frowned. "Well, to an extent," he agreed. "There's always luck to it, Jeremy. No system can be that perfect. It isn't all just numbers, no matter what Ish and Joshua say." They emerged onto Market Street, and the wind from the bay struck them, whipping into tangled curls Jason's reddish brown hair and snapping in the ends of the cravat he wore. The day was overcast; at the foot of the street, sky and water lay in varied tones of gray, broken by a spiky black army of masts. Across the water, the rolling shape of the hills was visible, greening now toward the emerald velvet of winter.

"A man has to know when to seize his luck, and make it work for him," Jason went on. "That's what's wrong with Ishmael—with Josh, too. They're cold-blooded. They hang back. They won't do it if it isn't in the numbers. They have the half-light, but they'll never have the sun."

"Now, I've seen Josh c—cut loose." Jeremy defended his middle brother. "You know he's got a hell of a temper when he's pushed."

"Most people will cut loose in anger if you push them," Jason replied. "Any dog'll bite if you kick it. But they won't cut loose in the other direction. Ishmael—he's a good man, but there's something uncanny about him. He doesn't drink, he doesn't fight, he's a vegetarian, he's a bookworm, he doesn't chase around with ladies—I've never even seen him lose his temper. He's inhuman."

Jeremy shrugged. "But he p—plays damn good poker."

"With a face like that he couldn't help it." Jason withdrew his hands from his pockets, to tip his hat to a pair of parasoled ladies making their way along the board sidewalk amid a soft rustling of taffeta and lace. "You know, brother, I would truly like to know what he was, and where he came from, before he showed up in Seattle. I'd even like to know *how* he showed up in Seattle. It sure as hell wasn't on Clancey's boat."

"He c—could have come overland from Olympia, or up from Portland," argued Jeremy, following as Jason stepped from the curb to the composite pavement of asphalt and boards that made up Market Street.

"Without bringing a horse with him? It's like he just fell out of the sky."

"Hey." They dodged a horse-car trolley and a cart-load of earth being hauled for fill to the harbor, and hurried up the pretentious marble steps to the carved portals of the Palace. "It's his b—business, Jason."

"I know," said his older brother conciliatingly. "And it's not that I want to pry. But I don't like not knowing about a man. I want to know what drives people, Jeremy. In most men it's power, or knowledge, or love. I don't know what it is that drives Ishmael. He's hiding something—and I'm just a little curious about what it is."

Elsewhere in the city, in the long gulf between the hills where the warren of alleyways began to grow tighter and more and more of the houses were built of paper, canvas and scrap; where signs were increasingly written in Chinese, Joshua huddled his plaid jacket more tightly about him against the damp cold of the afternoon. He felt as though he'd loitered on the slanted muddy street for hours, and knew every shop sign and shadow and flapping awning by heart.

Didn't they ever break for dinner?

St. Brendan's Hospital looked shabby and desolate, the bad grade of the lumber it was built of showing up glaringly in the streaky damp dark. One coat of cheap paint accentuated rather than hid the run of a poor grain that Josh's eye picked out almost automatically, from long experience. The place was a slapdash job— the first good earthquake would have them picking patients out of the ruins.

The door opened. A couple of women came out, one too tall and one too stout, dressed in faded calicos and hugging inadequate shawls about them as they hurried down the steps. The street wasn't paved hereabouts, and water ran down its center in a young torrent. Both women gathered up their petticoats in white handfuls as they hastened away. Josh tucked his cold fingers into his armpits, and backed a little more into the shelter of the overhang of the Li Chang Laundry, and went on waiting. The steam from within the little building breathed comfortingly on his face every time the door rattled a bit with the passage of feet inside, bringing with it the damp, mild smell of soap and clean linen. More women came out of the hospital, gesturing as they talked or pulling on mittens. None of them was the woman he sought. There was an air of downtrodden moneylessness to them. They looked tired, unlike the bright ladies who flocked around the gambling tables at night.

The day was darkening. A Chinese woman hurried by, clothed in dark, ragged cotton and bending her head against the eyes of the foreign devil in the laundry door. A gust of wind blew from the alley behind the laundry, bringing the stink of fish and garbage. Joshua glanced at the sky, found the muzzy blur where the sun should be, and calculated that he had two more hours until they'd be getting ready to hit the gambling halls again. His mind automatically began calculating odds, reviewing the system for blackjack.

The door across the street opened. Even hidden in shadows he knew her.

She paused in the doorway, head down against the wind, pulling on her gloves. She had a kind of shabby gray coat on, and long straight wisps of black hair trailed from beneath her bonnet. She came down the steps quickly, glanced up and down the street and started to walk.

Joshua cut across the sloppy thoroughfare at an angle to intercept her. He didn't call, but she stopped and turned as if he had.

"Sarah?"

"Josh." Her smile was hesitant, like sun after a dreary and bitter day. Self-consciously she pushed her spectacles farther onto the bridge of her nose.

"Do you mind if I walk with you?" he asked, as if he hadn't waited twenty-five minutes in the minimal shelter of the laundry doorway to ask her that question. "It's getting dark."

Diamond Lil's. The Orient. Montgomery Street, Kearney Street—gold dust from the Sierras and the Comstock. A merry-go-round of color and noise, darkness and gaslight, red and black cards on green baize, gold and silver coins. The blue haze of cigar smoke and the chatter of the Wheel of Fortune, the amber bite of liquor on the tongue and the shrill music of women's voices, the tinny rhythms of the piano and the soft rattlesnake rustle of shuffled cards. Men's arguments, the clink of coins, the flash of diamond cuff studs above the dealer's white hands.

Night turned to day by the deep gold of kerosene or the soft white of gas. Card laid on card, Jason Bolt in his black broadcloth suit and waistcoat of scarlet and gold that glittered like a king's robe, a cigar between his teeth and a young lady in yellow silk and black plumes holding his single whiskey and water. Joshua Bolt leaning in the doorway of the gambling rooms, watching, smiling, his blond hair falling in his eyes. Midnight suppers of steak and oysters; champagne breakfasts at dawn.

Winning and losing—but mostly winning.

Only twice did anyone attempt to rob them.

The first time was an attack on the four of them, as they emerged, flush and rolling in winnings, from Florinda's Place in the small hours of a rainy morning. They strode along Kearney Street as though they owned it, wet wind stirring in their evening cloaks and the lights of the gambling palaces flashing behind and around them. The fog was beginning to roll in, swathing the darker dens of the Barbary Coast and the wharves, then moving up to seep around the wealthier areas of town; and with it the fog brought men who felt safe in its invisibility.

It might have been worse had not Ishmael, striding along unobtrusively downwind of Jason's cigar, raised his hand suddenly; the others halted, and he stood for a moment, a dark cloaked form in the darkness, turning his head slightly back and forth as though listening. Very softly, he murmured, "There are men waiting ahead."

Jason looked from him to the thickening fog around the dark cliffs of buildings that hemmed in the slanted street. "How can you tell?"

"I can hear them. They're moving about a little but they're waiting. That corner up there, I believe."

"You can . . ." he began disbelievingly, then stopped, remembering the mineshaft incident. In the increasing dampness Ishmael's face, surrounded by its mane of Indian-straight black hair, had a strange cast to it, uncanny. Jason shivered without knowing why.

"We can go around by Grant," he said finally. "We're pretty much past Chinatown. We can get to the hotel through the back." But he knew they would be followed, the men cutting through the vacant lots and alleys between the saloons. All the climb up Pine Street and down the dark slope of Grant he could see Ishmael listening, tracking their pursuers by sound, and in time he could hear them, too. The fog had moved in, thickening closer and closer around them. He whispered, "Get ready," and hefted his ebony cane.

The fight, when it was joined, was short. One of the attackers fired a gun, but between the fog and the poor quality of the weapon itself the bullet went wild, and the man hadn't time for a second shot. Jason could see Ishmael duck under and aside from the big robber's arm, catlike and trained; in the fog and darkness the man bulked huge but Ish picked him up like a bunch of daisies and hurled him into the muddy mix of wood and asphalt of the street. That was all Jason had time to see. Another man seized him from behind and tried to cosh him, and Jason twisted away from the blow and tried to return it, using his own cane as a club. Even in the fog and darkness he could smell his attacker, body-dirt and grimy wool and booze. He got close enough to have to ward off a knee to the groin, clinched with the man and began slugging.

Someone grabbed him from behind, feeling for his

throat. Jason got a confused glimpse of Josh lying limp where he had been thrown, of Jeremy struggling to get another man off him, of Ishmael being grabbed from behind while another man came in on him with a knife.

What happened after that Jason was never completely sure, because it happened very, very quickly. What it looked like was that Ishmael twisted like a cat in the grip of the man who held him, dropped to one knee, hurled the man with impossible force over his shoulder and into his partner. Before the pair of them had unsorted themselves Ish was on his feet again. He made no move to go for a weapon or even close his fist. He just laid a hand on the shoulder of first one man, then the other, up near the neck. Their knees buckled and they went down like poleaxed steers. He took one step toward the men who were holding Jason and one of them threw himself at him, cursing in Italian. With that same lightness Ishmael caught him, picked him up bodily, and threw him into the foggy street; Jason could hear the clatter of his body rolling down the steep hill, and his yells of rage and pain. But it was Ish's face that drew Jason's eyes—absolutely calm and without a trace of either anger or exertion.

The man who had been holding Jason and the one who was working on strangling Jeremy had, by this time, not unnaturally, melted away into the fog.

The Bolt brothers and Ishmael were alone.

"What the hell did you do to them?" demanded Jason, rubbing his bruised windpipe as he came over to where Jeremy lay, gasping, on the boards of the narrow sidewalk. Ishmael was standing over him, looking at his hands as though he had never seen them before, as though he himself had been as surprised as his victims by whatever it was that he had done.

"I . . ." began Ishmael, and then broke off, his brow folding suddenly, as though with pain. Then he shook his head. "It's quite simple when you understand the principles," he said dismissively, in a very different tone of voice. Jason had the momentary impression that he had been about to say that he did not know.

"Come," said Ishmael. "Logic forbids that they will resume the attack, but I have never found logic to be the leading characteristic of the human species."

He turned, and helped Joshua to his feet, their black cloaks mingling into a single shape of darkness as he supported him along the steep sidewalk toward the back door of the Palace Hotel.

As they fell into step behind them, Jeremy said quietly, "Well, brother, now you know why he never loses his t—temper."

Chapter 13

THE SECOND ATTACK WAS AGAINST JOSHUA ALONE, but Jason always wondered whether the motivations for that attack were robbery, or something else.

"You have no idea," sighed Sarah Gay, "how good it feels to be walking around in the daylight, like a normal person."

Rare sunlight filled the city, turning San Francisco into a world of glass. The sparkle on the bay was almost blinding, the wings of the gulls flashing like distant pieces of mica, unbelievably bright against the blue. The air was cool and damp, and the smell of the sea filled the city with the strange wild yearning of far-off winds.

Joshua, walking beside her across the mud of Van Ness Street, felt there could be no more happiness in the world.

She sighed, the habitual look of worried exhaustion washed from her face by the light. "I feel positively wicked and abandoned, leaving the people at the hospital to fend for themselves this morning."

Josh smiled quietly. "I spend my nights in gambling halls and dens of iniquity, and here I am walking out with a wicked and abandoned woman from St. Brendan's Charity Hospital."

She laughed. They had left the city behind them to the east, where it clustered around the dizzy roll of its hills. Below them lay the sand dunes and rank sea grasses of the north end of the point, that grew below the heights. "And is it working?" she inquired, holding her petticoats clear of the sand as they climbed along the crest of the hills. "This mathematical system you have come to San Francisco to try. I understand that fortunes are lost by men who have systems."

"That isn't the fault of the systems themselves," said Josh. "Mathematics will always work if you are precise enough. It's just that most people's arithmetic isn't up to the concepts. Ishmael Marx is the only man I've met whose grasp of mathematics is such that he can make such a system work. And it is working. It's just that it works slowly, and that's the burr under Jason's saddle. He wants it quick and colorful, and mathematics doesn't work that way."

"Ah." Sarah smiled. "And that is the secret of gambling palaces and dens of iniquity. That something as precise and structured as the mathematics of the games themselves is hidden under a layer of jewels and brocade; and that most men see only the lights and brightness. Which is why the house wins. Aside," she added in mock disapproval, "from the copious amounts of strong drink served on the premises."

Joshua laughed again, and gave her his hand to help her over the rough ground. "You've got it there. But how would you know about dens of iniquity?"

She raised one curved brow over an eye cool and gray as rain. "You think respectable women are the only ones who fall ill?"

Joshua was silent for a time, walking in step along the crest of the heights, thinking about those brightly painted ladies in their gay silks. He knew how he felt after less than a week of this nocturnal existence, of the noise and the kaleidoscope of bright and dark, of waking in the afternoon and sleeping in rooms curtained to cut the sunlight through the day so that he might go back to that world of brightly colored night. Like the slender woman who walked beside him, he felt a kind of refreshed relief at being about in the daylight.

What would it be like to have to live that way all the time? To know the sun only as something you swore at when it leaked through the shades and woke you at four in the afternoon? The thought made him sick with weariness. He, at least, knew that he could go back to Seattle in time. Those ladies with their false smiles and their paint that covered the spoor of weariness had nowhere to go.

They found a boulder to sit on, at the crest of a particularly high hill. For a time they sat in silence, the city spread out below them and to their right, vast and jumbled, like the mounds of cracker boxes and paper thrown out behind a grocery store. At the waterfront the ships crowded at anchor, white sails furled like the wings of resting ducks; along the rocks by the Golden Gate the waves made tiny patterns of white against the slate color of the sea.

"Why did you become a nurse, Sarah? How did you go into that?"

She glanced over at him, the pale sunlight glinting on her spectacles, then looked away. She started to speak, changed her mind and sighed, as though deciding to trust him against a nature that did not easily trust. "I'm not really a nurse," she said. Her long hands were wrapped around her knees, and he could see that the backs of them had already begun to knot with manual toil. The long black tendrils of her escaping hair brushed her cheeks like cloud trails. "I'm a medical doctor. I read medicine under my Uncle David back in Philadelphia, and passed my examinations."

Joshua regarded her with considerable surprise. "A doctor?" And unbidden he remembered Sarah's wry smile at his own and Aaron's surprise when Ish had suggested it.

She nodded, and continued to look out over the city and the bay. "Does that shock you?"

"It's just that I—I didn't know women were allowed to be doctors."

"They're not." Her voice was thin and clipped. "It's perfectly legal—but it isn't really allowed."

"Hunh?"

She sighed, and turned to him with a trace of bitterness lingering on her smooth, wide lips. "If you were hurt, or ill—would you go to a man doctor, or a woman?"

He laughed uncertainly. "I'd go to any doctor I could find."

"But if you had a choice? Of several male doctors, or a woman?"

He hesitated, putting in mind his own automatic reactions. "I—uh—I don't know."

"Well," Sarah said, "I do."

To his shame Joshua knew she was right.

She went on, "That's why I came here to San Francisco. I was naive enough to hang out my shingle in Philadelphia. I was run out of business in a month. Oh, nobody wrote me threatening letters, or burned my house, or anything like that. But—weeks I'd sit, day after day in my consulting room, and no one would come. I applied for residency at the city hospitals and they assumed that I wanted work as a nurse—and offered it to me in the face of my medical credentials. They all seemed to find me a little amusing."

She sighed, and began her futile and never-ending task of readjusting her hairpins, tucking in the trailing ends of her hair, which were perpetually escaping from the darkness of the main mass. "Well, I came to San Francisco. I thought there were few enough doctors in this town that perhaps I might stand a chance of doing what I wished to do, of healing others and learning about the arts of healing." She shrugged. "I was wrong. Maybe in a town this size in the East I might have stood some chance, if there were so few doctors. But the town is still mostly men, and a man has to be in extremis before he'll let a woman near him with a scalpel in her hand. Your friend Ishmael is the only man I've met to whom it would even occur that a woman could be a doctor. Most of my patients in Philadelphia were women—those whose husbands would trust me with them, which weren't many. Women are thin on the ground, here."

She avoided his eyes, and tugged at the long weeds that grew in the cracks of the rock on which they sat. Her profile seemed to him thin and delicate, but those big hands were strong. They caressed the leaves of the weed she held more lightly than the wind. "So now I work as a doctor at St. Brendan's, though my title is Nurse. Dr. Killian knows, and Sister Sheila, but even if the board of directors of the hospital would sanction the hiring of another practitioner—which they won't, in spite of the volume of the work—they'd naturally hire a man." She shrugged again. "In any case I'm doing medical work, and I suppose it's all I can hope for at the moment."

Joshua took her hands in his. "What a waste. People are stupid. Sarah, I—"

She disengaged one hand, and touched a finger to his lips. "No, Joshua," she said quietly.

"But I—" he began, and she shook her head.

"I am what I am, Joshua. I am what I will be." Her eyes were gentle, understanding his words before he spoke them, knowing what he would say, and why. "I am a doctor, Joshua, and a woman in a man's business right now. Don't offer me the—respectable—womanly—alternative of marriage, for I would only turn you down."

He was silent, looking into her eyes with nothing to say. To have offered her marriage as an escape from striving would have been an insult, both to her pride and to her abilities, but the closing of that door stabbed him with a sudden pang of grief. He knew now that he wanted her—suspected that it had been so since he had first met her earlier that winter at the boardinghouse. And now he could not ask for her.

After a moment he sighed. "People are stupid. I think you must be a fine doctor."

"Because you find me fair to look upon?" Her voice was teasing, but her eyes were not—not entirely.

"Because you're honest," he said. "If you weren't good, you'd be too honest to try and fight the tide."

The slightly baiting look relaxed into a genuine smile. "Thank you."

He helped her to her feet. "Will you still have dinner with me tonight?"

She laughed. "Of course. It's rare enough that I am asked to dine with a gentleman, even one who does spend every spare evening he has in gambling dens."

"Good. I've told my brothers I'm taking a vacation. I'll come for you at eight."

She shook her head with mock dismay as they wound their way back down the hills. "Playing hookey from the gaming halls. I fear you are incorrigibly respectable, Mr. Bolt. I—what is it?" For Joshua had stopped as they passed the lee side of a hill, and was looking at the loose, sandy soil with a puzzled expression.

He reached down and brushed the smoothed depression with his fingers. "Someone's been here," he said. "For quite some time, it looks like, and very recently. Look, the kicked sand on the edge of these tracks here hasn't even settled."

Her lips tightened a little, but she only said, "So someone was here. We said nothing that could not have been overheard in mixed company—except for the shameful nature of my profession, that is."

Josh straightened up, and shook his head, as if trying to dismiss the thought. "But why would anyone have taken such pains to come and go quietly, so quietly neither of us heard?" He frowned, remembering what Jason had said at the outset of their adventure, about not going about the city alone; remembering also the incident on Kearney Street the other night. He scanned the silence of the hills around them. "I don't like this," he said at length. "Let's get back to town. I'll see you at eight."

"Got it!" Jason exclaimed, with an explosive crack of his fingers that made Jeremy halt in mid-motion of loosening his cravat and look over at him in the fashionable crimson gloom of the hotel suite.

"Got what?" Jeremy pulled off the red silk cravat and threw it on the sideboard, and began systematically emptying money out of his wallet and coat pockets onto it. The coins sparkled, gold and silver against the blood red of the silk and the shining black walnut beneath it, bright in the glow of the elaborately shaped lamp at his elbow. The curtains of the suite were, as usual, shut; even had they been open nothing but a wall of charcoal gray dawn fog would have been visible beyond. It was five-thirty in the morning, and cold as the Devil's icehouse.

"Those two fellows I saw in Florinda's Place the other night, remember?" Jason knelt by the well-laid wood in the hearth, and began scratching lucifers on the hearthstone to light it.

"I remember you spending half the evening fretting over where you'd seen them before." His tone was good-natured. Jeremy was long familiar with his oldest brother's memory for names and faces, and knew that nothing drove him so crazy as not being able to place where and when he'd seen someone. It was part, he supposed, of Jason's impulse to control things—the same impulse that made him so curious about Ishmael Marx. "Are we g—going out to breakfast or do we send for it?"

"They were the two fellows who came through Seattle last September," said Jason, ignoring Jeremy's question in the pursuit of his own mysteries. "You remember, Jeremy. They were dark and kind of strange-looking. I got the impression they were looking for someone—they asked a hell of a lot of questions. . . ."

Jeremy shrugged, and went to warm his hands before the young blaze on the hearth. "You g—got me."

Jason frowned at this defection. "It was at Lottie's." He pursued the issue. "Maybe you were over at the dormitory. Josh was there, he'd remember . . . I think that was a little before your time, Ish."

"D—does it matter?"

"Not really. I just wonder if they ever found the fellow they were looking for." Jason got to his feet, and prowled restlessly back to the sideboard, beginning to stack and count the coins that his youngest brother had left scattered in such carelessness. "San

Francisco would be the place to find someone, though. Everybody on the Coast comes through San Francisco, if you wait long enough. What'd you say about breakfast?"

"I suggest that we go out." Ishmael glanced up from his own silent brooding over a pageful of mathematical calculations that he'd made while observing the Wheel of Fortune. "It will take at least an hour to warm this room to acceptable temperatures, and there are better ways of passing the time than shivering over our coffee."

"Shall we wake up Josh, then?" Without waiting for an answer, Jeremy strode to the door of the room Ishmael and Joshua shared, his brown eyes sparkling with the relish younger brothers always feel about rousting their seniors out of warm beds on cold mornings.

Jason laughed. Ishmael began, "I hardly see that . . ."

Jeremy came back into the parlor. "He's not there," he said, puzzled. "His bed hasn't been slept in."

Jason elevated his eyebrows and whistled suggestively. Jeremy shook his head. "That doesn't sound like Josh."

"Little brother," Jason said, laying a patronizing arm over Jeremy's shoulders, "I ought to tell you a few facts about even that most respectable of men, your brother and mine . . ."

There was a deferential tapping on the door of the suite. The brothers and Ishmael exchanged an inquiring glance, and Ish rose to his feet and limped to answer it.

It was a hotel porter, a stocky middle-aged man with red muttonchop whiskers, wearing the brass-buttoned livery of the hotel staff.

"Mr. Bolt?" he asked, his eyes going from Ishmael to Jason and Jeremy. "Mr. Joshua Bolt?"

Jason stepped forward, "I'm Jason Bolt," he said. "My brother is out at the moment."

The man nodded, seemingly untroubled by the fact that Mr. Joshua Bolt would be out at that hour of the morning. "Well, sir, there's a lady downstairs asking after Mr. Joshua Bolt."

Jason cocked an eyebrow at Jeremy and grinned with ribald triumph; Jeremy shook his head impatiently and demanded, "Did she give her name?"

"A Miss Gay."

It meant nothing to Jason or Jeremy, but Ishmael said, "Is she in the lobby?"

"Yessir. Said she was on her way to work." His opinion of women who worked was patent in the inflection he laid on the word *said*.

"I shall go down." Ishmael handed the man a coin, and disappeared into the gaslit gloom of the corridor. As the porter turned to go Jason lifted a hand to stay him, and handed him another few coins.

"As long as Ish is going to be entertaining Joshua's lady-bird, we might as well send for breakfast after all."

Sarah Gay looked up quickly as Ishmael entered the lobby, and her normally severe face relaxed into a smile when she saw that it was someone she knew. Her plain, dark blue calico with its white collar looked somber and drab in the opulence of the Palace, which had been decorated, as the management was not backward about pointing out, with the finest of furnishings that could be brought around the Horn. Ishmael privately considered the dark crimson velvet of the wallpaper, the purple plush upholstery of the thickly carved furniture, the prism-encrusted chandeliers and perpetually velvet-shrouded windows as a particularly successful exercise in bad taste, but could not for the life of him remember what he had been brought up to think of as good taste. As when he had searched the woods in company with Aaron and Biddy, he had the sensation of almost being able to touch some different and unheard-of thing, aesthetic in this case instead of technological.

Then the feeling was gone, and he dismissed the question from his mind as he bowed. "Miss Gay."

"Mr. Marx," she said, without preamble, "please don't think that I'm trying to pry or meddle, but was there some reason Joshua Bolt couldn't leave the hotel last night?"

He raised one eyebrow. "On the contrary, Miss Gay. He left it at about seven-thirty, saying he had plans of his own for the evening. He has not returned."

Her eyes lowered briefly to her gloved hands, which rested, folded, upon her knee. The delicate line of her mouth tightened. "I was afraid of that," she said quietly. "He was supposed to come for me for dinner at eight."

They agreed that it was best to split up, Jason and Jeremy checking the police stations, Ishmael and Sarah the hospitals. "There's no way of checking the third alternative," said Sarah quietly, as she and Ishmael strode along the clammy dawn streets, their cloaks stirring at the fog that still clung to the corners of the buildings like ectoplasmic wool. "In any case the tide's turned."

Her cool voice did not fool him. Long used to reading the subtlest cues to hidden emotion, he glanced sideways at her, remembering what she had once said about the crimps that operated in any deep-water port.

"Surely there are far too many sailors in this city for professionals to kidnap an obvious amateur such as Joshua?"

She shook her head. "It depends on how many ships are in port short of hands. There's ways of finding out, but none that would do him much good if he's already on an outward bound vessel. The whole of the Barbary Coast is honeycombed with subcellars and tunnels, almost as bad as Chinatown. Anything could have happened to him. I . . . ."

From the fog a shape materialized, and a man's voice said, "Aha, Dr. Gay! We were just coming to seek you, but recognized your voice."

Much to Ishmael's surprise, Miss Gay halted and curtseyed to the man who emerged from the fog of a narrow street. "Your Majesty," she said. "Mr. Marx—permit me to present you to His Imperial Majesty Norton I, Emperor of the United States and Protector of Mexico, and his two dogs, Bummer and Lazarus."

Ishmael, who remembered very clearly Aaron telling him that the United States was ruled by a president and a democratically elected Congress, looked in some puzzlement from Miss Gay to the slender, dignified Englishman in the tattered crimson military uniform and flowing cloak who stood so haughtily before them amid the vegetable parings and horse droppings of the gutter. The aforementioned dogs—a pair of shaggy curs, one big and one small—slunk back snarling, and the Emperor Norton snapped his fingers preemptorily.

"Sirrahs, behave yourselves! You do us no credit." He turned back to Sarah, and bowed again. "When I passed the hospital the other day I saw you with a young gentleman. Since you have in the past done me many kindnesses, when I discovered that same young gentleman this morning lying unconscious in a doorway in Chinatown . . ."

"What?" cried Sarah, her usual cool poise deserting her as she caught at the elaborately braided sleeve.

The Emperor of the United States put a kindly hand over hers. "There, there, my dear. We assisted him to the home of some friends of ours in the district, then came to seek you. We were fortunate to find you so quickly."

"Take me there," said Sarah.

Joshua lay on a straw pallet in the back room of a noodle factory off Washington Street—a room whose broken windows has been mended with scraps of rotting cardboard but which was warmed by the steam from the kitchens next door. Ishmael glanced curiously around him as he and the Emperor of the United States escorted Miss Gay in from the noisome alley outside. The dozen or so Chinese who occupied the place all bowed as they entered, but he had the sensation of being observed by watchful eyes. There were several other pallets in the room, and the signs of occupancy by at least half a dozen; from the covered trapdoor half-hidden in the shadow in a corner his quick ears caught the vague sounds of movement underground.

"Please do not think that your young man is drunk, Dr. Gay," the Emperor Norton was saying. "I am completely familiar with the smell of alcohol, and there is none upon him. I am more inclined to believe he has been drugged."

She knelt beside Joshua's limp body, pulling back the velvet evening cloak that covered him, and one of the Chinese put in, "He not have poppy, either. No smell, no smoke." He shook his head and bowed, a thin ageless-looking little man with a long pigtail shot with white. "If he sleep in opium den, he no have cloak after, either."

"He has a point," agreed Ishmael, kneeling beside Sarah to feel Joshua's wrists. "Nor are his clothes damp. He would not have lain in the doorway long."

"Nothing on his breath," said Sarah, leaning over Joshua to sniff at his lips. "Not alcohol or opium."

"There was nothing in his pockets, either," added the Emperor, still standing among the cluster of Chinese at the door. "We sought for some means of identifying him, as all we knew was that he has walked you home from St. Brendan's these last four evenings. I thought he'd been slugged, myself," he added, less formally, "but there's no lump."

Sarah leaned forward, carefully lifting Josh's head and gently felt the back of his skull. She shook her head, puzzled, and lowered his head to the thin pillow again; then she brushed the ivory blond hair back from his temples and frowned.

The Emperor leaned over her shoulder to look. "What would have caused that?"

Sarah frowned. "Burns, it looks like." She glanced up swiftly, hearing the harsh draw of Ishmael's breath. "What is it?" she asked. "Is something wrong?"

In the dim daylight that came in from the alley his face looked taut; one hand was pressed to his temple, and perspiration gleamed thinly on his upper lip. But he shook his head, and the pain—if it was pain that he felt—seemed to pass. "Nothing," he said quietly, "Nothing."

On the cot Joshua moved convulsively; his eyes flew open in unseeing panic and he cried, "I won't!"

Sarah caught at his flailing hands. Joshua struggled against her for a moment, then gasped and lay still, his

177

face shining with a dew of moisture. Quietly, Sarah asked, "You won't what, Josh?"

He opened his eyes again, blinking up at her stupidly. Then with a faint moan he moved his head. "I won't what?" he asked. "What are you—Sarah—I mean, Miss Gay—where am I?" He moved his head to look past them at the dim door with its crowding shapes, and groaned again.

"You are in the Yee Han Song Noodle Factory on Washington Street," provided Norton.

"What? Aargh," he added, as another pang lanced through his skull. "How did I get here? I . . ."

"Joshua," asked Ishmael quietly, "what happened? The . . ." He paused, realizing how insane it sounded. "The Emperor of the United States found you about an hour ago on the outskirts of Chinatown, unconscious. Do you remember what happened?"

He tried to shake his head, and quit with a gasp. He gasped again when he tried to bring his hands to his throbbing temples, and touched the blistered squares of flesh there. "No," he said faintly. "Nothing. It's like—like it never happened. The last thing I remember was walking out of the hotel to meet Sarah—I mean Miss Gay," he corrected himself. Then, *"Who* found me?"

"I'll explain later," whispered Sarah reassuringly.

From the corner where he stood Ishmael watched them, the lunatic emperor in his gaudy uniform and the elderly Chinese, Sarah sitting on her heels and feeling Joshua's pulse with calm competence, the dim light reflecting like monster eyes off the lenses of her spectacles. His own head ached with a sharp stab of remembered pain. He put his hand to the small, square scars that marked his own temples, and reflected that Joshua was lucky to remember anything at all.

*   *   *

"And a two for the gentleman."

"Hit me."

"And a queen for the little lady."

"Hit me."

"And eight lovely clubs for the gentleman." The dealer's eyes, dark and cold as a shark's, gleamed flatly from a smiling face. "Bets up, folks, who'll buy another round?"

The gaslight gleamed soft and white above the tawdry blazon of the cards. One in the morning, the long drag end of the night. Joshua Bolt, standing shoulder-to-shoulder with Ishmael in the doorway to the billiard room, felt he'd lived his entire life in gambling dens. The tiredness he'd felt, walking with Sarah on the hills above the bay nearly a week ago, had grown to an all-encompassing sense of exhaustion. He felt it had been years since he'd seen daylight. Bridal Veil Mountain, the place they were doing all this to save, seemed like some far-off dream. But a dream close enough to touch, close enough that he could hear the unending whisper of rain on the pine needles, and the throaty clucking of the black, ice-choked stream that ran five feet from the kitchen door.

He glanced sideways at his companion in this combine of mathematics and glitter. Despite the shirtsleeves and rumpled hair, Ish looked capable of playing pool for the rest of the night. Jason was right. The man was inhuman.

Jeremy, faithful to the system, had folded on nineteen. Jason was still in, but if the card he pulled next round was three or over he must fold. And he did. They'd been losing all night.

That was the hardest, Joshua knew. The times they stuck with the system and lost. Even harder was to refrain from betting everything when the odds were that they would win, in order to recoup. Since his own interest in cards was almost entirely mathematical he knew that this was how it must be, but he knew that there was enough of a gambler in Jason's more extravagant makeup that every loss, especially the close ones, or the ones that could have been wins, rotted his soul.

It had, Josh knew, little to do with the money. Watching the angry glitter in his older brother's eyes, he knew this to be true without understanding it. Jeremy could win or lose with reasonable equanimity; the brief elation over his wins balanced the annoyance over his losses—and in any case in some things Jeremy was longer-headed than Jason. Jeremy could accept Joshua's and Ishmael's guidance and stick with the tedium of the system. Jason's bolder nature fretted under the restraint.

And it didn't help, Josh reflected, that they'd been losing for two days.

It was all in the odds, of course. He and Ishmael had explained it to Jason, and Jason had claimed to understand. But Josh didn't like the glint in Jason's eyes as he threw down an eighteen.

Behind them in the billiard room a man's voice grumbled, "Damn kid's game. Not a man's game in the place." The speaker intruded his wide shoulders between Ish and Joshua; a big man dressed in black clothing a bit too dandified for a rancher, a knight's head stickpin glinting in the dark silk of his cravat. The smell of whiskey hung faintly about him, but there was, too, an edge of danger, a readiness for trouble that said, Gunfighter.

At the blackjack table, Jason leaned forward, his red-and-gold waistcoat bright as blood against the white of his sleeves. He looked at his cards, leaned back, and folded.

Behind them, the big man grumbled, "About as

much skill and thinking as Faro. Spit in the Ocean! Acey-Ducey Under-My-Shoosie! Doesn't anybody in this Godforsaken hell play chess?"

Without so much as turning his head, Ishmael inquired, "At how much a piece?"

Mate was set at two hundred dollars. Queen went for a hundred ("About the price of any woman in this town," remarked someone), rooks seventy-five, bishops and knights fifty. Pawns were twenty dollars apiece. A mystified owner scoured the surrounding saloons for a chess set and finally came up with one that the owner of Florinda's Place kept for decoration in her parlor.

Ishmael beat the stranger in seven moves.

"By God!" roared the big man. "Let me see you try that again, stranger!"

He caught him with a reverse fool's mate, in three.

"But that," he said, pocketing his cash, "is a classic fakement."

The big man stroked his narrow black mustache and regarded his closed-in king thoughtfully through a haze of cigar smoke. Then he looked back up at Ish. "After I beat you this time," he said, "show me that one again."

Warned, stung and $600 poorer, the gunfighter settled down to grim play. Joshua stayed in the corner of the billiard room with the little knot of spectators who knew enough about chess not to be bored to distraction, watching the slow progress of the game. The man in black was no slouch; he studied every move carefully before he made it, working through in his mind possibilities that Ishmael clearly saw three and four moves ahead. Yet it was clear to Joshua from the outset that Ishmael would win.

In time the concentration was almost palpable in the air, like a vibration or a slowly intensifying light. There were less than a dozen spectators—an oddly assorted lot including two of the house gamblers, a dancehall girl in red silk, a rancher from Virginia City, a scruffy little man in checked pants who looked like a drummer and a thin cowboy in a trail-worn green shirt—and they were mostly silent. Occasionally the owner would come in, shake his head in mystification, and go out again to mind the progress of the gaudier pastimes in the gambling rooms outside.

Someone touched Joshua lightly on the arm. Jeremy's voice whispered, "What the hell are they up to?"

"Chess," said Josh.

Jeremy glanced past him at the tableau of still forms in the flickering halo of the gaslight, then back at his older brother. "Josh, listen. Do you have the rest of the money on you?"

That got Joshua's attention. "Why?"

"Jason's luck has turned—he's winning, and winning big. He's d—doubled what we came in with tonight; he must have picked up fifteen thousand dollars since he sat down, and it seems like the more he bets, the more he wins."

Joshua frowned, not liking the sound of this. "That isn't what he's supposed to be doing."

"But it is, Josh! He's going with his luck. It's what we came here for."

Joshua hesitated, and glanced back toward the unmoving circle around the chess players. Neither had stirred, nor had any member of their small audience.

Josh's mind raced, trying to decide what would be best. Ishmael had said that the essence of the system was not to be panicked, either by losses or by wins. Looking at that hawk-like profile bent over the hieratic ivory figures on the board, he wondered if Ish had understood how high gambling stakes could run. There were, Josh had discovered, some odd gaps in his friend's knowledge; curious, inexplicable areas of ignorance, and an odd sort of naivete. Joshua had no doubt that he understood the mathematics, but he suddenly wondered if Ishmael fully comprehended the human element of the game.

As he handed over the wallet containing their $8,000 reserve and watched Jeremy slip quietly away into the gambling rooms, he felt a sensation akin to panic intrude itself into the portion of his anatomy just above his watch pocket. At this time of night—it was now nearly three in the morning—the gambling rooms had an air of unreality anyway, ascribed by Ishmael to the cumulative effects of oxygen deprivation and nicotine poisoning. The colors seemed more intense through the blurring of blue cigar smoke, the noisier roar of the early night muffled down, with only an occasional, disjointed fragment of the dealer's voice coming through it, or a man's exclamation of triumph. Joshua left the group around the chess-game and made his way to the scrolled archway that led into the gambling room.

One glance told him that Jeremy hadn't been exaggerating. Jason sat in the middle of a small crowd, his red-brown hair tousled and falling into his eyes. Gold was stacked elbow-deep all around him; the glitter of it wasn't as bright as his eyes. He was riding his luck, and that, more than the aura of the gold, seemed to hang about him like a halo of fire—he was a man on a winning streak, twisting Fate into victory.

But what Jeremy hadn't said was that Jason had changed his game. He was no longer playing blackjack, but poker.

"Raise," said Jason in an emotionless voice, and Joshua felt his heart stop. It started again, racing—numbers would work in blackjack, a game of numbers played against the house's numbers. Poker was as unpredictable as the men who sat around the table: a calm-eyed gambler, a couple of ranchers, and a mining-man from Virginia City. The little money had all long since been run out of the game.

There was the soft, flat pat of folded cards thrown in. Jason scooped the money toward him; Joshua saw him smile.

At his elbow, Jeremy's voice whispered, "He's hot, Joshua. He's magic tonight. They c-can't stop him."

Joshua threw a despairing glance over his shoulder. In the brief gap between watchers he got a slim vision of Ishmael, brooding over the chessboard like an Egyptian cat-god. He looked back in time to see Jason draw two, raise, and raise again. And still he won.

It was like being in a nightmare, watching events in which he was helpless to interfere. Josh quickly calculated the sum on the table at Jason's elbow—about twice their total capital, some thirty thousand dollars. His brother was grim, the sweat trickling, shining, down his face, playing with an unerring instinct that was in itself almost a system. He was taking chances he couldn't possibly have taken, and winning, running the sum on the table up higher and higher and always getting away with it. Hypnotized, Joshua knew that was their entire fortune riding on those cards, riding on Jason's instinct, on that mysterious thing called "feel."

A harsh voice spoke in his ear, breaking the dreamlike spell. *"What is he doing?"* It was Ishmael, his face like something carved from rock.

"He's winning," said Joshua self-evidently, but his voice was shaky.

"He is gambling." Behind that neutral, expressionless tone that masked so much, Joshua could tell that Ish was profoundly shocked. "He has decided to trust his instincts, rather than the mathematics of the system."

"He has damn g-good instincts," said Jeremy softly, from Josh's other side. Jason stood pat, and won on three sevens; drew three cards on the next hand, and won again.

The stakes went up. There was close to thirty thousand on the table—Jason raised, and won. There must have been other noises, from the billiard room and the saloon, from the other tables. Joshua was conscious of none of them. He watched in horrified fascination as Jason disregarded every precept, every system, took chance after chance—won hand after hand. *We're going to do it,* thought Josh. *We're going to win the money, buy out our bet, go home . . .*

The weird elation went like fire through him. The closed-in room seemed hot beyond bearing; all the world was concentrated in the brilliance of the golden gaslight, and the glitter of the money; in the black-and-red magic of the cards. Jason drew two, and raised; one of the ranchers folded, the other met and raised. After a momentary, engimatic scrutiny of his cards, so did the gambler.

"Stand," whispered Joshua desperately. "Stand, for God's sake."

Jason raised a second time. The gold seemed to blaze like a mountain of fire in the lamplight. In a quiet voice, the gambler said, "Raise," and pushed forward the rest of his own pile, the equal to what Jason had left.

Josh whispered, "Fold on it . . ."

Jason, after a moment's thought, silently pushed forward the glittering stacks of gold.

Chapter 14

IT TOOK THEM THREE DAYS TO WORK THEIR PASSAGE
back to Seattle, on a cattle boat bound for Vancouver.
In that time Jason Bolt could barely be gotten to speak
to either of his brothers or to Ishmael. It was not that
they felt any animosity toward him; he was blistered
by his own shame. He knew what he'd done.

They trailed quietly off the gangplank in Seattle in
the early dusk, Jeremy carrying a new guitar case in
addition to his carpetbag, all of them back in the
familiar comfort of flannel shirts and Levi's, their
mackinaws buttoned against the raw evening cold.

On the wharf, waiting for them, were Candy Pruitt,
Aaron Stemple and Biddy Cloom. Candy and the Bolt
Brothers hugged each other, a round mutual hug, and
set off up the road for the mountain in the dusk.
Ishmael caught a last glimpse of them through the
trees, as Jeremy and Candy dropped back behind the
others, and Jeremy fished in his pocket and gave the
tall girl a small velvet box. He saw her pause in her
tracks for a moment, then take it and kiss him; then he
lost sight of them in the gathering dark.

He turned his steps thoughtfully after Aaron and Biddy, as they descended the muddy path toward the mill.

"I take it the expedition was less than a success," said Aaron with a wry expression.

Ishmael raised his eyebrow.

"You would have come home in a lot finer style than that garbage scow, if Jason Bolt had made a success of it."

"It was—fascinating." Ish paused, debating whether he should mention Joshua's inexplicable disappearance, then brushed the thought away. "Had Jason stayed with the system, he would have won his money in another ten days. He elected to try double-or-nothing, and he finished with nothing."

"Oh, *no!*" cried Biddy. "How *awful!* Oh, Ish, you'll have to tell me all about it—I've never been to San Francisco, or any big city, really. You must have had a *terrible* time, in all those *gambling palaces. . . .*"

"Indeed," said Ishmael, "were it not for the money I won playing chess, we would have been hard put to pay the hotel bill."

"Chess?" Stemple glanced sharply sideways at Ishmael in the gray dusk. "Who the devil taught you to play chess?"

"My—" began Ishmael, and the word dropped off into that white void, leaving him silent.

"I'll get this yet." Biddy Cloom straightened up, and surveyed her massacred forces on the chessboard with a critical eye.

"I believe you will," agreed Ishmael equably. "All that it requires is time and concentration."

Above the mantel, the camelback clock wheezed and thumped eight-thirty, and Aaron folded up his newspaper, removed his reading glasses, and went to fetch Biddy's cloak, to walk with her back to the dormitory.

As the dormitory had emptied over the last few months, Biddy had taken to spending more time at the big house near the mill. Several evenings a week she could be found there, usually cooking dinner for the two bachelors, often staying afterwards, sewing or knitting while Aaron handled the mill papers and Ish read. When she was in the company of people she trusted, like Stemple and Ishmael, Aaron was surprised to discover that Biddy was actually a fairly quiet girl. In fact, he had to admit that he had been wrong about her almost entirely, and was coming to enjoy her company, when she wasn't nervous and trying to attract men as the other girls did.

She was learning to play chess now, having watched his games with Ishmael in the last few weeks since his nephew had returned from San Francisco. Like most beginners she had no concept of strategy, nor any idea of why she kept losing, but Aaron noticed that she didn't make mistakes about which pieces made which moves, and didn't talk during games. She made up for this in between times with a spate of chatter and gossip—preparations for Candy's wedding, the fact that Jason and Joshua Bolt had had a fearful falling-out over some unspecified request that Jason had made of Joshua. Upon closer acquaintance with her, Aaron came to realize that one of the things that had earned Biddy her reputation for tactlessness was the fact that she was observant of those around her, and had considerable intuition about people's motivations.

He was even, he found, coming to miss her on those evenings when she wasn't around.

As Aaron left the room to fetch her cloak Biddy stood up, and as she turned away from the hearth Ish caught the faint clink of silver falling on wood. He reached to pick up what she had dropped—a tiny pendant that had slipped from its chain and fallen into the shadows by the fireplace. He angled it to the light, looking for something on its worn surface . . . difficult to see in this light, for the pendant was small, not much longer than his own thumbnail.

"Oh, Ish!" She came hurrying back, the silver chain loose in her hand. "I only just this minute realized it was gone."

"I heard it fall," he said simply.

"You . . ." she said disbelieving. Then, "No, you're funning me."

Ishmael started to object, then kept silent. There were too many things, he knew, that he took for granted. One day one of them would give him away; it was something of a tribute to human inability to believe the previously unthought-of that it hadn't already.

"It is very pretty," he said, holding it carefully on his palm. "It's a—a fleur-de-lys, isn't it?" The strange name came haltingly to his tongue. To his knowledge he'd never heard it before, and knew it was in another language. "A French lily?" He turned it over. On one side its center band bore a very small star, the thing he had been looking for in the firelight.

"Yes," said Biddy. "I think it's real silver."

Ish estimated its mass against its slight weight in his palm. "It appears to be," he judged. There was something familiar about the tiny thing, the sense that he'd seen it before. Someone had told him once that this shape was a French lily, a fleur-de-lys. A woman's voice, he thought. He could almost see the woman's face. "Where did you get it?" he asked, taking the chain from her hand and stringing it through the tiny wire hoop.

"Oh, you don't have to—thank you, Ish. It was

189

Grandma Larkin's. She said to pass it along to my daughters, when I have them." She smiled again, a wry, tired smile. "That may be a long time."

She was returning, Ish knew, to a dormitory all but empty, those few girls who were left humming with the preparations for Candy Pruitt's wedding. *An unnecessary cruelty,* he thought, maneuvering the fragile silver of the twisted chain-links together and pinching them closed with his fingernail. *One she does not deserve.* "Does it matter?" he asked, stepping behind her to fix the necklace round her neck again under the white lace of her collar.

She turned her head, startled, her brown curls falling over his hands where they rested at the nape of her neck.

"Is time so vital," said Ishmael, "that you would close the door to something important, only to take what was offered first?"

She regarded him, startled, and then he saw her eyes shine with sudden tears. "Are you only saying that," she murmured, "because Aaron has a bet on it?"

"Do you think that poorly of me?" asked Ish.

She tried to pull away from him, and he caught her shoulders between his hands and held her thus for the time it took her to think. When he felt her relax a little in his grip, he let her go.

"I'm sorry," she said quietly. She turned around to face him. "It's just—I'm glad you think I'd be worth two offers."

There was no logical reply. Aaron came from the other room, wrapped in his coat and carrying her cloak, and offered her his arm. They stepped together out into the snowy night.

Ishmael closed the door behind them, and sank back into his chair by the fireplace, staring at the gold light as it played over the chess pieces still scattered like footprints over the board. There was another way to play that game, he knew. A more complex way. He picked up two pieces, suspended them in the air above the board. Why did he think they should move up and down as well as back and forth?

Who was it that he so poignantly missed playing chess with?

Why did he sometimes have vague dreams about playing chess with a machine?

He set the pieces down. It was something he would not know until he saw it again, as he had known Biddy's pendant.

Not just another silver pendant of a fleur-de-lys, but *that one. I have seen it, I have held it in my hand,* he thought. *I know it, recognize it. Of all the things here that are strange to me, why do I recognize Biddy Cloom's French lily?*

It was clear, clear as crystal before his eyes. Lying in the palm of his hand, looking different, the star worn until it was no more than a fragile tracery, visible only in the strongest of sunlight. But undeniably the same.

But he could never have seen it, could never have held it before. He was an alien, alien to this planet, and the thing was part of Biddy's family and had been so for generations. Grandma Larkin's—even the name sounded an echo in his mind. Who had said they'd had—"Ever-so-great-grandma Larkin . . . ?" A woman's voice, a woman's face . . .

He knew them, knew them so well.

It is impossible. He raised his head to look in the mirror over the mantelpiece, and from it the alien face looked back, as it had looked at him every day since he had wakened at the cabin on Eagle Head Point, marking him as a stranger among these people, an impostor in human guise.

191

He ran his hands through his hair, shoving the black thick mass of it back away from his forehead, throwing into prominence the strange bone structure, the harsh slant of the brows. Very faintly he could see the marks on his temples still, the small greenish shadow images of burns. *What had that been?* Something that had wiped out his memory, as it had obliterated those few hours from Joshua's. Only Joshua had wakened with his friend and the woman he loved beside him. Joshua had wakened in a world that he knew.

Ishmael leaned his brow on his hands, his head beginning to ache excruciatingly, as it always did when he tried to see past that cloudy void of white pain. What had happened to him? he wondered.

And why had it happened to Joshua?

He was still sitting, staring into the fire, when Stemple returned an hour later. Stemple, too, had been doing some thinking on his way back up that dark, slushy road from the dormitory. He was uncomfortably quiet as he moved about, stripping off his coat and boots.

Ishmael glanced up at him. "It is unjust, what you are doing to Biddy."

Stemple laughed harshly. "I've as good as guaranteed her a husband before the second of January. And a good one," he added defensively. "Jason Bolt will do right by her."

"Indeed," replied Ish in a colorless voice. "Nevertheless, you wrong her."

"Ish," said Aaron, in the truculent tone of a man seeking to justify what he knows to be wrong, "if Biddy Cloom hadn't come to Seattle, and if there wasn't that threat of losing his mountain to push Jason into proposing to her—which he will do, New Year's Eve if I know Bolt—she'd die an old maid. I gave Bolt the chance to buy out of the bet and he muffed it. I'm not even sure letting him out of it at this point would be the best thing."

"For Biddy?"

Stemple went and hung up his coat.

"Aaron," said Ish, when he returned to the parlor, "one thing in all of this which I do not understand. What is so wrong with Biddy Cloom? This—beauty—that is spoken of, I do not understand. Perhaps because I am alien, I feel no desire for any of those girls, and I do not see—beauty. Are humans truly so blind?"

Stemple sighed. "I'm afraid so, Ish. I know what you're saying and that's why I think I'm doing—well, maybe not the right thing, but I'm not doing any evil in pushing Jason into marrying her. I like Biddy. She spent a lot of time up here while you were in San Francisco, and she's a good girl, when she isn't driving me crazy. I'm sorry I put her in the position of a laughingstock by making her the last girl to be chosen—the short straw—but I know Jason's going to marry her and I think he'll do right by her. She'll make him a good wife, too."

Ishmael raised an eyebrow at him. "Could you stand that?"

"Having Jason Bolt do me out of Bridal Veil Mountain?" Aaron shrugged. "I'll get over it." And he went up to bed.

"Ishmael!"

Ish turned, and squinted through the clammy drizzle to see Jason Bolt hurrying along the slush-foul mess of Madison Street after him.

It had, to the great delight of the girls in the dormitory, obligingly snowed on the occasion of Christmas. Ishmael had been mystified by their pleasure in the meteorological conditions, since Seattle weather had subsequently returned to its normal pattern and the streets were now calf-deep in a freezing mixture of ice, half-rotted snow, and rainwater.

He had just left the dormitory and the warm uproar there of preparations for Candy's wedding on the morrow, a pleasant atmosphere of lamplight and pine boughs and last week's Christmas tree still standing in the parlor, its slightly tattered finery reminding him for some reason of Emperor Norton I. Outside the evening was damp and depressing, and the cold made his leg ache.

Jason fell into step with him, as they continued along the street. Jason looked harried these days, more so than the flurry entailed in marrying off his youngest brother would account for. Ish guessed the reason, and it engendered in him both anger and distaste, as well as an obscure feeling that he should not be as concerned as he was about the emotions of others. It was, after all, their affair. The wind smote them, bits of sleet snagging in the fleece collar of Jason's jacket. It would be a miserably icy night.

"Ish," said Jason, "I have a proposition for you. A business deal, if you like."

"Your last business deal," replied Ishmael, "resulted in your losing $40,000 at poker and borrowing $700 from me."

"Which I paid back," Jason reminded him. "And I'm in a position to pay that again."

"Indeed?"

"Ishmael," said Jason, "you're fond of Biddy Cloom, aren't you?"

"I am."

"Are you planning to ask her to marry you?"

Ishmael looked at him, startled by the question, startled by even the idea of marrying here on this world at all.

Jason went on, "Because if your uncle has told you

not to ask her until after Friday, let me tell you that you won't suffer for it if you ask her tomorrow night."

Without thinking, Ish said, "No. I cannot marry Biddy Cloom or anyone else."

It was Jason's turn to look both shocked and startled, more at the vehemence in Ishmael's voice than at his words. "Why not? Oh, I know all the ladies in San Francisco said you were cold as a whale's backside, but . . ."

"It is true that I am—cold," said Ishmael quietly. "But it is impossible for me to marry. There is hereditary insanity in my family. My father, who married Aaron's sister, showed no taint of it, but two of my uncles on that side are in asylums in the East, and their children seem to be likewise tainted. I have known for a long time that I cannot marry. I would not do such a thing to any woman, to have her bear my children."

Not the best of stories, he thought, but true, after its fashion: for it was true that he could not take a human woman to wife, being what he was. He could see by Jason's shaken expression that the big man had at least believed him, and had realized that compared to some matters, the ultimate fate of Bridal Veil Mountain was of fairly small worth. "I—I'm sorry," Jason said at last. "I didn't . . ."

"It is not your doing," said Ish. "I have become accustomed to the knowledge, and only recently have I had cause to regret it. Could I do so, I would marry Biddy, for I can think of few women who would make as good a wife. But for me it is out of the question."

It was the truth, and Jason accepted it as such, and quickly turned the conversation to other things. Walking alone back toward the mill later on, the sleety wind driving against his back and the cold twisting the malformed ligaments of his bad leg with the familiar ache, Ishmael thought about that. As he had said to

Aaron once, he understood neither love nor desire for these soft, pretty alien girls. But as a companion in his exile he could do worse than Biddy Cloom.

I will be in this place, this alien world, until I die, he thought. *How long shall that be? How long do my kind live? Am I doomed to live all that time alone? Yet what is my alternative? For me to live here as an alien, an exile, is one thing. At least I know what I am and what I am not. But to father a son who will be half-alien, half-human—to be at home nowhere, and never knowing quite why . . . it would be a monstrous thing to do, not only to Biddy, but to the child.*

He knew that he could not afford to become involved in the griefs of humans, and their emotions were strange to him. Yet for some reason his heart hurt for that unborn child, half-human and half-alien, as he walked on down the slushy path in silence toward the dark house.

Chapter 15

"WILL THAT DO IT?" KIRK TAPED THE BUNDLE OF slick, semitransparent sheets of flimsiplast into a plastic sack, and turned back to watch Kellogg extracting the long, accordion-folded scroll which was extruding itself like some fastastic tongue from the fax machine.

"It better," remarked the base commander, as the last of the foot-wide ribbon collapsed at her feet. "Is this Library of Congress the same Congress Aaron Stemple was in?"

"It was back then," Kirk replied. "Like all bureaucracies it took on a life of its own and is still going strong."

She picked up the fax and began shuffling it into order. "Hell, Jamie, look at this." She held up the top end of the flimsy. "This stuff was just photo-duped into the record banks straight from the printed records. I don't think anybody's even looked at the stuff since 1867."

Kirk crossed the small transmission-fax cubicle to look over her shoulder at it. He had to admit she was probably right. Instead of the usual readout of computer-printed lines the fax contained what was clearly a page-by-page photoprint of the original volume of government transactions for Washington Territory 1860–1870. From where he sat at the table loading the plastic-wrapped bundles into quarter-meter cubical carrying boxes, McCoy growled, "I can understand why." After being photographed, reduced to microfilm, the microfilm screened and reduced to a graphic-image pattern which was stored for several centuries in a computer bank and then hyperspace-transmitted through four relay stations to be blown up again and xelo-faxed, the printing—like the printing of virtually everything they had received over the hyperspace beam from the Library of Congress banks—was virtually unreadable.

But Kirk only said, "Good. It means the Klingons didn't have access to this information. They could trace Stemple as far back as 1872, but no earlier. In 1867 they'll have to hunt for him, and the way people moved around on the frontier, that could take them a long time."

McCoy took the folded stack of fax from Kellogg, slipped it into another plastic bag and taped it shut. "Is this the last?"

"Should be." Kirk slipped over to the doorway of the cubicle and eased it open slightly. The corridor outside was clear. Removing the tricorder that was slung around his shoulder, he checked the readings. No one was closer to the transmission-fax cubicles than Corridor 16, the main artery of the base. It registered as a confused stream of life-forms, rather like an ant trail. The *Enterprise*'s big life-scan systems were so sophisticated that they could tell a cat from a fox in five square miles of territory, but the equipment filled several rooms. The most a hand tricorder could be set to tell you was that there were life-forms in the vicinity—it couldn't have distinguished a Klingon from a mollusk.

He leaned back into the room. "Coast seems to be clear."

"Good," grumbled McCoy. "About time something went right."

Kellogg was signing pink export-manifest slips. She handed them to Kirk to countersign, then stuck them to the lids of the boxes. On the sides the carrying-cases bore labels: LIVE TRIBBLES—DO NOT FEED.

As McCoy hefted the boxes, he grumbled, "I signed on as a physician, not a combination historical researcher and secret agent."

"How do you think I feel, turning fax-clerk at my time of life?" retorted Kellogg with a grin. As McCoy departed, she added, "Don't step on any Klingons on your way out."

"Most of the imp rep's agents are amateurs," she told Kirk a few minutes later, as they ambled along the corridors in the general direction of the transport chamber, far enough behind McCoy not to be obviously shadowing him but close enough to tell if anyone else was. It was early in the first shift. The corridors were alive with scientists, techs, clerical and security personnel, maintenance crew. "There aren't a lot of Klingon civilians outside the empire—ordinary civilians, I mean, not defectors—but there are some. The files on all of them are impeccable, naturally."

Kirk grinned. "And you checked them, naturally."

She shrugged, "What's the good of being BC if you can't get at classified files in the computer?" She hooked her hands in her belt, pacing along at Kirk's side with a preoccupied frown. "Jamie," she said after a moment. "Is what we're doing going to do any good? In the long run, I mean?"

He glanced over at her as they shouldered their way

through the usual crowd outside the canteen. A couple of Kzinti growled a greeting at her which she returned in their own language with a snarl and bared teeth. "We won't know that till it's over," he replied.

"What I mean is—hasn't it been over for centuries? It's all in the past, isn't it? If the Klingons have succeeded we won't know it, because we'll have grown up with it the other way, whatever the other way is going to be or was. Hell," she added in frustration, "we can't even *talk* about it without inventing a new verb tense."

"Well," said Kirk quietly, "that's the problem with time travel. Fortunately it's mostly a theoretical one, because we haven't got the capability to do it—yet. But what's so frightening about what the Klingons are doing is that there really isn't any way of controlling results, once you begin to tamper. There are legends of a civilization out in the galaxy of Kasteroborous that mastered time travel, and promptly stagnated because they never dared do anything again. If the Klingons succeed we may simply never have existed—or we may become worse than the Klingons themselves. The 1870s . . ."

"Commander Kellogg!"

Kirk and Kellogg halted, turning to greet the slender, nervous-looking man in the black-and-gold uniform of Klingon Imperial Service who came striding at them from the junction of Corridor 109. His formal black beard was thin and showed signs of both implants and dye, as did his hair—Klingon males being worse even than human males on that subject. He wore the harried expression of a man for whom it has long ago become second nature to glance over his shoulder, common to Klingon civil servants even of the highest degree.

"Colonel Nch'rth," Kellogg greeted him, producing

the correct glottal rasp and meeting his dark, haughty gaze with her own.

"It was my intention to send you a memo, Commander," said the imperial representative. "And I shall follow up this conversation with one, certainly."

"On what subject?"

Nch'rth's voice tightened, as if some internal tuning peg had been turned a fraction of a millimeter. "On the subject of the proper marking of containers in which dangerous fauna are transported." His eyes had, Kirk noticed, shifted from Kellogg to Kirk himself. Like any Klingon, he unconsciously turned to speak to a man rather than a woman. "The boxes used to transport dangerous or abominable creatures are clearly required to be marked as containing them. Yet one of the maintenance crew—a man who owes allegiance to the empire, and is thus under my protection—was badly bitten by a pelz that was being transported aboard the *Enterprise*. The bite of a pelz is a truly savage thing—the man could have lost a finger. The boxes should have been more clearly marked or the animal sedated."

"Whatever the boxes contained, they were clamped shut and, I believe, locked," said Kellogg, drawing the imperial representative's eyes back to her as a reminder that she was the one to whom he must speak regarding base regulations, not the captain of a starship. "And they were labeled, were they not, Captain?"

"Yes, they were," said Kirk. "I saw them myself, up in Dr. McCoy's laboratory later."

"The labels were not properly displayed," said the imperial representative stubbornly, still speaking more or less to Kirk. When Kirk made no response he turned back to Kellogg, his voice contracting until it threatened to go right up into the next register. "Believe me, Commander, this casual fraternization and tolerance of negligence between a supposedly neutral base commander and a high-ranking Federation military officer has not gone unnoticed and will not be tolerated. If such negligence had been on the part of a member of the Klingon military your reaction would be different. One of the other boxes in that shipment was marked as containing a Ceti eel. What if that had escaped? They breed like flies in the ventilating system. One of them could have wiped out this base."

"My attitude, Colonel, is hardly casual," said Kellogg, her voice suddenly hard. "And yours, if I may venture to say so, is scarcely professional. You have made your complaint and I will take action to see that such an incident does not recur. However, since your man had no right to be tampering with locked boxes no matter what they contained or how they were labeled, I suggest that you take steps to do the same. Good day to you, sir."

She turned, and strode briskly away, Kirk in her wake. Behind them, Colonel Nch'rth called furiously, "You shall receive a memo!"

She snapped back over her shoulder, "I shall read it!" and continued walking. "And as for you, Captain, regarding those boxes . . ." They turned a corner and passed out of earshot, and Kellogg grinned. "Where in the hell did you come up with a live pelz? I didn't know there were any on the base."

"We had one in zoological—Mr. Sulu smuggled it down as papers."

"Good God," said Kellogg, paling. "Don't tell me that was a real Ceti eel. . . ."

Kirk shook his head and grinned. "Just dirt, covering the fax-sheets. But I think after that, none of the imperial representative's amateur agents are going to be terribly anxious to snoop in any boxes we might be carrying on board the *Enterprise*."

"Would that it were live tribbles," Mr. Sulu sighed, as the door to the Officers' Conference Room on board the *Enterprise* zipped soundlessly open twenty minutes later to admit Kirk. "Better to perish smothered in fur than in flimsiplast. . . ."

"Hear, hear," muttered McCoy, from the pile of property transactions and licenses that he had been sorting through all morning.

"Where, where?" inquired Lieutenant Gilden, a thin, depressed-looking young man who had been drafted from his beloved Historical Section to catalog and help keep things in something resembling order.

"There, there," said Uhura in a comforting tone, following Kirk into the conference room with four velfoam cups of coffee balanced in her hands.

"Now, now," Kirk chided. Trae, who had been bent over the terminal that had been installed in the far corner when the conference room had been taken over by the inner circle of the Guardian Project, raised his head and regarded Kirk with the expression of a man who has, against his every inclination, expected better. He had obviously spent a great deal of time listening to Sulu, Gilden, Uhura and McCoy. The memory of Spock's voice drifted through Kirk's mind. *I feel as though I had been shanghaied by a shipful of Hokas. . . .*

It had been largely out of consideration for threats to persons and property that the headquarters for the paper-trailing of Aaron Stemple had been established aboard the *Enterprise* instead of in Trae's quarters on the starbase itself. Once quantities of duplicated records had started coming in from the Library of Congress, it would have been impossible to conceal from the imperial representative's agents on base that something was going on, and, after the attempt on Trae, Kirt put little trust in the predictability of the colonel's reactions. Likewise, for this reason, the research circle itself was kept as small as possible, including only those who had prior knowledge of events—Kirk himself, McCoy, Trae, Sulu, Uhura and Kellogg as their other duties would permit. Lieutenant Gilden was the only outsider to have been drafted in, to make sense of the random information gleaned by the others from their reading, to discard what was meaningless and catalog the rest.

Of this "rest" there was a vast deal. It had taken less than twenty-four hours for the Officers' Conference Room to take on the aspect of a combination lunchroom and library, with piles of faxed translations of the old Karsid intelligence reports, Library of Congress records on their long flimsiplast scrolls, faxed and photostated books interspersed with cups of dead coffee, candy wrappers, glasses of moxie that had long gone flat, and crumb-littered velfoam plates that Uhura had brought up from the mess hall as she came and went.

Uhura had taken over the post as outside contact for the Guardian Project. As communications officer she had less time to devote to it than Sulu or McCoy; her duties, unlike theirs, increased rather than decreased when the *Enterprise* was in port. It had been Kellogg's priority clearance on the hyperspace transmission channels that had gotten the Library of Congress information faxed through to the base, and Kirk's idea to establish a zoological research project that would both account for the *Enterprise's* continued presence in orbit and permit them to carry boxes from the base to the ship largely uninvestigated by agents of the Klingon imperial representative.

The only other people who knew what was going on were Mr. Scott and his people, who were engaged, under the supervision of Aurelia Steiner, in converting the *Enterprise* engines so that they could take the stresses of creating a time warp and then being kicked through it, and then—with any luck—reversing the process and getting back.

On the whole, thought Kirk, looking around the small, cluttered conference room, it was just as well. For three days now he had managed not to realize that Spock was dead more than five or six times a day—usually when he woke up in the morning, or stopped to rest. In spite of his grumbling about playing secret agents, McCoy was looking better, too. There was nothing like the pressure of knowing that your universe might be inerradicably altered to drive lesser considerations from your mind. After this was over . . .

He pushed the thought away. After this was over enough time would have passed so that the hurt would be a little numbed. And anyway, Kirk thought, watching them—Sulu thumbing through another slick, awkward-sized collection of title deeds from Portland and vicinity and groaning in protest, Gilden playing one of his arcane games of solitaire with note cards, Uhura talking to McCoy and even getting him to smile a little—*if we fail at this, we might not have an afterwards.*

Or even a before.

"Well, gentlemen," he said, taking a chair at the head of the table and removing a pile of translations interleaved with note cards and candy wrappers in order to sit in it, "what have we found?"

Sulu set down one of the heaps of fax sheets. "I think we've located him, Captain."

"In 1867?"

With a slight movement of his foot, Trae turned his chair away from the terminal, removing a sheet from the printer as he did so.

"Records of the town of Seattle, Washington Territory, show the purchase of town lots in 1856, 1860 and 1866 by an Aaron Stemple, listed as a sawmill owner. A man of some substance. He was a member of the first school board of the town in 1869, and the same Aaron Stemple is listed in 1869 as being elected mayor of Seattle, and in 1872 as running for territorial representative, a post which he evidently succeeded in attaining. He was noted for his philanthropy and for his undoubted ability to turn a dollar."

"You know," said McCoy thoughtfully, folding his hands on the untidy heap of flimsies before him, "that's what surprises me about this whole thing."

"That he was a well-off philanthropist and sawmill owner?" asked Kirk.

"That he suspected the Karsids in the first place. Trae here says they never presented themselves as aliens. They had an almost uncanny ability to pass themselves off as members of the same race as their victims. Why would Stemple suspect them of being extraterrestrials? Why would he jump to that conclusion, which it looks like he did almost immediately, judging from the date of the first contact-reports from the Karsids and Stemple's first letter to President Grant."

Trae said, "He is described as a shrewd man and an astute judge of character."

"Well, so was Charles Dickens, but I doubt he'd have come to the same conclusion. He was a Victorian—the Victorians were about the most pragmatic and hardheaded bunch of cutthroat businessmen you'd ever hope to find. Aliens from another planet? They'd never have believed it."

"H. G. Wells was a Victorian," remarked Kirk. "So was Jules Verne. The fathers of speculative fiction. Wells dealt in invasions of the Earth—not to mention time travel."

"Invasion," said McCoy. "Not economic servitude. And face it, Jim, it's something people in the twentieth century would have scoffed at, let alone the nineteenth. They'd never have taken it seriously. Only Stemple and, fortunately, President Grant, bless his boozy old heart. But for all he was shrewd—and if he ran a mill in those days he'd have to be—what would have tipped Stemple to the possibilities of alien infiltration? He was just a frontier capitalist with a flair for politics."

"Was he?" Kirk leaned back in his chair. "The frontier drew lots of people, Bones. People with all kinds of backgrounds. Dreamers, drifters, gamblers on ideas as well as crooks and grifters out to make a buck. Stemple may just have had a hell of an imagination, and the guts to back his convictions."

He extracted from the pile of papers before him the one picture that the faxes had provided, a fairly good copy for having been reduced to its component lights and darks and transmitted across centuries of time and light-years of space. A formal shot, probably an election photo, with that fixed, blank look common to the victims of long-exposure photography.

Kirk studied the fleshy, rather sensual face framed in its stiff white collar, black coat and subdued muttonchop whiskers. Dark hooded eyes with a calculating, almost ruthless expression. Almost a villain's face, he thought in surprise, remembering that Stemple was supposed to have been a humanitarian, not to mention a firm believer in extraterrestrials. This was not the face of a dreamer. There was no fancifulness in that closed, speculative gaze.

A frontier capitalist with a flair for politics, nothing more.

What would have caused a man like that to risk an evidently hard-won reputation by the assertions he had made before the secret Congressional committee set up to deal with the first of the Karsid contacts? What had caused him to be that sure of something that wildly improbable? What had given him the conviction to pursue it with the single-minded ferocity that the Karsid intelligence reports clearly showed?

Beside him, McCoy was saying, "H. G. Wells notwithstanding, from speculation to that kind of conviction is one hell of a leap."

"I wonder." Kirk set the fax down thoughtfully. "Are the Klingons out to kill him, or to prevent whatever incident it was that caused him to make that leap?"

Trae paused in the act of sorting through his reconstructions of maps made from Seattle property records. "Is it your supposition that Aaron Stemple may have had some kind of contact with extraterrestrials before the Karsids?"

"Only supposition," Kirk said. "He could simply have had a bolder imagination than his fellows, and a more stubborn disposition."

The Vulcan's long fingers twitched restlessly along the edges of the several maps he held, neatening the stack. Even the heavier grades of flimsiplast are far less amenable to tidy sorting than actual paper. "Your supposition could be correct, Captain," he conceded. "But in any case it is a distinction which I doubt the Klingons who conceived the project are capable of making. Like the imperial representative, they tend to prefer their solutions simple. If we cross this time warp, it will not be to aid in some problematical encounter, but to save this man's life."

Chapter 16

"WAS BIDDY GOING TO COME UP FOR DINNER BEFORE the dance?" Aaron Stemple peered sideways at himself in the small round shaving mirror as he tied his cravat.

"She had intended to," said Ish, leaning at ease in the doorway. He had donned a blue-and-black plaid shirt over his dark sweater for the occasion of the wedding and the dance, and dark Sunday trousers; his black hair hung down in a shaggy mane almost to his collar. In the two reflections side by side in the shaving mirror, Stemple could see nothing of that shocking difference that had first borne it upon his nephew that he was, in fact, a stranger in a strange land.

It was something he had almost forgotten, except for moments like this—that Ishmael was not his nephew, and was only passing for human.

Ish folded his arms in a very human gesture, and went on, "I believe that Jason Bolt is escorting Miss Cloom to the wedding, and to the dance afterwards."

Aaron turned, stung. Ish raised an eyebrow. "She is, after all, going to be his wife."

"He hasn't asked her yet," snapped Aaron irritably.

"That you know of," said Ish.

Aaron was still standing, staring silently into space, when he heard Ish's limping step retreat down the stairs.

The music of fiddles and banjos, the click of the bones and the brandy-colored lamplight against the clean pine of the walls. Wreaths of evergreen boughs jeweled with the ceramic-bright red of holly berries scented the air and transformed the long, barnlike dormitory parlor into a sort of bower, out of which Biddy's framed fashion prints peered with a kind of dignified incongruity. The air in the long, narrow room was warm with the candles and lamps, the press of people and the exertions of the dancers. The smells of it were heavy, wax and pine and cloves, and, whenever the kitchen door was opened, the sweet waft of baking.

All of Seattle seemed to be there. Lottie, decked out for the occasion in a gown of very bright blue taffeta, leaning laughing on the arm of an extremely rosy-faced Captain Clancey, in his Sunday best with his graying red whiskers trimmed. Candy Bolt, shining with wild, springing joy, her mahogany red hair twined with the white hothouse woodbine that Clancey had nursed all the freezing voyage north from San Francisco; Jeremy Bolt, looking ready to burst his brass waistcoat buttons from pride and happiness. Joshua, pale and solitary, standing near the refreshment tables and watching the dancers move through the first of the reels with a slight smile on his face. Biddy Cloom, pink and radiant with excitement, leaning on Jason Bolt's powerful arm.

Other faces—the loggers, the New Bedford girls either newly wedded or betrothed; the foundation of the settled town, as Jason had intended. The foundation of the territory. Stockholders in a brave new world, dancing in the lamplight while the snow drifted down outside.

Watching them, Ishmael thought, *they are one, they are whole. United as the—as the crew of a ship that sails the stars.*

And, oddly enough, for the first time since he had wakened in Stemple's cabin and seen his own reflection in the mirror, he felt a part of them. For better or worse, however he happened to come here and whatever he was, he was now a part of Seattle. There was no stricture that all members of a society had to be entirely human.

Someone touched his arm. "Will you dance, Ish?"

Biddy, her sallow coloring warmed by the dark blue of her bridesmaid gown, her eyes bright as Lottie's paste diamonds, stood at his side.

Couples were forming up for another reel, the tentative scrape and twang of the musicians half-buried beneath chatter and jokes. "I do not know how," he excused himself.

"Well, you can learn." She dragged him by main force into the line.

It required both stamina and concentration. Ignorance and a lame leg slowed him down, but there was a certain pleasure to be had in the measured figures, in the sheer swift joy of the movement itself. Dancing with them, moving up and down the lines, catching hands, catching arms, catching waists, Ish finally understood some of the beauty and fascination of these young girls, bright-eyed and lovely. He would never feel the irrational yearning of physical love for them, but he saw for the first time how others might.

From the opposite side of the room, Jason Bolt was watching the dancers, thinking to himself that it probably wasn't going to be as bad as he'd feared. Biddy

Cloom did improve upon acquaintance, and seeing her, flushed and giggling as she swung in the arms of Stemple's imperturbable nephew, he had to admit that there were times when she was almost pretty. He looked around for Stemple, but the mill owner had not yet come in. *Better,* he thought, *to get it over with before he does. He's got as much riding on it as I do, and he'll find a way to stop me if he can.*

As the music finished with a flourish he steeled himself to do what he had always suspected he would have to do, from the first moment Biddy Cloom strode down the gangplank of Clancey's boat.

The couples were breaking up, laughing their breathless way toward the bright-colored island of the refreshment tables. He went over to her and took her hand. "Biddy, can I have a word with you?"

There wasn't a lot of room to slip quietly away. The parlor was large, but milling with people; every corner seemed to contain either a refreshment table or another courting couple. Though the wind had changed and promised a break in the weather it was still cold outside. Jason reflected that he might have to propose to Biddy Cloom to save the mountain, but he wasn't going to acquire frostbite with matrimony if he could help it.

He finally settled on guiding her through the crowds to a quiet corner at the foot of the stairs, where the girls normally hung wet coats. The shadows of the banisters interposed themselves between the lights and crowds in the long parlor. Even twined with evergreen boughs they conveyed to Jason's present mood an uncomfortable suggestion of prison bars.

He held her hands in his. "Biddy," he said quietly, "I guess the time has come." He raised her fingers to his lips and looked down into her long, horsey face, banded with amber light and shadow. Bracing himself for the inevitable, he asked. "Will you marry me?"

Her homely face broke into a sunny smile. "Oh, Jason! How *kind* of you to ask." She squeezed his hands warmly. "Even though I can't accept it, I . . ."

"*What?*" gasped Jason. It had never, in his wildest dreams, occurred to him that any woman, least of all Biddy Cloom, would turn him down.

She blinked those long, perfectly straight lashes. "I can't accept it," she stated matter-of-factly. Then she smiled again, glowingly. "But thank you—thank you so much for asking. I've never had anyone propose to me before . . ."

I can believe that, thought Jason grimly.

". . . and I never suspected that you . . ."

"But—" This was not going the way he had planned it at all. "Why not?"

"Well," said Biddy simply, "I don't love you."

"What does love—" he began, and cut himself off short. "Biddy," he said, fighting for calm, "I mean it. I do want to marry you. Please say you will. If you don't . . ." He could not say, *If you don't I'll lose Bridal Veil Mountain to Aaron Stemple,* but neither, he found, could he say anything else.

Her face grew grave in the banded light. "If I don't, I'll be an old maid?" she asked quietly. "Maybe I will. I like you, Jason—I like you very much. And it's very noble of you to ask just to keep me from being an old maid. But there's only one person in Seattle that I love—that I would love enough to marry—and I . . ."

"Is it Ishmael?" he demanded. "Because if it is . . ."

"Ish?" Biddy looked surprised at the very suggestion. "Good Heavens, no. Oh, Jason," she added, seeing his expression grow grim. "I haven't broken your heart, have I?"

Struggling with shock and punctured vanity, Jason

would cheerfully have broken her neck, but at that moment she was distracted by a commotion at the outer door of the hall, by voices and the chilling draft of freezing wind.

"Oh," she said, as though the proposal had never taken place, "it's the passengers from Clancey's mail-boat!" And with a swish of lace-trimmed petticoats she skipped past him and out into the room again to be among the others greeting the newcomers, Jason at her heels.

Only one of them had come into the hall—a slender, dark-haired girl whom it took Jason a moment to recognize because she'd taken off her spectacles when the heat of the room fogged them. Joshua's voice cried, "Sarah!" over the din of the crowd and she looked up, myopia, trepidation and a hint of defiance in her enormous gray eyes. Joshua said, "Sarah!" again and fought his way through the press to scoop her into his arms. "Sarah, you came! I never thought—I mean—"

"Miss Gay, isn't it?" asked Jason, coming to her other side.

She looked up at him, that slight air of challenge back in her eyes as she put on her specs again. "Dr. Gay, actually," she said. "I'm a licensed medical practitioner."

If she was expecting patronizing amusement from this big, strapping man whom she'd met so briefly in San Francisco, she was disappointed. Seattle had been without a doctor far too long. Jason's voice grew eager. "Have you come to Seattle to practice medicine, then?"

She pushed nervously at the raveling trails of her escaping hair. "Well, I hope to practice here, yes. But I actually came to Seattle to be married. I think," she added, casting a worried glance at Joshua.

Joshua was blithering in a fashion totally unlike his usual calm self. "I don't have a ring but I'll get you one, I swear I'll get you one. . . ."

"Oh, don't worry about it, Josh. . . ."

Jason had to smile. Much was now explained that Joshua, usually the most secretive of men, had in the course of their earlier quarrel told Jason was none of his damn business. It stuck him with Biddy, of course—but it was almost worth it to see Josh broken out of his withdrawn coolness.

The subject of Biddy made him look down at her again, where she stood at his side, like the others babbling a welcome to this shy stranger. As he put his arm around her shoulders to lead her out of the group Jason saw that Aaron Stemple had entered the room, looking dark and somber and villainous as ever, and was watching him and the homely girl with narrowed eyes.

Jason said, "Biddy?" and she looked up at him again. As he steered her from the crowd he saw her sallow cheeks grow suddenly pink with confusion, and her hand instinctively sought his.

They were about halfway to the door when Aaron seemed to reach a decision, and crossed through the knots of people around the refreshment tables to intercept them.

Biddy halted, looking up at Stemple inquiringly.

Stemple said, "May I—speak to you first, Biddy?"

She glanced up at Jason, as having prior claim. Jason's gaze met Stemple's over her head, suspicious of some new mischief, but was met only by that enigmatic dark stare. He said, "By all means."

Stemple took Biddy's elbow, and guided her quietly to a corner.

He's up to something, thought Jason narrowly, watching them talk. *He's guessed I'm going to ask*

*her. But by God he won't get away with it. I'll keep
that mountain if it's the last thing I do—if I have to
elope with Biddy tonight to do it.*

Then, to Jason's lifelong astonishment, he saw
Biddy start, gazing up into Aaron's face. With a squeal
and a gasp you could have heard all over the room if
there hadn't still been such a row around Joshua and
Sarah, Biddy threw herself into Stemple's arms. Jason
stared, mouth open, as the two embraced, Aaron's
face buried in the girl's dark curls; then they disengaged briefly, and their mouths met in a long, satisfied
kiss.

They came back through the press of loggers and
girls as the fiddlers were tuning up for another square
dance. Aaron looked poker-stiff as usual, his arm
possessively around Biddy's waist.

"Jason," said Aaron quietly, "I concede that you
have won your bet. I—have asked Miss Cloom to
marry me."

Jason felt like he'd been hit between the eyes with
an ax handle. "You what?"

"I'm going to marry Biddy." The black eyes met
his, defiant, daring him to say something, anything,
*and by God I'll break you and your mountain and your
damn neck if you do.*

With an effort, Jason got his breath back. "I—I wish
you every happiness," he managed to say. "I—Aaron,
that's wonderful." Astonishment was giving way to
pure joy, and the magnanimous happiness with the
world that comes from being let off the hook. "Con-
gratulations—may I kiss the bride?"

Biddy presented a chaste cheek. Then she asked,
"What was it you wanted to see me about, Jason?"

"It doesn't matter now," he said. And, sincerely,
"Biddy—I'm happy for you. Not for any other reason,
just happy for you."

"Thank you, Jason," she said softly, and Aaron led her toward the dance floor.

One of the millhands came up quietly, and tapped Aaron's shoulder. "There's a feller asking to see you, up by the mill offices."

"Tonight?"

"Says it's important. Says he's down from Vancouver, with information for you about the disposal of the British timberland north of here. Needs to see someone about financing."

Aaron nodded impatiently. Ishmael had appeared out of nowhere. He said, "Would you mind if Ish deputized for me, Biddy? I'll be back."

She smiled, suddenly shy. "All right."

His eyes met his nephew's over her head. Ishmael tilted an eyebrow at him, and led Biddy onto the dance floor.

The fiddles struck up "Red River Valley." Aaron, wrapped in his mackinaw, paused in the doorway, watching the room, like an island of light in the wilderness. Saw them weaving back and forth in the dance: Ishmael and Biddy, like brother and sister, Ish's face solemn, though his eyes smiled. Joshua and Dr. Gay. Jeremy and Candy. Clancey swinging Lottie through the bright measures. Jason on the sidelines, a huge cup of punch in his hand and the relieved smile of a reprieved life prisoner on his face. Long skirts swished on the pine floor, their colors mixing and swaying in rhythm. Ish swung Candy in the center of the ring, and the formation dissolved into the grand right-and-left, men's hands and women's touching, swinging through the circle, the smiling faces flushed red with exertion.

His eyes followed one form around the circle, and he shook his head at his own folly.

At first he had only thought that his feelings had been because he would miss having her about the place—because he had gotten used to her. He had grudged to admit even to himself, let alone to anyone else, that it might be more than that. Maybe it was Ish's insistence that he treat her feelings with justice that had made him look at her differently than he had. He didn't know. He hadn't even been really sure what she'd say when he asked her—because there was seldom any telling *what* that maddening woman would say.

I must be out of my head, he thought, watching the couples work round the ring to one another again, and smiled. Homely, tactless, a girl no man in his right mind would consider marrying—except that, entering the room to see her on Jason Bolt's arm, he had known that he could not abide seeing her married to someone else.

The couples fetched up together again, after their circuit; he could see Ishmael swing Biddy in a circle on his arm, and laugh at something she said to him.

Ishmael would never be human, thought Aaron, but tonight, swinging through the figures of the dance, he was as near to it as he'd ever come.

Smiling to himself, Aaron hugged his mackinaw close about him, and stepped out into the night.

The music of the fiddles faded behind him. His breath steamed like a rag of silk on the still, frosty air. It had ceased snowing, and a thin slush lay underfoot. The clouds were breaking from the black sky, and stars were beginning to show, snagged in the dark tangle of the tree branches overhead, diamonds trapped in a lattice of black.

And amid that dark network of branches, Aaron thought that one red star seemed to be moving.

In the hall the dance finished, the men and girls laughing, holding onto each other to catch their breath.

Ish had seen Aaron leave, but knew, without being told, what had passed between Aaron and Biddy and Jason. There was a logic to it that pleased him. Biddy, holding onto his arm, was saying something to Sarah beside them, about coming to Seattle in the most awful time of year.

"It wasn't so bad," Sarah replied, worriedly pushing hairpins back into place. "Once we passed the Golden Gate we were able to make good time."

"Did you have to walk up from the harbor alone?" asked Biddy. "I remember when I first came to Seattle a year ago, it was like this, only there was mud. . . ."

"No." Sarah smiled. "Captain Clancey wanted to go ahead up to the wedding, but I came up with the other passengers. I don't see them—oh. There. By the door."

Ish looked over at them, two swarthy men edging their way out the door as he watched. He frowned, shocked and startled.

They were Klingons.

At first his only thought was, *What are Klingons doing at Candy's wedding dance?*

Then, as they vanished into the darkness outside, like a lead sledge it hit him: cold that stopped his breath, and the screaming echo of remembered pain.

Klingons.

The transport.

Aaron.

"Ish?" Spock looked down. The woman he held on his arm was gazing worriedly up at him. "Are you all right? You look absolutely green."

Without a word he broke free of her, limping swiftly across the room, maneuvering among the thick press of humans to the door. The Klingons were nowhere in sight as he stepped out into the freezing night.

It was deathly cold and still outside. Spock's breath

blew like a cloud on the icy air. Black and silver in the starlight the wide yard of the dormitory lay, patched with pools of golden window light. There was no movement visible up and down the muddy shadows of First Street, where it jogged down toward the harbor in the direction of the mill, and despite the cold enough people had been in and out of the dance to churn the new-fallen snow in the yard to a dirty and unreadable slush.

But Spock knew in what direction he must go. The logical place to ambush him would be the screen of the woods that separated the mill from the town. For a moment he debated about flanking wide enough to take the ambushers from behind, but discarded the idea. With his lame leg he could never move fast enough over the rough ground of the woods. So he started off along the road, hugging the shadows of the last few buildings of the town where he could, listening ahead for any sound, his mind a chaos of whirling memories.

They must have been hunting him for months, he thought. They had no record of where he was in 1867, and they had the entire Pacific Coast to search. But they had finally come to San Francisco, and everyone, as Jason Bolt had pointed out, passed through that city sometime.

They had missed him the first time. But small and clear he saw again in his mind Joshua Bolt standing, lamp raised, in the doorway of Mrs. O'Shaughnessy's the night of the first attack. Aaron had not returned to San Francisco, but Joshua had.

He left the last buildings of the town behind, moving stealthily through the freezing darkness. Wind cut through his wool shirt and the sweater underneath it as though they had been gauze. Aaron's tracks were clear here, in the slush and thin snow; none followed.

Joshua must have broken very quickly, he thought, when they put the Mind-Sifter on him. It surprised him a little that they had not killed him afterwards.

Non-interference? A ripple effect? Statistically the risk of ripple effect would increase exponentially, particularly with that much time involved. The Klingons would never have risked it. The historian Khlaru, whose name had been in the reports in the transport's data banks, might not have been able to dissuade the imperial representative from the plan, but he had at least accomplished that much.

He moved through the black shadows of the first trees of the woods, listening, as he had listened that night in San Francisco in the fog. That brought back other memories, of himself in San Francisco, the warm brightness of the gambling halls and the sting of champagne on his tongue. He had been a human among humans, betrayed into a maudlin concern for their stupid and illogical affairs. At the dance—memory of that understanding filled him with disgust and shame.

There is no time for this, he told himself, pushing the thoughts away. He paused in the inky shadows of a pine, his bare fingertips almost numb where they touched the wet roughness of the bark, each breath a spiked lance of crystal ice in his lungs. *They'll be waiting for him just this side of the mill yard.*

Silently, he resumed his course. He knew these woods, and the Klingons did not—he had walked through them all autumn, with Biddy Cloom, or Joshua Bolt, or Aaron Stemple, indulging in the murky sentiments of the humans among whom he had lived. He would not, he thought, allow that to happen again. And yet, whether he was able to stop the Klingons or not, he knew that he was destined to continue to live in this place among these humans. If in four months the

Enterprise had not made its appearance, it was not likely that it would.

He turned a corner of the path. Like something viewed through a gate, he could see the churned and sodden ground of the mill yard, under a thin sugaring of snow that was already melting; beyond the hill bulked bare and ugly in the starlight, a wasted stubble-field shorn by the reapers of trees. The roar of the tailrace drowned all sounds from the woods ahead.

Dark against the starlight of that gate Aaron Stemple stood alone in the middle of the road. Something must have alerted his suspicions, for he stood tense, ready. But even as Spock started to hurry up the path toward him, slowed by the cold that sliced into the wrecked muscles of his leg, he turned, shrugged and seemed to relax, and resumed his course toward the mill.

"Aaron!"

Stemple whirled, startled. At the same instant a glaring flash of greenish light erupted from the trees to his right. He dropped in the road as if he had been clubbed.

Spock took the only logical course. If the Klingons had not dared kill Joshua in San Francisco, they would not kill him—provided they assumed him to be human, and not a temporal anomaly like themselves. All this went through his mind in instants as he broke cover and ran to where Stemple lay in the slush of the path. The ligaments of his knee gave out and he stumbled as he reached Stemple's side, keeping the Klingons from firing again. Gently he turned him over in the mud and starlight, sickened by what he saw.

Klingon disruptors are messy weapons, designed to hurt, and to cow by fear, as well as to kill. Spock could see Aaron hadn't taken the main bolt, for he'd been turning back already at Spock's warning cry. But he'd been caught in the blast nimbus, and the right side of his face was a spreading ruin of ruptured tissue. Spock knew that his whole body must be torn that way, inside and out. Stemple's slow dragging breath brought the blood trickling from mouth and nose, black in the starlight against the marble whiteness of his face.

Ice rustled on branches. There was a thin, glassy crunch as a twig broke beneath a booted foot. Spock turned, the nerves of his injured knee screaming as they ground into the frozen muck. Like ghosts, the two Klingons materialized from the dark woods.

"Get away from him," said the shorter one in a thin, cold voice. Even with the disguise, the long straggly hair of the frontiersman and some minimal plastic surgery on the ears and brow, he could have been nothing but a Klingon. Spock wondered if his own disguise were that flimsy. The taller man he recognized vaguely, the shorter one not at all. Neither had been among those who had questioned him aboard the transport. He wondered whether they had listened to the tapes which he knew they'd made of the proceedings, and if they had, whether they would recognize his voice.

He lifted his hand from Stemple's face, his fingers a black smear of blood. "What have you done to him?" he asked, his voice a hoarse whisper.

"That does not concern you." Starlight slithered along the muzzle of the disruptor. At that range the blast would shred them both. This was not San Francisco, where the proximity of crowds had held them to the uncertain limitations of contemporary weapons.

Spock made no move to rise. "It concerns me that you have killed my uncle and my benefactor," he said, looking down the gaping black eye of the muzzle. "It concerns me that you have killed my friend."

The roaring of the tailrace was loud in his ears, and the far-off sighing of the wind. Behind them he could distinguish other sounds, the distant scrunch of boots in icy gravel, a woman's voice. The inky murk of shadows closed them in: the hunters and their prey in that long chase, and Spock kneeling between.

"Get away from him!" the Klingon leveled the weapon at him, knuckles moving as his hand tightened.

Spock said, "No."

In the harsh dialect of Klinzhai, the second hunter said, "You can't, you fool . . ."

"Shut up," snapped the taller one in the same tongue. "I know what they told us. No humans . . . but he doesn't know it."

Spock willed himself not to show any comprehension of what they were saying, though it must become obvious to them, logically, that he would not remain guarding a man already dead. Nor would it take them long to deduce that if he knew they could not shoot him, he must logically be a time-and-space traveler like themselves, and fair game.

"Get away," said the Klingon softly. "Or I shall send you with him."

Still Spock did not move. He could hear Lottie's voice clearly over the roaring of the millrace, saying, "I know he's in trouble, Jason. Those two men at the dance were the ones who came through back in September. . . ."

Jason's voice, indistinct with distance but sharp with alarm, said, "But they were in San Francisco. . . ."

"For the last time," said the Klingon assassin, "our business is with him. I think you would not put your life at risk for a corpse, my friend, but you waste your time. For he will die."

"Then let him die in peace," Spock rasped. "I do

not know what the range of that thing is, or why you want him dead, but I shall kill you if you come near." Spock had always been too logical to be much of an actor. He could never, he had always known, fake people out as Captain Kirk did. But the anger that shook in his voice was genuine. The Vulcan half of his mind reflected detachedly that they would never associate such emotion with the Vulcan prisoner who had escaped them; the human half knew that the words were not a threat, but a promise.

Clancey's voice was clearly audible now. "Steady, lass! Is it Aaron you're in such a taking over or Ishmael? You say . . . "

"I don't know—don't ask—for God's sake hurry."

The Klingons glanced at one another in the near-dark. The taller Klingon, the one who held the disruptor, said, "Kill him and let's go."

The shorter one turned back, and regarded Spock in the starlight for a moment, a dark shape in a plaid shirt, kneeling by the body in a black glitter of ice and blood. "We have killed him," he said softly. "He will not recover from the blast."

"And the other? He has seen us."

"What has he seen?" said that soft, thin voice. "Assassins are as common as lice on the frontier. As for him, he is fool enough with his own loyalties and life that his own place in this world cannot be a long one. Come."

"Aaron!" called Lottie's voice, harsh and piercing in the hard cold of the night. "Ishmael!" And he heard her running, her voice puffing and breaking. "Ishmael!"

The taller Klingon paused indecisively, disruptor still held steady upon them; toying, Spock's Vulcan mind was shocked to note, with the thought of momentarily disregarding the stricture against tampering with more than one element of the time-stream and making sure of Aaron and Spock as well.

He thought in disgust, *How typically Klingon*.

The shorter assassin caught his partner's arm, and said, "Come on, you fool! They're coming!"

"Ishmael!"

Spock swung his head around to shout a warning, and saw them at the top of the path, Lottie's stout silhouette between the bulky shape of Clancey and the tall shadow of Jason Bolt. Starlight flashed on the woman's dyed blond hair and the bunched taffeta of her skirts, and on the long muzzle of Jason's rifle. He heard the Klingons move, swiftly, and turned back to face them, ready to kill them or die trying.

But they were gone. There was only the blackness of the woods, and the faint suggestion of rustling in the trees. After a moment he heard the silvery whine of a transporter beam.

Lottie was running toward him, stumbling in the slippery muck of the road and gasping for breath, with Jason and Clancey outdistancing her up the long hill. Spock found that he was still kneeling, shivering, suddenly cold to the marrow of his bones with exhaustion. As the humans surrounded him he looked down at the body sprawled in the mud beside him, the gory ruin of the man he had crossed half the galaxy and centuries of time to save.

The Klingons had accomplished their mission, and departed. His own last link with his own time, his own world, was severed. He was alone, and he had failed.

Chapter 17

METHODICALLY, SPOCK PUT ASIDE THE HOLLOW
needles and the length of rubber tubing, and folded the
silk scarf he'd used as a tourniquet. His concentration
had narrowed with exhaustion to include only the
crude equipment Dr. Gay had lent him, and his own
hands. Automatically he registered this tunnel vision
as a symptom of fatigue and made a mental note to
compensate. He turned back to look at the tiny room
behind him.

Joshua Bolt slumped in the worn armchair beside
the bed. Aaron had sat there, doing accounts, when he
himself had first awakened to the sound of rain, the
emptiness of being no longer in pain, remembering
nothing. Existing, for one instant, in the absolute
present, utterly without past or future. Josh's face was
white from loss of blood, his eyes shut and a little
sunken-looking, his fair eyebrows looking almost
brown by contrast with the bloodless skin. On the edge
of the circle of lamplight Aaron lay, whiter than Josh,
almost as white as the sheets of the bed. His face was
changed, sunken and pinched-looking, half-hidden by

bandages that covered the ruined mass of wounds that would not heal.

Spock sighed. Fifty-one hours. Jason and Jeremy had given their blood already. Stemple was still hemorrhaging. How long would it take the internal damage, the lesions throughout the lungs, to heal? Would repeated transfusions carry him through until they did? His mind groped for a clinical train of thought, and found only emotional ones.

Wearily, he left the room.

The parlor of the little cabin on Eagle Head Point was dark. Spock leaned against the mantel beside the last embers of the fire, and numbly tried to piece together some kind of solution. He was aware that he was long past the point of even minimum efficiency, but there was no one else and he dared not let Stemple go unwatched.

Medical biology had not been his specialty, though he knew enough about it to understand the specialists under his command. Given even minimal facilities, he knew himself capable of saving Stemple's life. But without drugs, without life-support equipment, without electricity or even the means of obtaining it . . . He leaned his elbows on the mantel and rested his face in his palms, stubbornly fighting to remain awake and clear-headed.

Minor injuries from disruptors—grazes and flashcuts—would begin to heal in eight to a hundred hours, untended. This was epidermal tissue only. There was no recent report on untended internal human injuries, except, of course, somewhere in the files of some mercilessly curious Klingon laboratory. If he could stabilize Aaron's condition long enough to find nightshade and distill a crude heart stimulant of some kind—if he could maintain blood-transfusions to keep his heart going—if he could only get enough sleep to keep from making mistakes.

He shook his head, and pushed his fingers through his hair, trying to pull back some of his slipping attention. It would take very little, he knew, for him to drop off to sleep, and that would be fatal for Aaron. Fatal for the world, with the Karsid drones arriving in a matter of months—fatal for the time-stream, and who knew what other time-streams it would touch.

As he brushed back the untidy mane of hair that was his chief disguise among the humans his fingertips touched the small, faint squares of residual scar-tissue on his temples, and he shivered. After coming this far, he thought, and enduring this much, to fail in the end.

Behind him, Sarah Gay's voice said, "They're like Joshua's were, aren't they?"

He swung around, startled. He had been so tired he had not seen her, sitting in the dark corner beside the desk. Her hand was a white blur as it moved to turn up the lamp, and Spock knew that its light showed her more clearly what she had already seen: the stigmata of an alien that marked his face. The slant of the eyebrows, the long, strange shape of the ears half-revealed by the brushed-back hair. She said nothing, but regarded him for a moment in the stronger glow of the gold kerosene light.

He knew Dr. Gay's mind to be largely logical. She did not ask questions whose answers were obvious. After a long time she said, "How is he?"

"Joshua will be fine." It would, he realized, have been why she had come.

She shook her head. "I don't mean Josh."

Spock regarded her steadily for a moment, then shook his head. "I do not know," he said wearily. "I can keep him alive—I do not know for how long."

Their eyes met in silence again. There was another question to be answered, but the answer to that was obvious, obvious in Spock's mere presence. So Sarah asked instead, "How did you come to Aaron?"

"We were chance met," replied Spock quietly. "I did not bring this on him."

She got to her feet, and crossed the room to glance through the narrow door into the dark bedroom. Then she turned back to him, the lamplight flashing across her thick spectacle lenses. "What is it?" she asked. "I've never seen anything like that. The wounds in his face and chest haven't even begun to close, after all this time. The blood isn't even clotting. Is this something . . ."

"Not of this earth," replied Spock. "I am sorry, Dr. Gay. It has nothing to do with you, and little to do with me. I was drawn into it against my will. I would have saved him, had it been possible, and I still will if I can."

She looked at him in silence for a moment, then asked, "Where are you—from?"

He shook his head wearily. "The name of the planet would mean nothing to you. Your astronomers have not even discovered the star yet."

"I see." She looked down at her folded hands where they rested on the handle of the door. Then she looked up at him again. "I knew at the dance, you see."

Spock's eyebrow lifted, startled. Sarah smiled a little.

She reached out and took his hand in her long slim fingers; cold, as Spock had always found the hands of humans icy to the touch. Then she released it, and her fingers brushed lightly against his cheek. "That's fever-hot," she said clinically. "A hundred and three, a hundred and four. A—one of us—would be raving. You were clearly having the time of your life." She

230

took his hand again, and with her other hand pushed up his sleeve a little, to expose the scars on his wrist. "Those are recent, aren't they? An Earthman's scars will turn pink if he's flushed, when he's been dancing, for instance. When you took my hand for the grand right-and-left, I noticed that. The scars on your wrist had turned a sort of apple-green."

And yet, thought Spock, she had stood talking with him and Biddy afterwards. . . . He rubbed absentmindedly at the slick uneven blotch on the flesh. The Klingons had strapped his hands down, of course, when they'd questioned him. The straps had been high-density flexiplast, and had cut like metal when he'd struggled.

"In the future," he found himself saying tiredly, "I must remember to avoid dancing."

"Only with medical doctors," she replied calmly. "Will you be returning to your own world, now?"

Spock shook his head, exhausted and bitterly ironic. "For a long time," he said, "I did not even remember my—own world." For the *Enterprise* was his own world, and more than that would be far too difficult to explain to this woman. "I was injured. I had lost my memory, in much the same way that Joshua lost an hour or two of his. In some ways I wish that I had not recovered it, for I think that the memory of what I lost is worse than ignorance. But for me there is no way home."

It was easier, he thought, than explaining that his home did not yet exist and if Stemple died, it never would.

"I am sorry."

As he had to Jason, Spock said, "It is none of your doing."

She rested a hand lightly on his wrist. "It is precious little comfort to you, I know, for me to say so," she went on, "but your home is with us—all of us. Whether Mr. Stemple lives or dies, whether this—whatever happened to him—is over, or is only the beginning of other things, you are one of us now. Whatever you are or people think you are.

"We are all exiles here," she went on. "Lottie, Clancey, Mr. Stemple, the girls, myself. Whyever we left the places we left to come here, there is no way back to the past for any of us. This is our home, and we are all that we have. It is only that you are from farther away."

Uncertain footsteps came from the other room, and then Joshua stood framed in the dark doorway, rubbing his eyes. Sarah rose quickly and went to him. Spock stood in the shadows by the fireplace, watching them, listening to the voices; hers soft and querying, his tired as he nodded, the firelight catching a sudden gleam on that ivory-colored hair. She turned back to Spock, and pushed up her specs. "I'll be back in the morning," she said. "Will you be all right until then?"

Spock nodded, though his body hurt for sleep. He moved mechanically to fetch their coats, leaden with fatigue. As he watched them depart along the trampled track in last night's snow back toward town, the lantern-light bobbing around their mingled shadows, it was in his mind that Aaron would not live through the night. In the morning it would not matter whether Sarah returned or not.

He went back to the table where she had been sitting, and took her chair, and turned down the lamp again to rest his aching eyes. Leaning his head on his hands, he began patiently, wearily reviewing his options.

He was still reviewing them when he drifted into exhausted sleep.

Chapter 18

EARTH.

In the darkness it looked like a sleeper, helpless in innocence.

A very vulnerable Earth, thought Captain Kirk, standing before the main viewscreen on the *Enterprise* bridge. No gleam of lights from the swollen megalopoli of West Coast and East Coast. No strings of orbiting satellites, ship stations, docking bays. No silver bubble of defensive armament gleaming like a baleful eye on the moon, no ring of battle stations. No haze of the interstellar trash that any planet picks up in the first few decades of experimentation with spaceflight.

A pristine and beautiful Earth. Velvet continents, ebony seas. Somewhere down there his own ancestors were shooting Apaches in Arizona. McCoy's ancestors would be dressing up in bedsheets and hoods to pay a call on some Carpetbagger—or, he realized uncomfortably, perhaps to pay a call on one of Uhura's ancestors.

An Earth without defenses against the black, snake-headed ships of the Karsid Empire, and the insidious temptations of their trade.

Exactly the kind of world the Karsids liked, he thought. That ancient empire had known its economics well. A culture ripe for takeover, reaching out to the first potentials of science and industry; a developing machine-culture with a prosperous economy. Like Klinzhai had been, a long time ago.

Reasonably prosperous, defenseless and innocent.

"Well," said McCoy's cheerful voice behind him, "we made it."

Kirk glanced back over his shoulder. The doctor was standing, hands clasped behind his back, a few paces behind him, watching the screen with something of the same awe that underlay the feeling on the bridge as a whole. The trip had been a rocky and terrifying one. Over the intercom from the Engineering Section Mr. Scott's voice could be heard saying, "I dinna know how we made it, lassie, but it looks like you were right."

At the science officer's console, Aurelia Steiner extruded a mouth close enough to the comlink to say, "There was a 97.6 percent possibility of correct calculation." Her little white hands were playing over the buttons as she spoke, a half-dozen blue eyes on the end of long eyestalks hovered before the numerous readout screens. When Drelbs are busy they tend to forget how they look. Beside her, Trae of Vulcanis was watching the readouts over the equivalent of her shoulder, silent and thoughtful. He was one of a score or so on the *Enterprise* who truly knew what they had done, and what it had involved.

Slowly, the globe grew in the viewscreens. Mountains spread before them in the darkness, the shaggy pelt of forests on their flanks. Breaking sheets of black cloud promised cold and snow. Kirk returned to his command chair, keeping a weather-eye on the readings, but his gaze kept returning to that silent planet, that dark and sleeping world.

"Parking orbit achieved, Captain," said Mr. Sulu. "Transporter range of Seattle."

"Can you get a reading on the town, Lieutenant Uhura?"

Slim fingers played across the communications console. Kirk tapped into the circuit; McCoy, Trae and Aurelia moved up behind him to see.

Shapes faded slowly into being, faint images of the town, like things sunk in deep water. White patterns on the black of the glass formed and clarified themselves into recognizable trees, buildings, water. It surprised Kirk that the town was so tiny. He was used to thinking of Seattle as something that stretched from the Canadian border halfway to Portland. This composite image of infrared and ultrasound reflection and tricorder readings was nothing more than a shabby hamlet with mud streets, a clearing in the thick, surrounding trees at one end of the bay. They'd seen thousands of them on planets that the Prime Directive had forbidden them to touch because the cultural level was so woefully low.

Trae was comparing the screen image with his charts, glancing sharply from one to the other. "You put us down very precisely," he complimented Aurelia, who was dangling one of her eyestalks over his shoulder to look. "By the distribution of the buildings the date would appear to be late 1867 or early 1868. That rectangle there can only be Jason Bolt's dormitory, which was built late in '66. As you see, there is no sign of the addition that was made when it was converted to the town social hall in July of '68."

"Why a dormitory?" asked McCoy. "Dormitory for whom? Loggers?"

Trae by now knew the history of the town as well as any of its contemporary inhabitants. "In 1866/1867 a project was undertaken between Aaron Stemple and another landowner of the vicinity, a man named Jason Bolt, to wive the settlers. Thirty women were brought from New England, and the dormitory was built to house them until they married. The building later became the town social hall, and so remained until it was destroyed by fire in 1889. Evidently it was known as the dormitory to the end of its days."

McCoy chuckled. "So that's where Stemple got his reputation as a humanitarian. No wonder they elected him to Congress."

Trae regarded him severely; Aurelia flared a bright yellow with peppermint-scented amusement.

Kirk said, "Any sign of the Klingon ship, Lieutenant?"

"Negative, Captain," said Uhura. "Although we're picking up traces of antimatter exhaust that could have been a parking orbit similar to our own."

All Kirk's instincts leapt to battle alert. "Recent?"

"Within four days, sir."

"Origin?"

"Undetermined, Captain."

"Four days," whispered Kirk. There was momentary silence on the bridge, as those around him digested the implications of this.

Finally McCoy said, "So that means we're too late."

"No," said Kirk stubbornly. "The Klingons hadn't known where to look for Stemple. They could be anywhere on the West Coast, still searching. The ship could have gone off so as not to risk running into Karsid drones. And there's no telling when in 1867 the Klingon ship arrived."

"They have a week's lead on us," said McCoy. "In that time . . ."

"To us it was a week," said Kirk. "But with that time warp the Klingons could have reached Earth months ago—or only a few days.

"Lieutenant Uhura, run a tricorder scan of the entire area, twenty miles around the town. Screen it for non-Earth life-forms."

Uhura's hands passed rapidly over the board, the console bringing images to life, one after the other. A grid map of white shadows on black. Trees like little tufts of cotton, the faint squares of dead wood that marked isolated buildings, the small flickering lights that showed where foxes, deer or humans walked late in the night.

Then Uhura froze one image on the screen, a single green light among the fainter shapes.

"Alien life-form reading, Captain. Within a few miles of Seattle."

Kirk cursed, softly and fluently. This was going to be close. "Klingon?" he demanded.

Long fingers played over the board again, clarifying the database. Lights glimmered up onto her intent face. Then she looked up at him, her dark eyes wide.

"Vulcan, Captain."

The glare of gold light and the falling sensation of the transporter beams faded, and Kirk found himself surrounded by wild windy darkness and murmuring trees. Old snow blotched the ground; even under the thermal jacket he had donned in the transporter room he shivered. With the cold came the heady earth smells of water and pines, and the wild cold scent of the ocean. A fox's green eyes flashed briefly at them from the woods.

McCoy, who knew Seattle, said from the gloom, "According to Trae's maps we should be at about the northeast corner of the Grayson Plaza Building downtown." Kirk laughed. In the black silence of the woods around them only a single light burned, in the small, heavily glazed window of the little cabin in whose dooryard they had materialized.

McCoy checked his tricorder's faintly glowing readouts. "Two people inside," he said softly. "If Uhura's scan was correct, one of them will be Spock."

Kirk was angling one of Trae's charts to the reflected gleam of the window light. "The cabin is listed as belonging to Aaron Stemple," he replied quietly. "He found him."

Kirk knocked twice at the cabin door, but received no answer. He and McCoy traded a glance, then Kirk tried the latch. It lifted easily, a wordless comment upon the community of Seattle. The two men stepped inside.

The dying embers of a fire lay crumpled like a luminous scarf in the stone hearth at one side of the room. A kerosene lamp stood on the table at the other, its deep, sherry-colored light edging with ruddy gold the litter of what McCoy recognized as ancient, barbaric surgical and medical equipment that lay around it. At the table a man slumped, his head bowed on his folded arms, his breathing slow with sleep. From the dark mane of uncut hair and the plaid wool shirt McCoy assumed it to be Stemple, and started to turn toward the door to the other room. Kirk paused, recognizing something, even in sleep, in the attitude of the sloping shoulders.

He came back, softly, to the sleeper's side. "Mr. Spock," he whispered. "*Spock.*"

Spock raised his head. His dark eyes were clouded with a fatigue extreme even for a Vulcan; they regarded Kirk for a moment with a kind of blank incomprehension, then closed again, and for a instant Spock's crushing grip locked around Kirk's hands. He drew a long, shuddering breath, then opened his eyes again, and whatever had been in them—joy, relief, hope out of absolute despair—had been carefully wiped away and replaced with an unbreakable Vulcan calm that in an absurd way gave Kirk just as much joy to see.

"Captain," said Spock in his most formal tone, "I am glad to see you."

"Glad!" burst out McCoy, swinging back from the doorway at the sound of the voices. "*Glad!* Is that all you have to say, you rabbit-eared, fish-blooded . . ." Between his own joy and rage he could scarcely splutter.

Spock said quietly, "It is the literal truth, Doctor. I am glad, for I had despaired of your coming." He rose to his feet, and moved past Kirk toward the door where McCoy stood, his walk marred by the telltale catch of his limp.

McCoy's voice softened. "You big fake."

Spock merely raised an eyebrow at him. The gesture was a thoroughly Vulcan one, at odds with this strangely human Spock in Levi's and boots, the sleeves of his plaid shirt pushed up over the faded longhandles he wore underneath.

Turning back to Kirk, Spock said, "I presume that, since you have found me, you know what has happened?"

It was all the reunion, Kirk reflected with an inward wry grin, that they were going to get; for all the emotion Spock showed about it they might have spent the time since they parted in the Wonder Bar indulging in a little shore leave on separate planets, Spock undoubtedly with his nose in a technical manual. But that was Spock—and Kirk's wrists bore the red marks of that first, convulsive grasp. He said, "About the Klingon attempt to tamper with time-lines? The assassination of Aaron Stemple?"

Spock nodded.

"Were you able to prevent it?"

The Vulcan paused, then said, "Not entirely." He limped to where McCoy stood beside the half-opened door to the cabin's inner room. "It is up to you, Doctor, to do that." He pushed open the door and led the way in.

McCoy hurried past Spock as he turned up the lamp, Kirk at his heels. The unconscious man on the bed was breathing in slow, painful gasps, his sunken face the dead-white that marks internal bleeding. Gently McCoy removed one of the bandages over his face; standing behind him, Kirk heard him whisper "Good God!" at the sight of the characteristically savage wounds of a Klingon disruptor. Looking back toward the doorway, Kirk saw something he had rarely seen: Spock leaned against the doorjamb from sheer exhaustion.

The first officer straightened wearily up as Kirk took a step back toward him. "Stemple?" asked Kirk softly, pitching his voice for the Vulcan's hearing alone.

Spock nodded tiredly.

From beside the bed McCoy exclaimed, "My God, Spock, how long have you been keeping him alive?"

"Three days, four days." Spock's voice was a trifle unsteady. "I do not have your medical knowledge, but I thought that if he could be kept alive long enough for the lesions in the lungs to heal . . ."

Kneeling by the bed, McCoy passed a feinberger quickly over Stemple's chest. "You could never have done it," he said. "The damage is too extensive. We'll have to get him up to the ship. How you got him to last this long . . ." He looked up, his brows drawn together. "You must have been giving him massive transfusions." Even as he spoke his hands were busy with hypo and medikit.

"Everyone has been very helpful," said Spock. "The Bolt brothers, Captain Clancey, Lottie . . . he has blood in his veins from every compatible donor in Seattle. I did not know if it would work. I could only try, and hope."

The names were half-familiar to Kirk—property holders in the records, numbers on Trae's charts. It occurred to him that Spock must know all these people very well, for he had clearly been in the town quite some time. Spock must be at the end of his endurance, he thought, to admit dependence on a townful of frontier humans—to admit to the weakness of not knowing what to do.

"Hope—for what?"

Eyes shut with weariness, Spock only shook his head. He had expected to fail in the end; had known that he would fail. And having failed, he would be forever stranded in this place, with the knowledge that he had been unable to prevent whatever evils would now come to pass. Not knowing what else to do, Kirk reached out and laid a hand briefly on the Vulcan's bony shoulder.

From the outer door of the cabin came a quick flurry of knocks. A woman's voice said, "Ishmael?"

Spock turned, stepping into the brighter light of the parlor as the door opened and a young woman came in. She looked cold and scared, her curly brown hair lank with dampness, her mittened hands stiff where she clutched a cloak about her. Through the narrow door Kirk watched as Spock crossed the room to her, and the captain almost fell over in astonishment when his first officer put a gentle arm around the woman's shoulders, and drew her to him.

"He will be all right, Biddy."

"Are you sure?" She lifted her face from his chest, looking anxiously up into his eyes. A plain girl, Kirk saw, verging on homely, her nose red and swollen from crying. "Sarah said . . ."

Spock touched her cheek with his fingertips, a gesture as tender and human as Kirk had ever seen his friend make. "He will be well," he said again. "Trust me."

A half smile touched her long mouth. "Well, of course I trust you, Ish. But how . . . ?"

"Biddy," said Spock, breaking into what threatened to be a spate of questions with what was evidently the skill of long practice, "there are—friends of mine—who are going to take care of Aaron, make him well. Can you wait for three days?"

"But why . . . ?"

"Can you?"

After a moment she nodded, trustingly, like a child, and wiped at her reddened eyes with the back of her hand. "Can I see him?"

"No," said Spock gently. "That will not be possible. But when you return here three days from now, you will find him well."

"If you say so, Ish," she agreed worriedly. "It's just that—will you tell me then how it happened?"

"I fear not." Spock disengaged her grip from his arms and closed his hands around hers. "I will not be here. I am going away."

She stared up at him with stricken eyes. "Oh, *no!*"

Watching silently from the dimness of the doorway, Kirk reflected that there was no one in the world Spock had been born into who would speak to him that way—whom he would permit to clutch at his sleeves.

At his elbow he heard McCoy whisper, "Who is it?"

"He called her Biddy," murmured Kirk in reply. "Stemple's wife was listed as an Elizabeth, wasn't she?"

"But you can't go!" she was protesting. "I mean—who'll do the accounting at the mill? Who'll take care of Aaron?"

"You shall have to."

She lowered her head, her cheeks suddenly pink. "Of course," she murmured. Then, "Ish—what happened to Aaron—it didn't have anything to do with—with that bet, did it? The one he had with Jason Bolt?"

Spock's voice hardened slightly. "No. That was over."

She faltered, "I—I know it had something to do with me—with all of us getting spoken for by the end of the year. I mean, that was the whole idea, to get everybody married. I know they had a lot at stake. . . ."

"The bet was over," repeated Spock quietly. "Do you know what the stake was?"

She shook her head, her cheeks coloring with shame now.

"Bridal Veil Mountain. I believe Jason would have asked you to marry him at the dance, had Aaron not prevented him by asking you first. Aaron knew what he was doing, Biddy—but he would rather have given up all further chance to own Bridal Veil Mountain, before he would see you married to another man. I think that you should know that."

"Oh," said Biddy softly. An unexpected tear slid down her sallow cheek. "Oh, dear—oh, poor Aaron. That must have been *so* difficult for him—I mean, he *hates* to pass up a chance to make money," she added, with tactless frankness. "Oh, no wonder poor Jason looked so unhappy when I turned him down. . . ."

"You *turned him down?*" Spock's eyebrow went

up, and he reflected how much he—and everyone else, for that matter—had underestimated this woman.

"Well, of course. I love Aaron. I've always loved Aaron. He's comfortable to be with, even if he is grumpy—and he's only grumpy because everyone's gotten so used to thinking of him as a villain that he's too proud to change. And—well, I remembered what you said to me once, about closing the door to something important—and anyway I knew I loved Aaron. I would have waited."

Spock almost smiled. "But he did not know that."

"No," said Biddy, with a sidelong glance that made her look almost minxish. "And he never will."

"Take care of him, Biddy."

"Now, that's silly," she murmured, blushing again. "You know I could never do anything else."

With a touch she found surprisingly light for a man whose hands were so strong, he brushed the hair back from her forehead, and kissed her lightly on the brow. Hidden by the darkness, Kirk was aware of McCoy standing at his elbow, trying not to die of shock.

Impulsively Biddy threw her arms around Spock, hugging him close. "Oh, Ish," she said, "I'll miss you." Then she turned as if embarrassed by this expression of affection, for Aaron and for his nephew, and hurried through the outer door and into the night again.

When he turned back, only Kirk stood in the shadows of the bedroom door. McCoy's voice could be heard beyond, quietly signaling the *Enterprise* to beam four aboard.

Chapter 19

THE FIRST THING OF WHICH STEMPLE WAS AWARE AS he surfaced slowly from the black deep of unconsciousness was Ishmael's voice. The words made no sense, but the voice itself was clear—that dry, uninflected tone he used when discussing mathematics or logic. His "alien" voice, Stemple thought—only he had grown so used to it in the last four months that he had simply accepted it as part of Ish.

He was saying, "Tillman's Factor, combined with the gravitational fields of the Tau Eridani Cloud and the wandering dwarf star, would create a gravitational vector which would in turn cause a temporary time-slip if a ship of sufficient mass were accelerated through it at high warp speeds. An extremely rare phenomenon, and one that I doubt the Klingons would utilize again, even if it recurred, given the null, and possibly deleterious, results of the experiment."

So that was it—the content that had formed Ishmael's speech patterns.

Nothing, thought Stemple, *that anyone would have guessed.*

It came to him then that Ish had found his memory. Another voice with a slight Southern accent said, "Hoist on their own petard."

"Precisely, Doctor."

Southern accent? thought Stemple groggily, recognizing by the sweet fog in his senses that he was heavily drugged. *Quoting Shakespeare?* There were no Southerners in Seattle, no one to whom Ish would speak so in any case.

Another voice, lighter, still speaking English. A quiet voice, the voice of a friend, "We—missed you, Spock. We thought we'd lost you."

And Ishmael's again, "I admit to doubts in that direction myself."

An impression of light, of shapes in the fog, as Stemple tried to open his eyes. Three men in a lighted doorway, shapes that slowly cleared and focused.

Stemple knew then that Ishmael had not only found his memory—he had found his friends. This was Ishmael's world he was in, not his own.

No wonder, he thought hazily, that Ish had recognized nothing in the wild green beauty of the northern woods. This world was one of clean hard lines, of alien shapes and materials, of things he had never seen before and could put no name to. He remembered the fog lifting from San Francisco Bay, and Ishmael saying *I can see rooms . . . see inside the walls, even know the tiniest wire and microcircuit . . . but it all means nothing.* But it had meant something after all.

Ishmael himself stood in the doorway, hands clasped lightly behind his back in a familiar pose. A gold emblem gleamed dully on the breast of the blue uniform he wore. His hair, cut short now as it had been when Stemple had first found him, revealed the long alien curve of his ears and the strange cant of his brows. He had become, Stemple realized, almost entirely human there toward the end. Now that was gone.

But the men with him . . .

The men with him might have stepped off Clancey's mailboat, any day of the week. They were as human as the Bolt brothers. The younger of the two reminded him indefinably of Jason Bolt—had that same air of command, of being king-wolf of the pack.

It was he who spoke. "How did you escape?"

Ish—whose true name was evidently Spock—replied, "I have no recollection at all of leaving the Klingon vessel, Captain. I remember my—interview— with the Klingon captain up to a point, but past that point I can only conjecture. Since the Klingon transport was a jury-rigged ship they had two auxiliary-systems failures while I was aboard before my capture."

"That would have been the gravitational stresses of going through the time warp," said the man he had addressed as Captain. "We had a secondary-systems outage ourselves. Nothing serious—doors and lights."

"Indeed. I can only presume that the cell in which I was kept pending disposal had a lock which was linked to such a system. If the ship were not a proper battle cruiser they would not have had a special brig with independent door circuits. A third power failure would have enabled me to escape and make my way to the transporter room. But as I said, I do not remember anything between the Mind-Sifter, and waking up in Aaron's cabin."

"No bloody wonder," grunted the Southerner, a spare, middle-aged man in some kind of blue uniform. "You were probably running on autopilot at that point—autopilot and sheer cussedness."

" 'Cussedness,' Doctor, is not a logical . . ."

"No," said the doctor, "and that's my point. Logically, there wasn't a single way you could thwart the Klingons. Not in the shape you were in. But you were being human."

An eyebrow went up. "Humans are, indeed, noted for their illogical stubbornness."

"And without human illogical stubbornness, Mr. Spock, you would have been one dead Vulcan."

"But without Vulcan physical and psychic stamina, Dr. McCoy, you must admit that I would have been an equally dead human."

"Gentlemen," said the captain, raising his hands. "It doesn't matter—why—you did what you did, Spock. Only, you did succeed."

Ishmael—Spock—inclined his head. "Thank you, Captain."

After a moment the doctor added, a little truculently, "When this is all over and we're back on the other side of the time warp, come on down to sick bay and I'll fix that knee of yours. Do you remember how that happened?"

"Negative, Doctor. Since Klingons traditionally go armed with bladed weapons I presume that I encountered at least one between my cell and the transport chamber."

Someone called from outside, "Dr. McCoy?" The doctor glanced over his shoulder, excused himself and left. Ishmael—Spock—and the captain stood in silence for a time, the relaxed silence of old friends.

When the captain spoke his words made no sense to Stemple, unclear as they were through the dreamy fog of the drugs. "That explains it." He was talking half to himself, and Ish lifted one of those long eyebrows at him questioningly.

"It explains why he was so convinced of the possibility of alien interference in Earth's affairs. Why he was so sure that extraterrestrials could pass for hu-

248

man. Thanks to the Klingons, he was the only person on Earth with prior experience with extraterrestrial infiltration of society."

"Not the only person," said Ish consideringly. "But the only person at that time who could have been elected into the government. There were at least two others who knew—and I suspect that their support proved invaluable to him later on. The Karsids would have succeeded in their conquest of Earth simply because no one would question them until it was too late—and in such cases, 'too late' can be measured in months; weeks, sometimes. But in attempting to prevent that question from being asked, the Klingons planted the seeds of suspicion that was the Karsids'—and their own—undoing. Had they let well enough alone, they would have accomplished their goal. How long did it take you to find out what they were doing?"

"A little under a week. We had to extrapolate from Khlaru's original research—and Khlaru, it appears, succeeded in defecting from the Klingon Empire on his way back to the home planet after all. We received word of it just before we left orbit."

The eyebrow again. "Interesting. And it appears that you emerged from the time-slip at a different point than did the Klingons."

"How long were you there?"

"Four months. The Klingon hunters missed him the first time through Seattle, owing largely to chance. It took them almost that long to locate him."

"And you were with him all that time?"

"I was passed off as his nephew. I worked as accountant at the mill."

The captain nodded approvingly. "Good position. How much did you tell him?"

There was a long silence, Ishmael lost in his own thoughts. At length he said, "Nothing. I—I did not myself know why I was there. When I came to, on Earth, I had no memory. I remembered nothing of the mission, the Klingons, this. . . ." His small gesture took in the place where they were, wherever or whatever it was; that windowless, shadowy room with the faint sound of throbbing indefinably in the air. "I recalled neither my name nor my past. I only knew that I was an alien, and alone."

The captain was even longer silent, shocked and dismayed with the hurt of his friend. "They did that to you?"

"I did it to myself. It was the only way to block the Mind-Sifter. At the power levels they were using I could never have withstood it for an extended period of time. My only recourse was to self-induced amnesia and catatonia." A pause, before he went on in a neutral voice, "I think it just as well that I do not recall either the rest of the interview, or the circumstances of my escape."

"And he found you?" asked the captain quietly.

"Yes."

"And took you in?"

"Yes."

"And he knew no more than you—that you were an alien?"

"Yes," said Ishmael. "I was a stranger in a strange land, Jim. I had no hope, beyond what he gave me."

The man Jim was quiet. Knowing Ish—Spock—as he must, he would know the torture of loneliness in those four months of a hell of hopelessness on an alien world. It was in his voice when he spoke again. "Was it bad?"

Ishmael's reply was in that very formal tone that masked what in anyone else might have been termed impishness. "On the contrary, Captain, it was a fascinating experience to live as a human among humans. Rather like being a research worker on an anthropological field assignment."

Their eyes met, human and alien. *Give me a straight answer,* said the captain's gaze, and Ishmael's, *You know the answer.*

The captain turned, and came to Stemple's bedside, Ishmael limping quietly behind him. The captain was startled, Stemple saw, to find him awake—if he was awake, and this wasn't some pain-induced dream. Ish moved up beside him, and reached down to take Stemple's hand. "You're among friends."

Stemple nodded, almost too weak to move. "You—found your friends." He was surprised at the faintness of his own voice, but Ish heard. Of course, Ish would.

"Yes. And my memory, and my home."

"They aren't—like you—either."

"No," said Ish softly. "I have always been a stranger, an alien even at my mother's breast. But I had a home among you. I will never forget."

"Nor we." He looked cloudily up at the alien face—human and familiar to him now. He knew he'd never see him again.

"Tell Dr. Gay that I have gone home. She knows."

"Ah," whispered Stemple. "Sorry—to lose you. Glad . . ." Ish's hand tightened over his, telling him that he understood this very human piece of illogic. After a moment's rest he murmured, "Why? You know why, now?"

Ish nodded. "I cannot tell you," he said. "But everything will be well, now."

Aaron managed a crooked grin. "Just my luck. Curious—the rest of my life. Itch—I can't scratch."

It was the nearest Kirk had ever seen Spock come to that sudden tangle of human emotion that is between laughter and tears. There was a break in his voice and a soft chuckle, as near to human as Jim had ever seen him. "I'm sorry, Aaron. I would tell you if I could."

"I know." The drugs were pulling him down, dragging him, as if weighted, into dark waters again. "Take care of yourself, Ish."

That surprising grip tightened over his hand again. "You, also. Good-bye, Aaron."

Kirk started to say something else to Spock, but his first officer straightened up quickly, and without a word walked from the room.

"So they really were hoist on their own petard." McCoy drained his glass, and picked up the brandy bottle, offering more. Kirk held out his; Spock shook his head, nursing the half glass or so that he had left. It was the first time Spock had consented to drink with them. Though the alcohol had no visible effect on him, the social implications were interesting. Spock had, McCoy concluded, learned something of humans on Earth after all.

"Not only that," said Spock, after a moment's consideration. "Their experiment in retroactive tampering with history was not only a failure, but a warning. When their mission logs are analyzed, I believe they will come to realize that not only did they not achieve their ends, but in attempting to achieve them, they in fact precipitated the very chain of events they sought to stop. We are, in fact, the product of a tampered time-stream already. The Klingons were attempting to prevent the tampering caused by my presence, but as they were not aware that they were looking for an alien, they made Stemple their target."

McCoy regarded the Vulcan over the rim of his glass. "So by attempting to thwart history, they actually served it, by bringing you there."

"Precisely," said Spock.

Kirk tilted his head to one side, caught by some thought. "Then—you're almost implying a sort of—predestination. That historically, you *had* to be there."

"Historically, I *was* there, Captain. You will find in the town records of that time an Ishmael Marx listed as accountant for Stemple's Mill; and, did the mill records still exist, you would find that they are in my handwriting."

"That's prepostrous," said McCoy uncertainly.

Spock only cocked an eyebrow at him.

"You're implying a predestination," said McCoy, "a—a purpose—about the whole thing. That's a little illogical for a Vulcan, isn't it?"

"Not at all, Doctor. Philsosphically, the concept of holistic unity of all things would include unity of past and future, as well as of space, personalities, energy and matter. And as for a specific intentionality about so-called random events—it would be illogical to conjecture without sufficient data."

"In other words, God can be presumed to exist in the absence of solid evidence to the contrary." Kirk leaned back in the more comfortable of the two chairs in Dr. McCoy's rather Spartan quarters. Spock, out of deference for the awkward sheath of the lightweight cast on his leg, sat on the edge of the bed.

"If you wish to speak anthropomorphically," Spock conceded, in his most Vulcan tone.

"But what about the others, Spock?" asked Kirk, holding up his brandy snifter to catch the warm, dimmed light of the shadowy lamps. It was late in the watch—he knew they'd all have to turn in soon, if they were going to be on the bridge at 0800 the following day to leave orbit around Starbase Twelve.

"Others?"

"The Klingons were seeking to halt one chain of

events, the one that prevented the Karsid infiltration of the Earth in the 1870s. But doing that, how many other chains of events got started, that would not have been started had the timestream not been tampered with? How many people did you influence besides Aaron Stemple, Spock? You said that there were two at least who knew what you were. How many other people's lives did you change?"

"Seven, directly," replied Spock, with his customary precision. "Not counting the ripple effect. Influence is an incalculable quality, Captain. Events of major significance can last for a few seconds only. That is why I say that I was an integral part of the history of the town; that is why I say that we ourselves are the product of a tampered time-stream."

"How do you mean?" asked McCoy.

Spock glanced over at him, and set his empty brandy glass down on the edge of the table. "I mean that I have reason to believe that Biddy Cloom is an ancestress of mine," he said. "Had I not lived in Seattle, had I not been there when I was, I doubt that she would have married, or borne sons. Because of my influence, she—did." There was an almost imperceptible pause in his voice as he spoke.

Watching his face, Kirk saw that he realized, perhaps for the first time, that Aaron Stemple, and Biddy Cloom, and the Bolt brothers and Lottie and Candy and Dr. Gay, were dead now. Had been dead for centuries.

Kirk returned to his quarters in a meditative mood. The room was comfortably dim after the daylight glare that eternally brightened the corridors. He made a final check on communications with the base, and confirmed clearances for the *Enterprise* to depart at 0800. A recorded message from Maria Kellogg further informed him that Trae and Khin Khlaru had departed Starbase Twelve for Vulcanis, where the Klingon historian was applying for Federation citizenship; and that the imperial representative Colonel Nch'rth had been recalled to Klinzhai, where, Kirk presumed, he would have a lot of explaining to do.

He stripped mechanically for bed, his mind on all the things that had been said that night in McCoy's quarters, and on the plain, brown-eyed girl he'd gotten such a quick glimpse of in the cabin on the mountain, homely and anxious, with a small silver pendant gleaming on its chain at her throat.

A thought came to him, and he went to the small terminal in the corner cubicle, and tapped quickly into the personnel records of the ship's central computer. As Maria Kellogg had said, what was the point of being commander if you couldn't pull classified files now and again?

White letters formed up on the dark screen before him.

> SPOCK, S'chn T'gai—S179-276-ST
> Lieutenant Commander.
> Science Officer, Starship Enterprise.
> b. 3492.6, ShiKahr, Vulcanis.
> Parents: S'chn T'gai Sarek,
> Hgrtcha Clan, ShiKahr, Vulcanis.
> Amanda Stemple Grayson,
> Seattle, Washington, Earth.

DON'T MISS
THE NEXT

STAR TREK®

NOVEL

BLOODTHIRST
by J.M. Dillard

A class one medical emergency summons the Enterprise to the Federation outpost Tanis. There, a grisly surprise awaits them. Two of the lab's three researchers are dead, their bodies almost entirely drained of blood. There are no clues. No records of their research. No remnants of their work.

There is only the outpost's sole survivor, Dr. Jeffrey Adams. A man with a secret that will rock the very foundations of Starfleet...and a terrible, all-consuming hunger that will bring death to the crew of the Starship Enterprise.

Look for
BLOODTHIRST
coming in December 1987 from Pocket Books

POCKET
BOOKS